Love is
a time of enchantment:
in it all days are fair and all fields
green. Youth is blest by it,
old age made benign:
the eyes of love see
roses blooming in December,
and sunshine through rain. Verily
is the time of true-love
a time of enchantment — and
Oh! how eager is woman
to be bewitched!

THE GUARDED SOUL

Angus and Donald Fraser were brothers who loved one another with a love as deep as it was unusual. Angus was a sensitive, highly-strung boy of twenty. Donald, the elder, was practical and purposeful. Both of them loved Sheila McLeod, but it was to Angus that Sheila was engaged — and Donald kept silent, fearing to break the happiness of his brother and the woman he loved, hiding his secret even from his brother. But Sheila's heart began to grow troubled; soon she realised that it was Donald she loved and not Angus . . .

ALAN DARE

THE GUARDED SOUL

Complete and Unabridged

ULVERSCROFT
Leicester

First Large Print Edition
published 1998

British Library CIP Data

Dare, Alan
    The guarded soul.—Large print ed.—
Ulverscroft large print series: romance
1. Love stories
2. Large type books
I. Title
823.9′14 [F]

ISBN 0–7089–3987–2

Published by
F. A. Thorpe (Publishing) Ltd.
Anstey, Leicestershire

Set by Words & Graphics Ltd.
Anstey, Leicestershire
Printed and bound in Great Britain by
T. J. International Ltd., Padstow, Cornwall

This book is printed on acid-free paper

1

The Frasers

The two sons of John Fraser opened their luncheon packets on the heather-clad side of Ben Tavis, and let the shaggy highland ponies find what grazing they could along the beautiful shore of the mirror-like loch. They were engaged in rounding up the sheep for clipping, and already some three hundred of them were penned against the slope of the mountain, under the vigilant eyes of the two men.

'Good lot of wool,' said Angus. 'Never seen them better.'

Donald nodded as he turned his critical eyes on the flock. He was three years older than Angus, and as different from him as one brother could be from another. Both of them had been given the best education that their father's meagre means would permit, and both had done well at Glasgow University, where Angus had finished up but a bare year ago. But temperamentally they were poles asunder. Angus had something of the artist about him. He could be dreamy at times, and terribly impulsive at others. This impulsiveness had landed him in many troubles, from the majority of which his stalwart brother rescued him. Donald had none of Angus' dreaminess. He argued from the head rather than from the heart, and was practical and purposive. In stature he was bigger — and more rugged — a man's man from his fine reasoning head to his firmly planted feet.

'What a day, Angus!' he said. 'The loch's like a piece of glass, and there's old Tavis all blue and mysterious. I've got an appetite like a horse.'

'You always had. Don, I can never understand why you stay here.'

'It's home.'

'I know, but things are not too prosperous. I remember you used to ramp on about distant countries, where a fellow could stake off a square mile of land and grow fine crops, or break in wild horses. I used to imagine you in buckskin breeches and with two six-shooters in your belt riding over the never-never land.'

Donald laughed as he, too, recalled these boyhood fancies.

'And you were going to be a musician — conducting huge orchestras all over the globe, your portrait in the papers, and ladies flinging bouquets at you. Oh, Angus! and here we are eating ham sandwiches.'

'Well, there is no livelihood in music — father was right about that, but there is a future in the Colonies. You're the sort of chap who could make a success of anything, Don,' he added seriously.

Donald's eyes twinkled.

'What's the idea, Angus? Trying to get rid of me?'

'Don't be an ass. I was just thinking that Culm doesn't give you much scope, and that there isn't anything here to hold you — not even a lass.'

At this Donald's expression changed. There was a momentary twitching of his mouth, but the next moment he was smiling again.

'I'm not a ladies' man, Angus. A girl can't open her mouth without me putting my foot into it, as O'Neill would say. Besides, you inherited all the family beauty.'

Angus gave him a push and he all but rolled down the mossy bank.

'Steady, old boy!'

'Then stop your rotting. There was Mary Keen, who thought you were the handsomest boy in the old Grammar School.'

'That was when I had my hair parted in the middle, and nicely plastered down with goose-fat. No, Angus, I shall be for all time a fat and contented bachelor.'

'Not you — you old humbug. I say, we must hurry or the sheep will undo all our work. Idiotic things — sheep. No sense of discipline at all.'

'Nor would you have if all your future spelt 'mutton.' But I'm ready when you are.'

Donald stood up and stretched his big frame. It was mirrored in the water below — a magnificent figure of a man, perfectly proportioned and alive with immense energy. Angus admired him as he stood there — an admiration dating back to when Donald had fought and beaten a lad four years older than himself. Between these two the blood bond was tremendously strong.

A few minutes later they were astride their wiry ponies, collecting the scattered parties of sheep from glen and hill. By the time the flock was penned it was dusk, and both were aglow with the rude health engendered by their open-air life. Gray-haired Mrs. Fraser welcomed them back to the farm.

'All in, Donald?'

'Every mother's son — and daughter. Oh, for tea! Where's father?'

'He had to run into Culm. Angus, Sheila called this morning to remind you about the dance tonight.'

'Forsooth!' said Donald. 'As if Angus is

likely to forget that.'

'Why don't you come too, you old bear?' retorted Angus. 'Think of all the poor 'wallflowers,' and you sitting at home doing nothing.'

'I shall be with you in the spirit,' replied Donald, with a solemn expression. 'Mother, why didn't you inculcate dancing into me when I was young and tractable?'

Mrs. Fraser smiled fondly. She loved her two boys as a woman does who has watched them from the cradle to manhood. Her husband had been inclined to be a trifle harsh, but she saw now that this was a good thing. Had she been left to bring them up alone, she might easily have spoilt them by over-indulgence.

'Why not go, Don?' she asked. 'I'll warrant you could put Sheila through her steps as well as Angus does.'

But Donald was adamant. He had a job to do in the house and he meant to do it that evening. As for Sheila — her very name caused his heart to flutter. She lived on a neighbouring farm, and she and Donald and Angus had been friends since childhood. Donald had secretly worshipped her, and once he had been near to telling her so. But his departure for Glasgow had been the means of separating them for a long period,

5

and when he came back to work on the farm, he found Angus as deeply in love with Sheila McLeod as he himself had been.

Time passed and the two drifted closer and closer together. Angus, as usual, had confessed to the 'big brother.' He was in love with Sheila — ought he to tell her so? Did Don think he stood any chance? Don thought he did, and advised him to go ahead. The upshot was an engagement ring, and a very excited Angus.

'She — she listened to me, Don,' he babbled. 'I can scarcely believe it even now. I'm to see McLeod to-morrow and tell him — or rather ask him. That'll be an awful business, but I feel as courageous as any lion. Still, I hope he won't kick me out.'

'Why should he? He and father are the best of friends.'

'That is true. Don, I'm the luckiest devil on earth.'

'I agree.'

McLeod on hearing of this raised no objections. He had a deep regard for the Fraser family, and believed in early marriages. When next Donald saw Sheila her eyes were bright with happiness. He congratulated her warmly, and her blushes were like red roses.

'I'm very happy, Donald,' she said.

'Be sure you always remain so, Sheila. But you will be. Angus will see to that.'

'What a pair you are,' she mused. 'If there is anyone Angus loves more than me, it is you, Donald.'

This had caused Donald some embarrassment, but he had passed it off with a deep laugh, and thereafter he put himself to the task of bottling up his emotions so far as they affected Sheila. That was over six months ago, and now he was complete master of himself. But he was wise in avoiding any situation which might fan into flame the spark within him, and for that reason he chose to stay away from the dance at Culm. Talking with Sheila was one thing, and dancing with her — holding her in his arms, quite another.

'Are you calling for her, Angus?' he asked.

'I wanted to, but she insisted on calling for me because we are nearer Culm, and it will save time. She is going to bring the dog-cart.'

'Then hurry up and get into your glad-rags. If you keep her waiting I'll break your neck.'

Angus grinned, and threw a small piece of bread across the table at Donald, to his mother's annoyance.

'Will you two never grow up?' she asked.

'Angus will,' replied Donald. 'When he is married and has a large family to support. Can't you imagine Uncle Donald hobbling along to put oil on the troubled waters — about every fortnight?'

'I'd wallop you for that, Don — if you were not so elephantine. Lord, is that the right time?'

'It is, and if you are going to use the bath have the decency to leave me a little hot water.'

Angus finished his tea and ran upstairs, whistling blithely. While he was busy at his ablutions John Fraser came home. It was easy to see where Donald got his big and intelligent head, his wide, thoughtful eyes, and his stubborn jaw. He was the perfect reflection of his father. Angus' rather softer features were inherited from his mother.

'Well, Don, did ye get the sheep in?' asked Fraser.

'Aye, and they're fine and heavy with wool. We'll start shearing to-morrow.'

'Good! Where's mother?'

'Upstairs, I think. Shall I make you some fresh tea?'

'No, thanks. I had a cup in Culm — with McLeod. We've had a talk about Angus and Sheila.'

Donald looked at him questioningly.

8

'McLeod's for an early marriage,' resumed Fraser. 'His man has left him, and his idea is to take Angus into partnership — when he's married.'

'Hm!'

'I'm not sure about it myself.'

Donald shook his head.

'It would be a mistake, father. Angus is marrying Sheila — not the family. They ought to have a little place of their own. It might be hard work to start it and make it pay, but they'd be happier that way. When a man's married he doesn't want his mother-in-law on the spot. Relatives are all very well, but are better visited than lived with.'

'You're right, Don. That's exactly how I feel about it. I'd like to see Angus pushing his own plough, and facing his own responsibilities. Independence is what matters most. When I was his age I was breaking up stony soil to win a home for your mother. The hardest battles bring the pleasantest victories. I'm not averse to Angus getting married this year, but I'm all for his starting off his own bat.'

Donald smiled a little wistfully as he reflected how wonderful it would be, fighting for Sheila. So far Angus had not done much fighting, but Donald felt that he had plenty of grit under his care-free exterior, and that

Sheila would be the driving force. Lucky Angus!

As usual, Sheila arrived before Angus was ready. When she turned her fine dark eyes on Donald he felt the old passion striving for expression, but he kept a tight check upon it. Sheila was going to be a kind of sister to him. He meant to be content with that.

'He won't be a minute,' he explained. 'We were a bit late with the sheep-drive. You're looking well?'

'Of course. I'm always well.'

'And your feet are tingling?'

'Just a little. Don, why don't you come with us?'

'I'm no dancer. Besides, there are one or two jobs I want to do.'

'You never seem to have any relaxations.'

'More than you know of. I'll go and rout out Angus — he ought to know better.'

'Oh, please don't trouble. I'm a little early.'

So they sat and talked and laughed until Angus came down and apologised. He was in the gayest of moods, for he had looked forward with the keenest delight to that evening.

'So-long, Don!' he said. 'I'll be home about eleven-ish.'

'Take care of him, Sheila,' said Donald.

10

'He's all hot and excited.'

'I will,' she promised with a laugh. 'Good night, Don!'

Her hand seemed to quiver in his, but he paid no heed to it, for he could not possibly guess what great secret lay in her warm young heart.

2

Doubting

June came to the highlands, and the banks and braes were purple with heather. High up on the side of Ben Tavis, Sheila rode under a perfect sky, her hair streaming in the wind, for she had let it down in the absence of any observer. Away beyond the blue loch lay the Fraser farm. She stopped and gazed at it reflectively. Up there were Angus and Donald — the playmates of her youth.

'Donald!' her lips framed the name, and then she lowered her head in shame.

That was her secret — the thing that rankled and hurt her to the very soul. She recalled the day when Angus had come to her with his eyes nervous and his hands trembling. He had talked to her of love and she — she had listened, because her own heart was greatly stirred. Then the happiness of being engaged, the wonderful visions of the future. She had not wanted that dream to end, but of late it had been far less potent than of yore. When Donald had come back, the little seed of doubt entered her mind. These two brothers had been, and were, so dear to her, she had scarcely troubled to treat them as separate entities. But now things were changed — one was to be a brother-in-law, and the other a husband. No longer were they like Siamese twins. And as the weeks went by Donald's great personality obtruded over everything. She tried to persuade herself that this feeling for him was but the natural affection that a girl might reasonably have for the beloved brother of the man she was going to marry. Once, in the past, she had thought that Donald loved her. Then he had gone away and she dismissed the idea from her mind, for the difference in their ages had appeared greater in those days. Never since then had she been given cause to believe that her intuition was correct. Donald's sense of chivalry and honour was as firmly rooted as the everlasting hills.

This new whispering of her heart troubled her deeply. It was like the utterance of a caution — warning her against the misunderstanding of her own desires. She did not want to think of Donald in the way she did. Angus was to be her husband — Angus of the sunny smile and high spirits. Why did Donald's image always creep into her dreams?

With a plaintive sigh she set the pony moving down the steep side of the mountain, and found a spot where it could drink from the enticing loch. When she was about to leave Angus came galloping up — hatless and perspiring.

'I saw you from the house,' he said. 'I had a bet with Don that it was you, and here I am to prove it.'

'You shouldn't have left your work, Angus,' she protested.

'Father's away, and Don didn't mind. Dear old Don — he'll do my share and more.'

'But it isn't fair — to him.'

'I'm not going to stay long. You look beautiful this morning, Sheila.'

'Flattery — so early!'

'It's never too early to tell the truth.'

'Where did you read that?' she said teasingly.

'It's original.' His eye caught the glint of her engagement ring. 'Sheila, when are we going to get married?'

'There's plenty of time, isn't there?'

'I begrudge every second of single life now.'

'But you are not yet twenty-one.'

'I shall be in three months, and then I come into some money left to me by my

14

aunt. Can't it be then, Sheila?'

She hesitated.

'How impatient you are, Angus! Aren't you happy in being engaged to me?'

'Of course, but think of marriage — a home of our own! You know, sometimes I think it can't be true — that no girl ever loved me, and that I'll end up my days a crusty old bachelor like — like Don.'

'But why should Don — '

'He doesn't seem to have the slightest desire for marriage. No girl ever succeeds in arousing his interest. It's strange when one considers what a splendid fellow he is — big-hearted and most lovable, and so jolly fond of kiddies. Perhaps if he found a girl like you, he'd change his ideas. Sheila — say yes.'

She laughed though her heart felt unaccountably heavy, and told him she did not intend to be hustled. At the same time she promised she would think it over seriously.

'I'll be satisfied with that,' he said. 'Now kiss me and I'll hurry back to the grindstone.'

She did so and then watched him riding madly over the strewn boulders towards the distant farm. Again she sighed — the sigh of a girl who finds herself wedged into a cleft.

Angus reached the farm and found Donald

with his sleeves rolled up and his shirt open at the neck, repairing a broken stretch of fencing.

'You owe me sixpence, Don,' he said.

'So it *was* Sheila?'

'Yes. Did you think I could be mistaken?'

Donald laughed. He knew perfectly well it was Sheila, for he had eyes like a hawk. But the little wager afforded Angus an excellent excuse to leave his work. Donald handed over the coin.

'Put it in your money-box for the rainy day,' he said.

'There aren't going to be any rainy days, you old dismal Jimmy.'

'Oh, Angus, there's a man been hanging about here, asking for you.'

'A man!'

'He wouldn't give his name — a dark little chap with a small moustache. A bit impudent too. I very nearly kicked him out.'

Angus bit his lip, and then shook his head.

'There must be a mistake,' he said. 'I can't recall any such person.'

But Donald thought his manner was strange, and later in the day he saw Angus talking with the man in question. There seemed to be an altercation and Donald wondered whether he ought to intervene, but on second thoughts he stole away unseen. When Angus entered the house he was obviously a trifle depressed. Donald said nothing, but he wondered what had happened to cause Angus to exhibit a mood that was by no means natural to him.

As the days passed Angus recovered his habitual care-free demeanour, and Donald forgot all about the incident. But at intervals Angus displayed signs of distress — agitation, and Donald thought that Sheila was not seeing as much of him as she was wont.

'Are things all right, old boy?' he asked one evening.

'All right!'

'With Sheila, I mean?'

Angus laughed.

'Why, of course. We had a bit of a tiff, but it was my fault, and I'm just going over to tell her so.'

'That's certainly the best thing you can do.'

Apparently Angus' apology smoothed away the trouble, for on the morrow he was full of fun again.

'You're mighty pensive these days, Don,' he said. 'What is it — a girl?'

Donald shook his head and gazed across the tumbling moorland to where old Ben Tavis reared his great bulk above the loch.

17

He saw there not the beloved mountains of his youth, but the wide Canadian prairie that offered him scope for his tireless energy.

'You've often teased me about carrying out the dreams of boyhood, Angus,' he said. 'Well, at times they are reborn. Maybe I'll never see anything more beautiful than this, but I feel cramped at times — terribly cramped.'

'Don, you're not thinking of — of going away?'

'It's no new thought, old boy, but a very old one revived at intervals. You remember the picture you drew — two six-shooters in my belt and buckskin trousers — '

'I was only rotting, Don.'

'I know. But there was sense in what you said. There are big lands waiting to be developed, and the call is for men who can do the work.'

'But we'd miss you dreadfully. Why, when I get married father will need you more than ever.'

'That's the rub — the constant obstacle.'

Haymaking came with its gruelling work, and Donald had no time to think about distant lands. Rain was threatening, and it behoved them to get their hay in while the sun shone. Like a young giant he toiled, and the thing was accomplished.

'Donald's a rare worker,' admitted his father. 'Angus is all right, but he hasn't Don's sense of responsibility. What a pity Donald doesn't hang up his hat to a good lass, who would make him a fit wife. He's restless, I'm thinking.'

Mrs. Fraser nodded, but she did not worry greatly about Donald. Her perception told her that Donald could be trusted to find his own happiness. He had always been the same since he was a lad in knickerbockers — self-reliant to the last degree — sure of himself, and a little masterful. Angus was a bird of another colour — good metal, but needing tempering.

'Perhaps Don knows best,' she said.

Meanwhile Sheila was still wrestling with her doubts — still putting off the wedding-day on the plea that both she and Angus were very young. McLeod, however, was intent upon accelerating the union.

'I'm thinkin' it would be a guid thing to have the bells ringing on Angus' birthday,' he hinted.

'Perhaps. But I want to be quite — quite sure, daddy.'

'Aren't ye sure, lass?'

'Yes — yes, of course. But — '

How could her father understand this storm within her breast? How could she find the courage to tell him that she was daily warming towards a man other than the one to whom she was plighted? It might be better to let things run their normal course and to keep her painful secret to herself for all time. It would save a lot of pain to others.

Before she could bring herself to accept this easy way out something happened at the Fraser farm which was destined to change the whole aspect of things. John Fraser came home from a visit to Culm, with a face that was drawn and haggard. Mrs. Fraser found him in the sitting-room staring woodenly through the window — hands clenched on the table before him, and a pile of cancelled cheques lying under a brass candlestick.

'Is — anything amiss, John?' she asked.

He still stared into space.

'John, why do you sit like that?'

His head came round, and in his eyes was an expression which caused her heart to quaver.

'The worst thing in the world has happened, Jane,' he said. 'We've a thief under this roof — a common forger.'

'John!'

'Aye, but it's true.'

'I — I don't understand. Who is there here but you and I — and the two boys?'

'Aye, the two boys — our sons for whom we have worked and worried these twenty-odd years.'

'But John — you don't mean — you can't mean that — ?'

'One of them is skunk enough to rob his own father.'

'No — no!'

'Would that I could harbour the slightest doubt.' His voice nearly broke, but the next moment he was master of his emotions. The granite hardness of him came uppermost.

'Find them — bring them here,' he said harshly.

'John, you are not going to accuse my boys of — of — ?'

'Bring them here. You will see for yourself the kind of viper we have reared. Go, mother. We have to face this thing. It is not time for sentiment.'

3

The Cheque

Donald and Angus entered the old oak-beamed room, Angus neatly attired in anticipation of a meeting with Sheila, and Donald in his rough working garb — covered with sawdust. They saw their father, with his broad back towards them, staring out of the window, and from behind came their mother looking pale and ill. It was perfectly plain that a storm was brewing, but for the life of him Donald could not imagine what it involved. Angus had a strained look on his handsome face and glanced at his mother nervously.

'John, they're here.'

Fraser turned round, and waved his hand towards the couch.

'Sit you down!'

The boys did as they were bid, but Mrs. Fraser remained standing, with her hands clasped before her.

'One of you wonders why I have sent for you, the other one knows,' said Fraser, gazing at the two boys in turn. 'There is

22

a thief in this house — one of my own family.'

Donald started.

'Father — !'

'Wait! I know what I'm saying. I've done my best for you two lads. Maybe you'll never know the struggle it was for me and your mother to bring you up and give you a good schooling. I've denied you nothing that was in my power to give, and now one of you has turned upon me like a snake. Look at this cheque!'

Donald, in a state of bewilderment, took the cheque. It was dated three weeks back, and was for the sum of fifty pounds, payable to bearer. At the bottom was his father's signature. He could see nothing wrong with it, and passed it to Angus.

'W-well?' stammered Angus.

'Forged!' rapped Fraser.

Donald's brow came down, and his mouth twitched. Fraser's eyes switched from his elder son to his younger, but the mother averted her eyes. She did not want to know the culprit.

'Are you — sure, father?' asked Donald hoarsely.

'There's no doubt. I never signed that cheque. It was done by someone who knew my signature — someone who had access to

23

my cheque-book. I've been to the bank in Culm. The cashier remembers paying the money.'

'Yes — yes.'

'It was to — to one of my sons. It was on market-day, and he was very busy, but he remembers it was one of you. I — I pretended it was all right — to stop the scandal. Now I want the truth. Which of you presented this cheque. Which of you is a thief and a forger? Speak, for the love of God!'

Donald was about to utter an indignant denial, but he closed his mouth before the words were uttered, for Angus was sitting like a figure in stone, with the cheque fluttering in his hand. Fraser took it from him, almost savagely.

'Are you both dumb?' he demanded.

A sob came from the distressed mother. It changed Fraser's programme. He had intended to force a confession there and then, but now —

'Listen!' he said. 'I'll not ask you to humble yourself before your mother — whichever of you is guilty. But I'll not harbour a thief under my roof — not even though he be my own son. Let him who is guilty leave this house to-night, for ever, and my curses go with him — '

'John!'

Fraser would not look at his wife. He feared the depth of his own love for his sons. It was duty now that swayed him, and like the granite man he was he meant to go through with it to the bitter end.

'I was wrong,' he said. 'I will not curse him, but he shall be my son no longer. I will leave twenty pounds on the mantelpiece — to help him on his way, and may God forgive him for bringing disgrace on this household.' His big voice almost broke. 'Go now, the pair of you.'

★ ★ ★

Donald saw little of Angus that evening. With his father's terrible accusation ringing in his ears, he went over the hills to reflect. There must be some mistake, he thought. Someone from outside might have stolen a blank cheque, and knowing Fraser's signature — But the cashier — was he too, mistaken? Then he remembered Angus' intermittent fits of depression, and the visit of that impudent stranger — He tried to rid his mind of the conclusion it was rapidly reaching . . . He was passing the hayrick on his return to the house, when he heard voices from behind it.

25

'You are troubled, Angus?'

'Foolish Sheila! Why should I be troubled?'

'You have spoken so little all evening.'

'I am just a wee bit tired. Did you see Don when you came along the glen?'

Donald walked on with his fists clenched. To think of the delightful Sheila with all her dreams shattered! No, no — that must never happen. Her happiness mattered to him no less than Angus'. Before he sought his room his mother came to him. She took him by the shoulders as if he were a child instead of a strapping man, a head taller than herself.

'Don — Don — was it — ?'

He wanted to look into her kindly brown eyes and tell her that his conscience was clear, but he recalled Angus and the girl that Angus loved. Kissing her hand, without a word, he went upstairs. Angus came up later — to his bed in the opposite corner to that occupied by Don. Slowly he undressed, looking at intervals at Sheila's portrait on the mantelshelf. At last he blew out the candle and slipped into bed.

Donald lay wide awake, listening intently. An hour or so passed, and then a slight noise came from the opposite corner. He heard the scratching of a match, and the candle was lighted again. Looking through his half-closed eyelids he saw Angus reaching out for his clothes. He sat up.

'Don!'

'What are you doing, Angus?'

'I'm — I'm — Don, I've got to go. You heard what he said. It was true — God help me!'

Donald got out of bed and sat by the side of his dejected brother, his right arm round Angus' shoulder. There was no contempt in his face — just sympathy mingled with astonishment.

'Tell me, old boy?' he begged.

'It started a year ago. I began to back horses with a bookmaker in Culm. For a time I had good luck, and won a pound or two. Then I lost my head and plunged — and lost . . . What's the use of going into details? I got involved and the bookmaker never worried me to pay up until I resolved to stop that crazy game. Then — then he began to threaten me. Three weeks ago — no, nearly a month — he came here — you remember the man you saw? — and told me that unless I paid within seven days he would come and tell father everything. You know father, and his hate for gambling? I was at my wits' end. One night I drank more than was good for me, and — and I forged that cheque. I meant to repay the money — when I came into Aunt Janet's legacy.'

'But you could not have hidden the — the business?'

'I know. I just wanted to postpone the evil day. Reason deserted me, Don — the devil saw to that. It was decent of father to give me this way out. I — I simply could not confess before the mater. What a mean skunk I have been — to hurt them — to bring shame upon them — !'

There was a queer catch in his voice. Donald stood up and looked at his brother.

'Get back into bed, Angus.'

'But I'm going — now.'

'Do as you are told. Get into bed!'

'I tell you — '

'You'll tell me nothing. You are not in a position to handle this problem as it must be handled. There is Sheila — have you thought of her?'

'I — I tried to tell her this evening, but could not. She — she — it would break her heart.'

'Enough hearts have been broken already.'

Donald turned away and began to dress. Angus gaped at him, and then jumped up and caught his arm.

'Don, you — you aren't — ?'

'One of us must go, Angus. Don't worry, old boy. You know I've always had a desire to spread my wings a bit. Here's an excellent chance — '

'No — no. I wouldn't let you do that. Do you think I am such a miserable creature as to let you — ?'

'You are going to do exactly as I say,' interrupted Donald firmly. 'See nothing — know nothing. Marry Sheila and make up to father and mother for all they've done for us. I'm going to have my own way, old boy, whatever you may say.'

'But Don — I should hate myself eternally.'

'Reason it out for yourself, Angus. If I go two people will be made a little unhappy. If you go there will be three.' He laughed. 'Why, this is a blessing in disguise. I'm simply aching to get away.'

Angus began to argue anew, but Donald lifted him bodily and put him back into bed. In a few minutes he was fully dressed, and had a small suit-case packed. He held out his hand to Angus.

'Here we part, old boy.'

'Don! Don!'

'Sh! Your promise now. Swear you will keep silent?'

'How can I?'

'Swear! Word of honour.'

Angus hesitated for a moment.

'Oh, Don — you make it so hard. I — I swear.'

A handgrip and Donald was gone, with the lighted candle in his hand. He crept down the stairs and smiled as he saw the pile of notes on the mantelshelf. Kissing his hand at them he unlocked the door, and went out into the still and peaceful night.

4

Facing Facts

John Fraser slept ill that night. At intervals he awoke to full consciousness and strained his ears to catch any unusual sound. Once he thought he heard a door creak, but that was all. He knew that his wife was equally wakeful, though she preferred to feign sleep. And so the long night passed.

Just before sunrise he rose, dressed and went downstairs. The first thing he saw was the pile of treasury notes on the mantelshelf exactly as he had left them. He took them up and counted them. Not one was missing. He went to the door, and found it unlocked. But he now remembered that he had omitted to lock it the previous night.

He sat down and stared at the notes. It meant — it could only mean — that his command had been ignored. The guilty son was bold enough to face things out. Fraser's lips curled contemptuously. He had hoped that a painful scene might be avoided — that his wife would be spared humiliation and pain, for sooner or later the truth must come out.

31

As he sat there, deeply depressed by the horrible revelation of the day before, he heard the bang of a door, and then a creaking of old stairs. He raised his head and waited anxiously. A few seconds passed and Angus entered the room. His habitual care-free expression was gone. Usually he leapt down the stairs — three at a time, but now all the healthy spirit of youth seemed crushed out of him. He halted and looked at his father.

'Good morning, Angus!'

'Morning, father!'

'Is Don — is Don — ?'

Angus winced and bit his lip.

'Don — Don has — gone.'

'My God!'

He had not expected that — quite. Donald the apparently trustworthy! The big, happy-go-lucky Donald, whose needs had been so notoriously few — !

'Are you — sure?'

Angus nodded. He could scarcely speak for the emotion and shame that combined to choke him. Too late he realised his promise to his brother — his word of honour. Even now he wanted to blurt out the truth, to remove for ever the cloak of shame from Don's shoulders. But when Don had made that appeal for silence he had meant it. Weak

32

as he had been in this matter, a promise to
Don was like an oath taken before God, for
these two had never broken faith with one
another. He saw his father's head droop.

'Don! To think it was Don!'

'Is mother — ?'

'She doesn't know — yet.'

Angus saw the wad of notes, still crushed
in his father's hand.

'He left those — of course,' he said
thickly.

'Why 'of course'?' snapped Fraser. 'It was
not my wish he should go without a shilling.
It was my right to help him — even after
— this.'

'Yes, father,' said Angus meekly. 'But then
— but then — '

'Go — start the milking! We have to forget
it. He is gone and may he fight down the evil
that is in him.'

Angus went out into the bright morning
sunshine. He breathed in the keen air as if
he were suffocating, and saw himself reflected
in the water-trough near the pump as an ugly
monster supported by another man's broad
shoulders. What would Sheila think of him
if she only knew? But it was just because of
Sheila that Donald had done this thing, and
because of Sheila he, Angus, must let things
take their natural course.

While he was busy Mrs. Fraser came downstairs. She looked round for her sons, but saw neither of them. A little later she saw Fraser by the sheep-dip and also heard the rattle of cans from the dairy. With palpitating heart she prepared breakfast, and when it was ready she banged the gong outside the kitchen door. Fraser came in first, with his lips strangely compressed.

'A bit early, mother.'

'No. It's just half-past seven.'

'Angus will — '

'Angus! Then he — he — ?'

She faltered, and her husband put one arm round her frail shoulders.

'Angus is here, mother. But Donald — '

'Yes — yes?'

'Donald left — last night.'

'Donald left — last night,' she repeated in a dazed way. 'My Donald a — '

'S-sh! We must face hard times as well as pleasant ones. There's good in the boy. He left my money — untouched.'

'And he never said — good-bye!'

'Maybe he wanted to spare you — pain.'

'Yes, it was that. Oh John — to bear a son in suffering, to watch him grow into manhood, to be so proud of him — so vain of one's own — motherhood, and then to — have him go into the night without a word — a kiss — in shame — '

'We must be brave, mother. Who knows but one day he may come back — redeemed in our eyes?'

Her eyes glistened at this wonderful prospect.

'Yes — one day,' she murmured. 'But what are we to tell folk? How can we explain his absence?'

Fraser winced, for he too had foreseen this difficulty. Not for anything in the world would he have his neighbours know the real truth.

'It will look like a quarrel,' he said. 'Aye, let them think that. And now — here comes Angus. Don't let the boy see you crying.'

No word was spoken anent the drama during breakfast, and Angus realised that the ban had fallen. The chivalrous Donald must live now only in unspoken memories. He feared to see Sheila — feared her very natural questioning, because of the impossibility of answering them truthfully.

Two days passed before he saw his sweetheart. She rode up to the farm on her highland pony and found Angus working in an outbuilding. He thought she looked a little wistful as he kissed her, and that her response was colder than usual.

35

'You're just in time for a cup of tea, Sheila.'

'Oh, don't trouble. I was on my way home and — '

'Mother will be disappointed if you don't stay a little while. I'm finished now.'

'Very well.'

He wanted to tell her about Donald, but feared he might bungle matters. It was better she should hear it from his parents, he thought. While he made himself presentable Sheila went into the house. Mrs. Fraser welcomed her warmly, for she had a great appreciation for her prospective daughter-in-law.

'You've seen Angus?'

'Yes. I ought to have gone straight home, but Angus begged me to — '

'Quite right, too. Tea is all ready. Father — here's Sheila,' she called.

Fraser's eyes glistened as he gazed on the alluring form of Sheila. At least Angus' future was safe! He saw in Sheila an admirable wife — the sort of woman upon whom a man could rely in fair weather or foul. But the look of pleasure faded out when he realised that Sheila must be told about Donald's departure. Delay might cause her to suspect trouble other than a family quarrel.

'You — you haven't heard about Donald,

Sheila?' he said in a low constrained voice.

'Donald! He's not — ill?'

Fraser shook his head slowly, and Mrs. Fraser moved her hands nervelessly.

'Donald has gone away.'

'Gone away! Not — for good?'

'I fear so.'

Sheila tried her best to hide the stab of pain, that was even more intense than she herself had imagined it could be. She gazed from Fraser to his wife questioningly.

'There was a bit of a quarrel — two days ago. Don considered it best to carve his own path in life.'

'But — '

'Perhaps it was wisest,' resumed Fraser. 'He was a strong-willed fellow. He'll make good wherever he goes.'

'Yes — yes. But don't you know where he has gone?'

'Not — yet.'

'I'm so — so sorry.'

Instinctively she found Mrs. Fraser's hand and pressed it gently, for she saw in her kindly eyes the depth of the sorrow which she felt.

'Ah, here's Angus! Sit you down there, Sheila!'

Tea was not the pleasant thing it should have been. Conversation was fragmentary and forced. Angus seemed nervous and utterly unlike his usual self. Sheila was glad to get out in the open air.

'Angus! What — what happened?'

'You heard.'

'But Don was never quarrelsome. What made him go off like that — without a word?'

'I'd rather not talk about it, Sheila. We're all depressed — miserable. This place will never be the same without dear old Don. But he was always keen to go abroad — you know that.'

'He might have said good-bye — to me and father.'

'He acted on a sudden impulse. It's best not to mention the matter to mother or father. You see — they feel it very deeply. No doubt Don will write soon and tell us what he is doing — and where he is.'

This was poor consolation for Sheila, with her own heart in a turmoil. For her the crisis had arrived — accelerated by this astonishing news. It was as if Donald had taken with him some part of her own being. Now she knew without any possibility of mistake, that it was Donald that she loved and not Angus. Little by little this truth had been welling up, until now it overflowed her consciousness. Even to think of it caused the blood to mount to her cheeks.

'Was it — was it all Donald's fault?' she asked.

'No — no. It was all a dreadful mistake. I — I can't go into details, but Don was not to blame.'

She wondered at his irrepressible emotion, until she recalled how close these two brothers had been to each other since the old boyhood days. Then her heart quaked as she remembered the pressing need. Angus must be told that her love for him had faded. To go on pretending things were the same as ever was out of the question. Angus must be told, and then her own father.

Summoning up her courage she tried to commence, but the words were hard to come. She delved into her vocabulary to find expressions that would lessen the blow, but Angus gave her no chance. He wanted to keep his mind from the little drama in which he was so deeply involved — and in this endeavour he poured out all his heart to Sheila.

'We'll be married soon, Sheila, and start a small place on our own. Old Don will come home one day to find us with heaps of cattle and maybe a fam — '

'Angus!' she pleaded.

39

'Sorry! But can't you imagine how fine it will be to see Don, strapping as ever, entering our home? Perhaps he'll make a fortune, and then they'll have the streets hung with flags and a brass band to welcome him home. He's the sort of chap to run up the ladder of success, three rungs at a time.'

'Angus — if — '

'You were a bit fond of him too, weren't you, Sheila? Now own up — you couldn't help yourself.'

'You don't know what you are saying.'

'Yes, I do. Why, if you didn't love Don I don't think I should love you — as I do. He's the finest — the most dependable chap that ever lived. The thing I'm most sorry about is that he won't be here for the wedding.'

A convulsive choke came from her. She could not tell him now, for she was on the verge of tears. Every word he uttered made it harder for her. She stayed but a few minutes longer, for she felt like a traitor, though her good sense told her that the greater sin would be to marry one man while every scrap of her consciousness — every beat of her heart — told her that she loved another.

'I'll call for you to-morrow evening, Sheila.'

Those were the last words she heard as she rode away. But in the intervening twenty-four hours she had to find the courage to act in the way which she believed was right.

5

Rumour

Gavin McLeod, though a man of meagre education, was as shrewd and observant as any person within fifty miles of Culm. Having lost his wife he lavished all his abundant affection on his only child — Sheila. But of late there had been a great change in Sheila. The high spirits which had been so outstanding a characteristic of her temperament were no longer in evidence, and any reference to Angus brought a queer flush to her cheeks. McLeod, putting two and two together, reached the heart of the problem with his habitual promptitude.

'Lass — ye're fretting,' he said. 'I'm no likin' to see your sweet eyes dull and moist. Come — out with it!'

Sheila turned her rather pallid face to him.

'It's — Angus, father.'

'Has he been upsetting ye — the young scoundrel?'

'No — no. It's — about our engagement. Father, I can't go on with it.'

McLeod opened his eyes wide.

'That's bad,' he said slowly. 'Where's the hitch?'

'I — I've changed my mind. I thought I knew it a year ago — but I realise now that I was too young. Being engaged was — attractive. I scarcely stopped to think that marriage was the natural outcome. But lately — I'm fond of Angus. He has done nothing to cause me to change my mind. The change is in myself. I am powerless to help it. It's just as if I had grown out of childhood and am looking at things from the viewpoint of my real self. I — I can't marry Angus because I don't love him as a woman should love — her husband.'

McLeod sat with heavy brow and compressed lips. He had long since taken it for granted that there would be a union between his family and Frasers, and that Sheila should change her mind was so remote a possibility that he had never even considered it.

'Maybe — maybe it's just a phase,' he said.

'No. For weeks — months — little doubts have been creeping in, and now I know beyond all doubting that I should never be happy as the wife of Angus. You don't know — how hard it is to say this, when I know that it is your great desire.'

'He's a braw laddie, Sheila.'

'I know. If he were not it would be easy to — to undo what has been done. It is the fear of hurting him terribly that has stilled my tongue for so long. And you — '

'You can leave me out of it. I'll admit I wanted this marriage to take place, but it's your happiness that is nearest my heart. I'll not have ye marry a man ye don't love — as your mither loved me.'

She flashed him a look of the deepest gratitude for his sympathy and understanding.

'And what about the lad — does he no suspect?'

'I fear not. We have been friends for so long. It is this friendship which he takes for love. It deludes him as it deluded me. He is calling to-night, father. I must tell him. I can't go on letting him believe — letting him dream of — of impossibilities. I wanted you to know first.'

He walked across to her and patted her shoulder paternally.

'It's going to hurt him, lass, but there's no help for it if ye feel as ye say you do.'

'I am quite sure — now,' she replied huskily. 'But how crude words are! If only I could let him see just how I feel about him. I want his friendship even though I

44

cannot give him love.'

'Why not — why not?'

But she knew as he knew that the blow would fall with appalling force on the sensitive Angus, and she prepared herself for the ordeal. Again and again her mind turned to the departed Donald. Both Angus and his father had asserted there had been a quarrel, but she found it exceedingly difficult to imagine Donald quarrelling with his own kith and kin — and with such apparent vehemence as to cause him to pack up and leave instantly. Never in all her life had she known Donald lose his temper. Angus in the heat of his excitable nature might do so, but Donald always seemed to have his emotions well in hand. It was strange — so strange that her mind kept reverting to it.

It was ironical too, that this should happen just when she had discovered herself — when the very sight of Donald was causing her to feel that at last the goal was clearly illumined. The knowledge that Donald had gone out of her life was like a deep knife-wound. It threw her back upon her own resources, and slammed a heavy door in her face. Possibly Donald would always remain a delightful memory, with himself ignorant until the end that a woman in the remote highlands had found her true love too late? Still, it made no difference to her resolution concerning Angus. Angus must not live in a fool's paradise. Friendship was going to be tested that night.

By the time Angus arrived her mind was as inflexible as the granite rocks that strewed the towering hills. She meant to be strong with the strength that her great revelation gave rise to. But she prayed that Angus would feel and understand how difficult her task was. She met him some distance from the house.

'I'm a bit late,' he said. 'It looks like a storm brewing, and I ran back for my coat.'

Sheila nodded as she looked across the hills at the brooding sky.

'Let us walk,' she said. 'Not far.'

He looked at her sharply, for her voice seemed a trifle strained and shaky.

'Is anything wrong, Sheila?'

'Yes. Everything is wrong. Angus, we have been friends for a very long time, haven't we?'

'What a question!'

'Much hangs upon it. I have something to tell you, Angus, that may break that friendship for ever.'

'Sheila! It isn't possible.'

'I trust not. It depends upon you — and you alone.'

'I tell you — What strange words you say, and how strangely you look at me. What is the matter? For God's sake tell me.'

'Angus, I want to be freed from my engagement.'

'Freed from — ! You don't mean that — you can't! It's just a joke to — to scare me. Sheila — !'

Her steady, somewhat sad, eyes gave him the definite response. A great shudder went over him. For a moment he could not speak, and then his words came falteringly.

'You — mean that?'

'Yes. It isn't you, Angus, that is the cause. You've done nothing to merit — this. I — I can't explain. All I know is that I — I am different. I tried to tell you yesterday — and many times before, but I lacked the courage. You've been good to me, considerate in all things and yet — I recoil before marriage. We shouldn't be happy, Angus — I know it.'

'Happy! Why, I would die for you.'

'I don't doubt even that. But love cannot be controlled — ordered into desired channels. I want you to free me, Angus. Won't you take back — your ring?'

He stared at the small hoop of gold and brilliants.

'Is this — the end?'

'Not of friendship,' she pleaded. 'If you

wanted that, it — it would break my heart. All that I have the power to give, I give. But love — Angus, will you try to understand?'

'Yes,' he replied stoutly. 'You must do what you think is best for your own happiness. You know how I've cared — how I've dreamed about the future — But that is like chiding you, when you have done your best to lessen the blow. It — it must be as you wish.'

He took the ring from her, gazed at it for a moment, and then slipped it into his pocket.

'And now — am I to go?'

'Angus, does this cancel the years and years of friendship?'

'Not on my part.'

'Then let us walk, and talk — as we used.'

'Yes — yes. But I warn you, Sheila, I am not giving up hope. I'll not pester you — but at least permit me to hope that things may change — one day.'

'No one has the right to try and drive out hope,' she replied softly. 'I admire you more than ever, Angus, for the way you — you've helped me,' she added.

Half an hour later the storm broke. The thunder rolled over the hills and a great deluge of rain descended. Through a welter of water Angus led her home, and then went back to his own farm with a heavy heart.

★ ★ ★

Weeks passed and every day the Frasers waited on the postman, each anxious for a word from Donald, though Fraser himself would have died rather than admit it. Then at long last came a post-card for Angus. It was headed 'S.S. *ORINCO* — at sea!' and contained but four words, '*Going strong, old boy.*' Angus cunningly left it lying on the table after breakfast, and later he stole in and saw his mother with it in her hand. Her face became pink with embarrassment.

'All right, mother,' he said, kissing her. 'It came this morning. I thought you might like — '

'God bless you! At sea! How did he get the money to — ?'

'He's working his passage.'

'Yes — yes, of course. But where to?'

Angus shook his head. He had no doubt that his first conclusion was correct. He imagined Don, swabbing decks, perhaps stoking furnaces. He saw in every detail that fine healthy face — so full of determination. Don on the wide, free seas — bound for some distant port, and he, Angus, eating out his heart amid the old surroundings.

'Wherever he is bound, mother, it is to a land of promise.'

'Yes, Don will succeed — he must!' she said emphatically. 'Angus, I've never asked you before, but did he never — did he never confide in you about — about — ?'

The hands of Angus closed until the knuckles grew white under the tight skin. For the twentieth time he was near to breaking his promise to Don, but the old loyalty triumphed. Don had made that noble sacrifice — for him and Sheila. Until Don gave him permission to divulge the truth he must be silent, though this silence caused him to feel, at times, a contempt for himself. With the engagement broken the argument was less strong, but Don must be obeyed even against his own burning desire to vindicate his brother.

He refrained from replying to his mother's question, for never in his life had he lied to her. As for Sheila, there still remained a small spark of hope. No longer they talked of love, but friendship remained. The news had come as a surprise to his parents, but like wise folk they let the matter drop. Sheila was always welcome at the farm, and never by an indiscreet word did they cause her to feel embarrassed.

'I've heard from Don, Sheila.'

Her brown eyes opened.

'He is on a ship — working his passage, I think. Can you imagine him as a sailor?'

Sheila could have imagined him as anything in which courage and purposiveness were needed. But she said nothing. Angus never guessed the secret that was locked up in her breast, and she saw no need to reveal it since she felt that Donald had vanished for ever.

The summer passed into autumn and winter's edge was felt. The long-threatened snow now lay on the summit of Ben Tavis, and thin ice formed on the still marges of the lock. One day, while in Culm, McLeod heard a strange rumour. It was to the effect that Donald had been sent from home in disgrace. McLeod forcefully denied it, but the gossiper stuck to his guns, and his auditors seemed more inclined to believe him than they did McLeod.

'I'll no listen to sich scandal,' said McLeod. 'For shame on ye all.'

But in his own heart there were doubts. Fraser had certainly been most secretive about his elder son's sudden departure, and if ever Donald's name was mentioned there was a noticeable tightening of his face.

Christmas came and passed and a New Year dance was announced to take place in Culm. Angus wondered whether, in the circumstances, Sheila would go with him. He hesitated about asking her, but at last put aside his qualms. To his delight she agreed to go.

'Splendid!' he said. 'I haven't had a dance for months.'

The local function was well-attended, and Sheila found herself in great demand, for in Culm the male element predominated. She was relieved to find that Angus displayed no aversion to her many partners, and she admired him more and more for his sensible behaviour. Her last partner was a young clerk employed at the local bank. He was a garrulous individual but a very fair dancer.

'Who is the girl Angus Fraser is dancing with?' he asked.

Sheila shook her head.

'Rather pretty. I heard that Angus was engaged to a girl. I suppose — '

Sheila's mouth twitched.

'I wonder what became of his brother — Donald?'

'I think he went abroad.'

'Hm! He didn't look the sort of fellow who would turn out — that way.'

'What do you mean?' she asked, trying to conceal her surprise at the remark.

'He got into awful trouble. His father tried

to hush it up, but of course you can't hush up a thing like that in a small place like Culm.'

'Hush up — what?'

'Surely you must have heard?'

She shook her head, fearing to say a word.

'It was to do with a cheque. Donald got into a mess — financially — and — and forged a cheque.'

Sheila's heart seemed to turn cold in her breast.

'Of course everybody knows — though they pretend not to. They say it nearly broke Fraser's heart.'

'I — I don't believe it,' she said chokingly.

'It's true. I happen to know it's true.'

'How can you — ?'

'It was at our bank.' Then, fearing that he had said too much, 'Please regard that as confidential.'

Fortunately the music stopped at that moment. He led her back to her seat, and then apparently alarmed at her obvious agitation, beat a quick retreat. Angus came up and found her staring into space, wide-eyed and trembling.

'They're going to play 'Auld Lang Syne' and then break up,' he said. 'Come on — join the circle.'

Sheila was aware that her hands were being pumped up and down, and that there was great laughter and rejoicing. She herself tried to laugh — but the effort was like a great pain. What she had heard was so unexpected — so unbelievable — it stunned her. On the way home she made monosyllabic responses to Angus' remarks, for her mind was far away. When they reached her home she bade him good night automatically. McLeod was sitting up, waiting for her, for he had seen the new year in in his own fashion.

'Enjoyed yourself, Sheila?' he asked.

'Yes — no,' she stammered.

'Eh!'

An impulse came to confide in him — to discover if he had heard anything of this foul rumour.

'Father, I've heard something — something awful to-night. They are saying that Donald — Donald left home in disgrace — that he — that he forged a cheque.'

McLeod started, and in an instant she divined that he too had heard this outrageous calumny.

'It isn't true?' she said hoarsely. 'It can't be true.'

'It sounds — incredible,' he replied slowly.

'Even you believe it. I can see it in your eyes.'

'Lass, I would have been the last man in the world to believe it if his own father had denied it.'

'What do you mean?'

'I saw Fraser to-night. We toasted the new year. I thought it my duty to tell him — what I too had heard.'

'Yes — yes. Didn't he say it was a lie?'

McLeod shook his head sadly.

'He wud speak no word,' he added slowly.

'Then — then — !'

Her throat seemed to close up at the significance of her father's remark. Fraser had not denied that allegation. His own father had remained dumb! Could anything be more damning than this? And it seemed to explain so much — Angus' agitation whenever she mentioned his brother, Mrs. Fraser's sad eyes, the sudden flight from the old home, the lack of correspondence. She would have to be without sense of reason not to draw the inevitable conclusion. Yet something within her rebelled against the idea of such a possibility. Stubbornly she shut her mind to all the evidence of guilt. Until Donald himself told her with his own lips she would not believe it. Faith — illogical faith — remained yet.

That night she knelt by her bed and

uttered the first spoken prayer that she had given voice to for many a month, in a voice that was vibrant with emotion.

'O God — be good to him. Be good to him, O Lord!'

6

The Land of Promise

In a small shack situated in the foothills of
the Rocky Mountains, Donald Fraser sat and
smoked over a blazing log-fire. His features
relaxed into a smile as he thought he saw
in the flames little visions of another land,
nearly five thousand miles away. Over two
years had elapsed since he had stolen away
from the old home at Culm, and during that
period he had experienced many vicissitudes.
The little farm which he now ran was the
result of enormous energy and unrelenting
thrift. It was still heavily mortgaged, but
month by month the incubus was being
reduced.

He had started from home practically
penniless, working his passage out from
Greenock. On touching Canadian soil he
had found a job of sorts, changing it shortly
after for another which offered bigger scope.
No amount of temporary set-backs could
quell the indomitable spirit within him. He
aimed at one thing and kept that objective
constantly before his mind's eye — a farm

of his own in the beautiful West.

The worst was now over, he thought. He had got a foothold and meant to hang on with the tenaciousness of a leech. The previous owner had made a hash of things, and had sold out for a song — glad to touch Donald's dollars. Little by little this hard-bitten son of the highlands was succeeding where the lesser man had failed. To his neighbours — men who farmed on a much larger scale — it was a miracle, for the land he held had long been voted a 'bad patch.' But Donald had ploughed out the rocks, and blown up the tree stumps while other men slept. Where half a dozen cattle had grazed there was now half a hundred.

Railhead and market was ten miles distant — at Albany, whither the main line of the C.P.R. went westward to the Pacific coast. Looking from the window Donald could see the wonderful bulwark of the mountains against the sky, with snow on the higher peaks and pine forests climbing to the timber-line. It was much like his native land on a vaster scale, and at times he imagined he was back in Culm, amid the scenes of his childhood.

Loneliness! Yes, he had suffered that at first. But nostalgia had now worn off. Before him dangled that bright jewel — Success.

His one aim was to achieve that — and then to steal back to the old home and have a look at things there. He imagined that Angus must be married by this time. Dear old impetuous, scatterbrained Angus! Well, Sheila would make him a good wife — bless her sweet brown eyes!

Then he grew very reflective as he recalled the days when he too had dreamed a wonderful dream — with Sheila at the back of it. Of course, it had been presumptuous on his part. He was not the sort of man that a girl like Sheila would lose her heart to. Women liked vivacity. Yes, Angus had that.

A knock came on the door, and a queer individual entered. He was a half-breed man — a mixture of Cree and something else, with a dash of Gallic blood in his make-up. Possessing a name which few persons could pronounce with ease, he was known locally as Slocum, the origin of which Donald never discovered. He was Donald's trusted hired man, and was as capable as he was unprepossessing.

'Hullo, Slocum! Anything wrong?'

Slocum pulled at a lock of his lank hair which depended over his frost-bitten ear.

'Wanna go Albany. Daughter ver' sick.'

'That's bad news. You'd better take Sally — but don't over-drive her.'

Slocum nodded and went out. It was true he had a daughter in Albany, but Donald rather suspected his excuse was a fabrication, and that Slocum's real object was a game of faro or poker. He settled down to a book, but was aroused a little later by the arrival of a horse. He thought it was Slocum, returned for some reason, but the subsequent rap on the door was unlike the half-breed's summons.

'Come in!' he shouted.

A woman of about twenty-two entered, clad in riding skirt and long boots. She was dark as a Spaniard, and had large and very bold eyes. Donald put down the book and stood up.

'Hullo, Rose! This is unexpected.'

'I've just come back from Albany with father's mail. There happened to be a letter for you, so I thought I'd bring it and save delay.'

'That's good of you.'

'Here it is.'

It was the first letter he had received for months, and it was nothing more important than a notification that his insurance premium was overdue. Rose settled herself in a chair and rubbed her hands together before the fire.

'All alone, Don?'

'Yes. Slocum has just gone to Albany.'

'I passed him on the road. Gee, the winter's coming.'

Donald nodded. He wanted her to go, for she had a habit of getting on his nerves. It was so obvious that the letter she had brought was of no importance — since it bore the address of the insurance company — that her two-mile ride from the Willeton ranch seemed quite unnecessary. He had no great love for Willeton or his daughter, and had not been averse to letting them realise it. Willeton was a blustering man of fifty, mean and grasping, and Rose was much the same, with a lot of feminine faults thrown in. On one occasion she had — under no provocation whatever — called Slocum a 'dirty Indian' and struck him with her riding-whip. But to Donald she was all sugar-candy.

'How are things?' she asked.

'Not too bad.'

'Father was saying he wouldn't mind buying your farm.'

'It isn't for sale — thank you.'

'Doesn't it depend upon price?'

'Not in the least. There are many things in the world that money cannot buy.'

'I've never seen anything yet,' she retorted.

'You may — one day.'

'You are very short with me to-night, Don,' she said. 'You're the worst-tempered man for miles.'

He laughed at the rebuke. Of late he was quite aware that she was paying him marked attentions. Though she had known him for less than a year it was 'Don this' and 'Don that' regardless of the fact that he had done his best to steer clear of her. Moreover, it had come to his knowledge through Slocum that she was not averse to giving people to understand that she and her big neighbour were on the most intimate terms. This nocturnal visit to his shack was not an act of which he approved, and it aroused in him mild resentment.

'Is your father at home?' he asked.

'Yes.'

'And he knew — you were coming here?'

'Of course not. I should have been a fool to tell him.'

He frowned at this, and filled his pipe reflectively, while Rose watched him from the corners of her dark eyes.

'Father's an idiot where — where men are concerned,' she volunteered.

'You must go back at once. It is very late.'

'Of course I am going back. What else did you imagine?'

Donald felt, and looked, as if he would like to administer a sound spanking for this naïve retort. He was fast coming to realise that Rose was an audacious man-hunter, and that he in this case had been chosen as the victim. So far as he was concerned his heart was absolutely untouched by her, and on more than one occasion he had been near to telling her exactly what he thought of her.

'When are you going to call on us?' she asked.

'I'm a busy man.'

'You aren't very busy now,' she said, glancing at the book which he had picked up.

'I am busy trying to improve my mind.'

'Does it need improving?'

'Most of our minds need improving.'

She laughed and shrugged her plump shoulders. Time after time she found herself up against an iceberg, and it rankled in her mind.

'It's your manners need improving — not your mind, Don,' she said tartly.

'I'm sorry. I had no intention to be rude.'

'But you are. You are so horribly brusque — and after I have risked father's wrath by coming across to you.'

'It was foolish of you.'

'There you go again! Oh, you bear! I won't stay a moment longer.'

Donald sighed with relief when at last the door closed after her, and peace was ushered in. He had no wish to appear unneighbourly, but Rose made any kind of intimacy dangerous. She wanted to play with fire, which was not at all Donald's intention. He tried to give his mind up to reading.

Slocum returned in the early hours of the morning, but despite this he was up and about at sunrise. In reply to Donald's enquiry he asserted that his daughter was not so bad as he imagined.

'How much did you lose?' asked Donald.

Slocum opened his mouth, and then grinned.

'Not lose — make six dollar.'

Donald laughed and started the daily spell of unremitting toil, snatching but an hour for a meal at noon. From the top of the hill on his small patch of land he could see the big Willeton ranch in the distance, with cattle grazing up the valley, and he wondered if ever his own holding would be as imposing. A few days later business sent him on a trip to Albany, where he was successful in disposing of some produce at a good price. While he was there he met a neighbour from a farm to the east of Willetons, with whom he was on very friendly terms.

'Well met, Fraser! You don't often come to town.'

'As little as possible. I prefer my shack.'

'You're sure a modern Diogenes. But maybe there's another reason, eh?'

He prodded Donald in the ribs, playfully, but the significance of the remark was lost upon him.

'There's a good reason, Gillet — I can't afford the time.'

'Exactly!' responded Gillet. 'And how is she?'

Donald stared at him.

'How is — who?'

'You sly oppossum! As if everybody doesn't know!'

'What does everybody know?' asked Donald, raising his eyebrows. 'Let's get down to bedrock.'

'The Willeton girl. You can't hope to go on throwing dust in our eyes.'

'Rose Willeton!' Donald's normally calm eyes blazed. 'Gillet, you don't imagine that I and Rose — ? Great Scott! You must be crazy.'

But Gillet still believed he was being hoodwinked.

'It won't do, Donald,' he said. 'Rose has got one in before you. She told us last Sunday.'

'She told you — !'

'Yep. Maybe it was intended to be confidential. Anyway, there is no harm done. My congratulations!'

He wrung Donald's hand, while Donald gasped for breath, and then went off to intercept a friend, leaving his late auditor still dazed with what he had heard. When at last his brain functioned he thought he saw Rose's scheme. Shamelessly she was hinting to her neighbours that an understanding had been arrived at between herself and Donald. At first it looked like sheer foolishness, but a little reflection led him to conclude that her first object was to warn off any other female admirer — leaving the field clear for a straight hunt.

It aroused Donald's deepest resentment, and his first impulse was to see her and demand how she dare utter such abominable falsehoods. But on second thoughts he took pen and paper and wrote a letter that was calculated to knock some sense into the conniving Rose. It was neatly done, and ten minutes after the last word was written Slocum was on his way to Willetons.

Rose was alone in the house when Slocum arrived, and the half-breed handed her the letter with a scowl that was engendered by his memory of the insults she had laid upon him. She waved him away haughtily and went to her bedroom to peruse the epistle.

DEAR MISS WILLETON, —

It has come to my knowledge that you have been making certain statements — coupling my name with yours — for which there is positively no foundation at all. I must ask you to cease making such wild assertions, or I shall be reluctantly compelled to announce broadcast that I have never had, and never shall have, such intentions as you impute to me.

Yours faithfully,
DONALD FRASER

A little hiss of rage left her lips, and she crushed the letter in her strong hands. There was no regret, no sorrow at receiving her congé — merely hate for the man who had written those stinging words. She was used to getting her own way — especially with men, and this blow to her pride was deep. Love was off now. The dominating passion was hate. She wanted to humble this new arrival who had been proof against her blandishments. Immediately she looked about her for the means to do so.

7

Humiliation

Though Willeton exercised a rigid supervision, his ranch was actually run by his foreman, Aldous Lee, who hailed from Arizona and knew all there was to be known about stock. Lee was a man of considerable ambition, but he possessed a weakness for gambling which had had disastrous effects upon his career. He was a sour individual, hated by most of his 'boys' and by some of his neighbours. Yet it had to be admitted he was efficient to the last iota.

In the course of his duties Lee had fallen foul of Donald, and the trouble had arisen through the breaking of the boundary fence that divided the two holdings. Lee had ridden out one morning to find some of Donald's stock calmly grazing on Willeton's succulent grass — a mile from where they should have been. He drove them off and met Donald near the boundary.

'Keep your damned cattle off our land,' he shouted.

Donald drove the roving beasts through

the gap and then walked up to Lee.

'There's no need to use violent language,' he said. 'I'm not responsible for the wind.'

'Wind! Yah!'

'Do you suggest I made that gap?'

'I shouldn't be surprised. The same thing happened a month ago. I'll shoot 'em if I find 'em here again.'

Donald's face tightened up.

'I should walk warily, Mr. Lee,' he said cuttingly. 'You don't own the earth — yet.'

Lee glared at him and, with a savage curse, rode away. Since that day Donald had met Lee at intervals in various circumstances and always Lee had scowled at him. He did not know that at the back of Lee's mind was a burning hatred caused by Rose's infatuation for her neighbour. But Lee had eyes to see, and knew what was going on.

It was to Lee that Rose turned in her unrelenting animosity for Donald. With feminine intuition she had summed up Lee's feelings and knew she was safe. The desire to humble the proud man who had cast away the pearls which she offered, was now an obsession.

'What do you think of Mr. Fraser?' she asked Lee one morning.

'Darned upstart!'

'Evidently you don't like him?'

'One of these days I'll break his blamed neck.'

'I wish you would, Aldous.'

He stared at her in amazement.

'I suppose that surprises you? You thought I was very friendly with him?'

'Wal, I kinder — '

'I was — until he insulted me. Now I hate him.'

Lee gave her a side glance, and saw the trembling bosom and the flashing eyes.

'Guess we've a whole lot in common,' he said.

'What has he done to you?'

'Stung me with his darned tongue. But I'll get quits with him — one day.'

'One day! Why one day?'

'When the chance comes.'

'One should make chances, Aldous. Suppose the chance was here now — what would you do?'

'What are you getting at?'

She looked about her furtively.

'It's just a simple idea,' she said. 'But I think it might work.'

* * *

To Donald's great joy he saw no more of Rose. Apparently the letter had served its purpose, and this means was much preferable to angry words. He went about his work, feeling that he had choked her off definitely. Since taking over the farm he had sent no word to his people. Prior to that he had scribbled a card from time to time, informing them that he was well, but giving no address to which they might reply. That stratagem gave them a way out — he thought. Possibly they would not feel like writing back. He knew the old stubborn pride. But now the desire to hear the news from home was strong within him. He wanted to hear that they were all well — that Angus was happily married, and that a certain memorable incident was in process of being forgotten.

He sat down and began to write. Skilful with his pen he drew an alluring picture of his present surroundings — the rolling foothills, the vast bulwark of the mountains that backed them, the big winds that came shrieking down the valley, the flowers in summer, the wonderful colourings of the beeches and maples in the fall. Then followed a humorous description of Slocum, and an impression of Albany's big cattle market. Love to them all, especially to any possible niece or nephew! That made him wince, but he smiled again immediately. There must be no jealousy — no envy where Angus was concerned. Lucky Angus!

On the following morning he received a great surprise. Aldous Lee rode up to the shack, and Donald could see half a dozen of Willeton's 'boys' in the background. He strolled out and looked up at Lee's leather face.

'What's the trouble?'

'We've lost six head of prime cattle.'

'Well?'

'There still a hole in your fence. They may have got through.'

'They haven't. My land's not big enough to conceal strayed cattle. You ought to know that.'

'I'm not so sure.'

The innuendo was plain enough, and Donald's face flushed angrily. He pointed to the gate.

'Get out!'

Lee's mouth became twisted in a sneer, but he rode away the next instant, mumbling something unintelligible. Donald turned to the waiting Slocum.

'You heard what he said?'

'Yes, boss. But Slocum count cattle jus' now. He big dam liar.'

Donald forgot the incident during the morning, but an hour after the midday meal Lee rode in again, with Willeton himself and some 'boys.' Slocum ran round to the corral where Donald was working.

'Lee come again, with Willeton — big trouble.'

'Confound them and their cattle! I'll go and talk to them.'

When he reached the group of riders he saw at once that Willeton was out of temper. His neighbour had never been very friendly but at this moment he looked absolutely murderous.

'Good morning, Mr. Fraser!' he said with cutting emphasis. 'We're hunting up some cattle that is missing.'

'I've heard that. But I told Lee — '

'I know what you told Lee, but it doesn't go.'

'What do you mean?'

'Maybe you'd have no objection to coming right along, and seeing for yourself?'

'I've no time to waste,' said Donald curtly.

He was turning on his heel when a rope spun out and he found his arms neatly lasooed to his sides. Lee sat grinning at him with the other end of the rope in his hands.

'Forward!' said Willeton.

Lee heeled his mount forward and Donald was nearly jerked off his feet. Speechless with rage he half-walked, half-ran over the rough ground, with the tight lariat biting into his flesh. The faithful Slocum tried to get near him to cut the lariat, but a horse was driven into him and Slocum measured his length on the ground.

Willeton's party made for an old disused quarry that lay at the farther end of Donald's land. It was now much overgrown and had a depth of about thirty feet. At the entrance Willeton held up his hand and the riders stopped. He turned to Donald.

'Look over there — you liar!'

A jerk on the lariat projected Donald forward. To his amazement he saw Willeton's lost cattle, all tethered to a stout stake.

'I lost a bigger bunch two months back,' said Willeton. 'Now I know where they went.'

'This is a dirty conspiracy,' said Donald in a hoarse voice. 'I told you the truth. I know nothing about this.'

'Don't you? And who has been trying to obliterate the brand? Are you asking me to believe it was a ghost?'

Donald remained silent, but his expression betrayed his real emotions. To be branded as a common rustler and a liar in the bargain was exasperating to the last degree. He smiled under his suppressed anger.

'Laughing, are ye?' snapped Willeton. 'I'll

give you something to laugh about. Twenty years ago we shot cattle-thieves on sight. But there's another kind of medicine to-day. Set those beasts free, Lee, and make him fast to that stake.'

Lee dismounted and did as he was bid with the tethered cattle. Then he turned to Donald. Donald swung away from him and faced Willeton.

'You wouldn't dare,' he said hoarsely.

'Wouldn't I — by God! This is a law-abiding country, I guess, and fellows who break it have only themselves to blame for anything that may come to them. Get him, Lee — and you, Dave!'

A second man dismounted, and Donald was seized roughly. He made no resistance, since it would be useless, and a few minutes later he was lashed to the stake, back towards the stockmen. Willeton handed his quirt to Dave.

'Give him a dozen of the best,' he snapped.

Dave complied and the tough thong bit through Donald's shirt. But he did not feel any physical pain. The thing that hurt and enraged him was the bitter humiliation that Willeton in his fiendish rage was subjecting him to. Everything went red before his eyes.

'Twelve!' said Willeton ultimately. 'That'll do, Dave. Maybe he'll think twice before he attempts rustling again. Leave him there. That dirty breed will cut him down.'

Donald heard them ride away. A few minutes later he became aware of Slocum's presence. There was a flash of steel and the bonds fell away from him. He turned round slowly and saw the half-breed's eyes focussed full on him.

'All right, Slocum,' he said, forcing a smile. 'No bones broken.'

'The dog! One day I keel him, by gar!'

Donald laid a restraining hand upon him and shook his head.

'You can leave it to me, Slocum. I'll settle this little matter before very long.'

'Better to keel —'

'Come, we are wasting time. There is work to do.'

'I come, boss.'

They walked back to the shack in dead silence, Slocum aching for blood, and Donald smarting from a sense of injustice. What to do in regard to the matter he scarcely knew. He had no doubt that Lee would publish the news broadcast. Before justice could be done it was necessary to discover who had engineered the plot. That Lee was in it he had no doubt, but at the back of his mind there lurked another figure — Rose. He was reluctant to think that Rose, even in her outraged vanity, could sink to this, but he had to admit that with her passions mounted high. If she hated she would hate with all the intensity of her unrelenting nature. With her there were no half measures.

It was only now he realised that his lacerated back was bleeding badly — and that his shirt was saturated. Rose, or Lee, or the pair together had drawn first blood. It was not revenge he craved for, but the satisfying of the deeply implanted sense of justice that was the keynote to his nature. He dispatched Slocum on a job and walked towards the shack with a view to attending to his injuries.

But a surprise was in store for him, big enough to sweep from his mind even the recent humiliating incident. He saw a brown mare tethered to the railings and a woman apparently coming away from the entrance. For a moment he thought it was Rose, until her face came round fully. Then recognition leapt to his eyes, and with a shout he ran forward — hands outstretched.

'Sheila!' he gasped.

8

Tragedy

Donald's surprise at meeting Sheila is better imagined than described. He stood wringing her hands for a moment, letting his eyes range over the soft alluring face, that was now crimson with blushes. Then, to his embarrassment, he saw her eyes go to his bloodstained shirt.

'Don! Why, your — '

'I had a bit of an accident,' he prevaricated. 'I was just about to look to it when you — But, Sheila, this is wonderful. It must mean that — that Angus — Come, where are you hiding, Angus?'

Her mouth twitched and she shook her head slowly.

'I am here — alone, Don. I am staying with Rhoda Fergusson at Black Rock. She came to Canada with her father five years ago, and quite recently she begged me to come and stay with her. Don't you remember the Fergussons?'

'Yes, but I didn't know they were in this part of the country.'

'Less than five miles away. It is strange you haven't met them.'

'I knew there was a Fergusson living at Black Rock, but never imagined it was anyone I had known in Scotland.'

'They were equally ignorant. But Rhoda in one of her letters mentioned your name and I — I wondered — '

He let the hiatus pass, for his mind was busy with other things. To him this meeting was a remarkable coincidence, but he did not know that Sheila's acceptance of a long-standing invitation was due to causes other than a desire to see her old school friend again.

'Why have you never written, Donald?' she asked reprovingly.

'But I have.'

'Just a card — from nowhere. Two years have passed and we — we have wondered — '

He winced at this, and then smiled.

'Well, I have made amends. I have just written a long epistle home — telling the old folks all the news. You see, Sheila, I left home under rather unhappy circumstances. It was necessary to — to let time pass and bury the enmity. In addition I wanted to be able to say that I was making good. Will you, will you wait a few minutes while I change my clothes?'

'Yes — yes. I had forgotten your injury. How selfish of me to keep — '

'It's nothing — just a scratch. Come right inside — and don't look too closely at my humble abode.'

While he made himself more presentable she gazed round the shack, but the place was by no means repellent. It was essentially a man's abode, but as clean as a new pin. Here and there were the products of his industrious hands — a home-made woollen rug, a neatly carved bookcase carrying some good reading matter, a low stool fashioned from a solid block of red pine. In a corner were fishing rods, a gun, and some skins. Beside her, on the table, was a long corncob pipe which he smoked in the long evenings. She took it up and smiled as she gazed on it.

'Hope I haven't been long,' he said, entering the room.

She dropped the pipe hastily.

'You are quite a quick-change artist. And this is where you live?'

'Most of the time. At intervals I go out adventuring.'

'Aren't you lonely?'

'Not now. I have a hired man — a curious specimen whom I call Slocum. We get on very well together.' There was an awkward silence, and then he put the question which she feared. 'Is — Angus all right?'

'Yes. He was when I left.'

'I suppose — I suppose you are married now?'

She shook her head and tried to avert her eyes.

'But — !'

'It — it never came to that, Don,' she added huskily. 'We — we talked it over and decided that — that we weren't suited.'

Donald's amazed eyes swept her fair form. Such a possibility had never even entered his mind.

'Not suited!' he repeated. 'But you — and he — '

'I can understand your surprise. Don't think it was Angus' fault. It was I who — who broke it off, because I felt — '

She was obviously very distressed, and he realised it was cruel to dwell on a subject which must be painful to her. But at the same time his sympathy went out to Angus, who for years had dreamed of the future and all that it held.

'Perhaps — perhaps it may yet come right,' he ventured.

To this she made no response, and he wondered what Angus could have done to bring about this unexpected situation. Had it happened soon after his departure from home he might have ascribed it to a lover's tiff, but more than two years had passed since he had made the sacrifice for Angus. And during most of that time he had had visions of Angus and Sheila happily married, building a family . . . Yet in his heart he felt that the end was not yet. Sheila would come to realise that the old love was very strong. Perhaps even this temporary parting would result in rehabilitation. But all the same two years — two precious years — of happiness had been lost to them.

'How long are you staying with the Fergussons?' he asked.

'It depends upon many things. You know that my father has never really prospered at Culm. For years he has been thinking of emigrating. He looked upon this visit of mine as a chance to discover what kind of prospects there are here. I am to write him and give him full details, and then he is going to decide whether he will come out and join me.'

'So it is possible you may not return to Scotland?'

'Just — possible,' she said brokenly.

'Does Ang — ?' Again he was thinking of the beloved brother, but he checked himself to avoid causing her pain. 'How long have you been here?'

'Only a week. I think I am going to like it. Of course Culm was beautiful, but here are new interests — a new world. One feels there is so much to be done — that the next-door neighbour is not crowding you out.'

He laughed at the idea, and tried to get rid of the vision of Angus.

'You've changed, Don,' she said.

'I wasn't aware of it.'

'But you have. I always thought you were just a little reserved — almost shy at times. That has gone.'

'Has it? Perhaps you are right, Sheila. The world is a big place, and I knocked around a bit before I settled here. I've added a little to a half-baked education. I've lived with men in strange circumstances, listened to queer tales, and realised that life can hold some pretty awful blows.'

'And no rewards?' she asked sharply.

'Aye, rewards in plenty — but not immediately. You see, up there in Culm we were just a small family — we and our neighbours. We jostled each other and could, more or less, tell where we would be and what we would be doing the following week, or the following year. I suppose we grew a little stale just because of that. I was content to jog along, looking forward to old age and — and the inevitable. I vegetated. Yes, Sheila, I almost grew into a vegetable.'

'Not you, Don. You were always active — alert.'

'In body, but not in mind. In this big land of possibilities a fellow gets a new outlook. He has to go up or go under. There's no standing still.'

He was the living illustration of his own assertions. She thought he seemed to vibrate under the quick pulse of abundant life, and she read in his steady blue eyes the reinforced determination that had always been his outstanding trait.

'Show me your holding,' she begged.

A glorious hour was spent in her company, during which she appraised the work of his hands. When at last she departed she cajolled a promise from him to call at Fergussons soon and make the somewhat belated acquaintanceship of Fergusson and his daughter. Her coming had shaken him deeply, for it was the last thing in the world that he had expected. He recalled the day when he had nurtured the hope that his secret love for her would bear fruit, then the repression of that desire — because of Angus. Now, for some reason, Angus had lost the love he had so swiftly won, and the field was clear — He shook his head and frowned at his own thoughts.

On anointing his lacerated back that night his mind turned to the Willeton incident, and his blood ran hotly at the injustice and humiliation that he had suffered. The desire to get this wrong righted was an obsession. But in his dreams he forgot all about it. There Sheila held the field — a radiant vision towards which he found himself fighting his way — until the shadow of Angus intervened.

It was on the morrow that Sheila heard a distressing and almost incredible rumour. Rhoda Fergusson had questioned her about her visit to Donald, and nodded her head strangely when Sheila told her, with unconcealed excitement, that their neighbour was the man who had vanished from Culm two years before.

'You — you were great friends, weren't you?' asked Rhoda with raised eyelids.

'Yes. We have known each other since we were children.'

'Hm!'

'Aren't you very friendly — with Fraser?' asked Sheila.

'I have never seen him — except at a distance. He doesn't appear to seek any kind of social life. I heard he was very friendly with Rose Willeton, but that is all over now — I imagine.'

'Why?'

'I — I scarcely like to tell you,' demurred Rhoda.

'Is it something detrimental?'

'Yes.'

'Then I shouldn't believe it — about Donald.'

'Lee swears it is true.'

'Then I may as well know in order to be forearmed.'

'Lee says that Fraser stole some cattle belonging to Willeton — that Willeton and some of his boys found them hidden away in an old pit. Willeton was so enraged he had Fraser lashed to a stake and horsewhipped him.'

'Horsewhipped him!' gasped Sheila.

'Yes. It sounds brutal, but — '

'There is some mistake. Donald couldn't do a thing — When did this happen?'

'Yesterday.'

Sheila winced as she recalled the injured back of Donald. He had told her it was due to an accident, and now — Meeting him again had had the effect of dulling her recollection of another incident in which Donald's name was mentioned. Her old stout loyalty suffered a heavy blow.

'It — it sounds incredible,' she said.

'I am afraid there is little room for doubt. Willeton wouldn't have gone to such extremes if he were not positive.'

This left Sheila in a difficult position, since she had asked Donald to call on Fergusson. She wondered whether she ought to ride over and explain the state of things. With this ugly story going round Fergusson would certainly not give Donald a warm welcome. While she was still procrastinating Donald decided to pay the promised visit. Fortunately Sheila saw him from a distance, and instantly went to intercept him.

'So — so you've come?' she said lamely.

'Yes. I managed to snatch an hour or two.'

'Don, I — I think it would be better if — if you didn't call on Fergusson.'

He gazed at her confused countenance, and at once he divined what she was concealing.

'I understand,' he said. 'I gather that our friend Willeton has been talking?'

'Yes — at least Lee has. It would be better not to bring about an embarrassing situation.'

'I agree. Well, I had better get back. Thanks for coming to — to warn me.'

He turned his horse, but she caught the bridle before he could get moving.

'Don, you do me a great injustice,' she said. 'Why are you so cruel?'

'You mean that you — you don't believe that story?'

'Not unless you tell me with your own lips that it is true.'

'Part of it is true. They found the cattle on my land — hidden away. They — they took the law into their own hands.' She saw his mouth twitch and the fine eyes narrow. 'But I had nothing to do with that. If ever I discover who planned that dirty scheme — '

There was no need to finish the sentence. In every line of his face the burning sense of injustice was expressed. She caught his hand and pressed it.

'All right, Don. That's good enough for me. Tether the horse and let us walk.'

So for a blessed hour these two revived the past, but at times there were awkward pauses, and Sheila was compelled to recall Donald's flight from home, and the accusations that had been made. It was significant that he never mentioned that memorable day.

9

Doubts

With Sheila living within easy reach of him, Donald found life a very different thing, but there were several big flaws in his happiness. The largest was due to the fact that the news of the alleged cattle-stealing had been spread far and wide by the hateful Lee and his associates. When Donald next went to Albany he found himself under the lash of scornful eyes. He tried to be indifferent to this clearly expressed animosity, but did not quite succeed, and on one occasion when he overheard one of Willeton's men retailing the story anew he lost his temper completely.

The upshot was a brawl in which the cowpuncher was laid out on the floor of the saloon. Donald hurried away, regretting the incident, for he realised that the gossiper had only narrated things as he saw them. Resorting to brute force was no solution. On the contrary it helped to place him further and further beyond the pale. Lee heard about the brawl and passed on the news to Willeton.

'That darned rustler been beating up one of our boys,' he snarled.

'Fraser?'

'Yep. It's time we put a spoke in that fellow's wheel for good.'

Willeton gnawed at his moustache. To him Donald's name was like a red rag to a bull.

'I'd buy him out even now, to get rid of him,' he muttered.

'He wouldn't sell. He's as stubborn as a blamed mule. Better shoot him out.'

'Can't do that. But give him long enough rope and he'll hang himself.'

'I wish he'd make a start.'

It was inevitable that Sheila should meet the Willetons, for the Fergussons were on very friendly terms with their prosperous neighbour. She went as a matter of duty, but her heart was opposed to it, for it seemed like disloyalty to Donald, who, she was convinced, had been unjustly treated. Rose Willeton was quite effusive.

'I've heard so much about you from Rhoda,' she chirped. 'Fancy your spending the whole winter here.'

'Why not?'

'Most visitors leave when the maples change their colour.'

'Is the winter so hard?'

'One gets used to it — even to welcome it, but to a stranger the cold is inclined to be discomfiting.'

'You forget I came from the Scotch Highlands. Mr. Fergusson swears that Scotland has Canada easily beaten in that respect. But I am rather anxious to find out for myself.'

Rose's bold eyes roved over Sheila's beautiful face. She had already heard that Sheila was 'scouting round' on her father's behalf, and that that was her excuse for spending so long a sojourn at Black Rock. But she had also come to learn that Sheila was seeing a great deal of the man who had jilted her, and putting two and two together she arrived at the conclusion that Sheila's object was other than it was purported to be.

'Rhoda was telling me that you knew Donald Fraser before he came to Canada,' she said mischievously.

Sheila nodded.

'His family and mine were close friends,' she added.

'What do you think of him?'

'Ought you to ask me that — in the circumstances?'

'Isn't it a fair question?'

'No, for you believe him to be what he is not.' Rose laughed scornfully.

'He scarcely deserves your loyalty. Don't

let him trade upon your sentiment and good nature, Sheila.'

'I know you dislike him.'

'Yes, I hate him. I hate him because for a time I thought he was straight. But my father caught him red-handed, and made him smart for it. I've no use for dirty thieves.'

'I would rather we did not discuss him.'

'Then we won't. I only wanted to open your eyes to facts. He is the sort of man to play on a girl's emotions — and steal her sympathy. But at last people's eyes are open and — '

'Please — please!'

Rose said no more just then. She was satisfied in having had another dig at the man who had turned her passionate love to bitter enmity. To Sheila these constant castigations were most painful. At times she wondered whether she was quite justified in believing in Donald. It was a fact that he had run from home, under the most suspicious circumstances. It was a fact that never did he attempt to clear himself in that respect. When she was apart from him little doubts arose in her mind, but when next they met these were swept aside like morning mists under the mounting sun, and she saw Donald through the reflecting mirror of her heart.

A week passed and snow came — fine dry

snow that sprinkled the poplars and conifers, glistening in the sun like a million jewels. It was the prelude to winter in the north, and was not unwelcome to Sheila, who had always loved to watch the change of the seasons. When next she saw Donald he was driving a dog-sled back from Albany.

'What do you think of them?' he asked, pointing to the six huskies.

'Lovely. I suppose they are more useful than horses — in winter?'

'Yes. So you are staying on?'

'That was always my intention — Rhoda insisted. My father is still hesitating.'

'If he decides to come out you — you will not go back at all?'

'No.'

This caused his heart to beat quickly, for it signified that her parting from Angus was final in her eyes. It meant that the past was dead, and that the part he had played in that old romance was unavailing.

'Poor Angus!' he murmured.

'Don!'

'I — I can't help it, Sheila. I know where all his hopes were centred. Why did he bungle things so?'

'Bungle!' she gasped.

'Isn't it bungling when a man has Paradise within his grasp and then loses it? There wasn't — there wasn't another girl, was there?'

'No — no.'

'Just — incompatibility?'

'Call it that, Don, I've told you it wasn't his fault. It was my own blindness that led me to believe that — that friendship was love. Don't ask me any more — if you have any regard for my feelings. You don't know how it hurts.'

'I'm a blundering fool, Sheila — always interfering. Please, please forgive me.'

When she was alone she marvelled at his obtuseness. He didn't know — he couldn't understand — that all the love in her heart was directed towards himself, despite the shadow that hung over him, in the face of all reason. This love for his younger brother was so big a thing in his life it clouded his otherwise brilliant vision. But it did achieve something. It increased her love and trust in him, even when others were doing their best to undermine it.

One morning a bombshell was burst upon Sheila and her hosts. Rose rode over in a state of great agitation, and Sheila came in from a walk to find Rose and Rhoda together, awaiting Fergusson, who was busy in his small office.

'Is anything wrong?' she asked, noticing

their tense expressions.

'Something dreadful has happened,' blurted Rose.

'Rose!'

'I am sure of it. My father left home last night to call on your father. He said he might be a little late, and I went to bed at ten o'clock. This — this morning he had not returned.'

'But he didn't call — '

Fergusson entered and greeted Rose cheerily, stopping short as he divined the brooding atmosphere.

'Have you seen my father — since yesterday?' queried Rose huskily.

'No.'

'Then — then — !'

Fergusson caught her by the arm, and looked at her keenly.

'What's the trouble?'

'He is missing. He left home last night at seven o'clock, to call on you — '

'Call on me! I never expected — '

'I know. He received a letter which he wanted to see you about. This morning his bed had not been slept in.'

'Great Scott! Did he come on foot?'

'No, on horseback. I saw him ride away.'

'There may have been an accident.'

'We have searched everywhere along the

trail. Now Lee has gone into Albany, in case my father changed his mind. I left word for Lee to come here when he returned.'

Fergusson walked up and down the room, stroking his chin in perplexity.

'You are sure he rode in this direction?' he asked.

'Yes — yes. I watched him for a few minutes, until the darkness hid him from view.'

'You don't know what the letter was about?'

'No.'

'Was he excited?'

'Oh no. I don't think it was very important. I concluded he wanted a chat more than anything else. During the day he was a little moody.'

'Strange!'

'I shouldn't worry, dear,' said Rhoda. 'He may have met some neighbour and been enticed to play a game of cards.'

'But he wouldn't stay away all night without letting me know. He has never done such a thing in his life.'

'Have you tried to follow his tracks?'

'Lee tried early this morning, but it snowed a little during the night, and we had to give it up. I have sent some of the boys to neighbouring farms, but I know it is useless.

He said he was coming here, and if he never reached you — '

She shuddered, and then started as she heard the dull thud of hoofs on the snow outside. Fergusson peered through the window and ran to the door.

'Lee!' he called over his shoulder.

A minute later Lee and another man entered. Rose looked at the foreman anxiously.

'He never went to Albany,' said Lee.

'Is Rogers back?'

'Yes.'

'No — no news?'

'None.'

'What the devil is one to make of it?' mused Fergusson.

'He may have lost his memory,' suggested Rhoda for the sake of making a consoling remark.

Lee uttered a short laugh, causing all eyes to switch to his grim countenance.

'There was never a more level-headed man than the boss,' he averred. 'He left home with the intention of coming here, and returning pretty early, for he told me he'd see me before I turned in — about some stock we were selling. If he never got as far as this there is only one reason, I'm thinking.'

'You don't suggest — foul play?' asked Fergusson in a hoarse whisper.

98

'I do, and there's a fellow savage enough to be capable of it. Do you get me?'

Fergusson bit his lip, and Rhoda started. In an instant Sheila divined what Lee intended to convey. Rose took the cue immediately and her eyes blazed with hate.

'I — I believe you're right, Lee,' she said. 'He has never forgotten the chastising father gave him. Father had to pass close to his place to get here. It was dark and — '

'Wait!' interrupted Fergusson. 'That is a serious allegation. I'm all for justice, but we mustn't let our prejudices run away with us. If Fraser — '

'It's true,' said Rose almost hysterically. 'There is no one else who had cause to hate my father. I know it — I feel it in my bones. My poor father is dead and Donald Fraser is the culprit.'

Sheila was trembling with mingled horror and resentment. She tried to speak — to utter an indignant denial, but the words stuck in her throat. Rhoda too was so aghast she did nothing but stare from one to another.

'We're going to get Fraser,' said Lee thickly.

Rose concurred. It was real hate now that obsessed her, for with her the blood bond was very strong. She wanted a hanging — a lynching, and without delay. But Fergusson's cooler brain was brought to bear upon the hot-bloods.

'It may be as you say,' he admitted, 'and it may not. But to go and bring this accusation against Fraser without a shred of real evidence is sheer madness. Listen to me, Lee. I'm older than you and no less keen on justice being done. Put that gun away and don't be a damned fool. I'll ride into Albany and put this matter in the hands of the Sheriff. In the meantime, continue the search, but steer clear of Fraser.'

Lee scowled and hesitated, but Rose was quick to see that Fergusson's advice was sound.

'It is wisest, Aldous,' she said. 'But we will watch him. He shall not escape.'

'Don't draw premature conclusions, Rose,' begged Fergusson. 'Your father may yet turn up — alive and well.'

Rose shook her head. In her imaginative mind she could visualise what had happened on the preceding night. She saw Fraser with blood on his hands, and her father's dead body somewhere under the snow.

'Lose no time,' she begged. 'I want justice done.'

When they had gone Fergusson gave orders for his horse to be brought round. Sheila still sat still, as if stunned by what she had heard.

'A bad business,' mused Fergusson as he put on his coat.

Sheila turned her eyes to him.

'You don't think that — that Don — Mr. Fraser — had anything to do with — with Willeton's disappearance?'

'It looks bad.'

'Horrible!' ejaculated Rhoda. 'All this time he must have been waiting his opportunity — nurturing hate and — '

Sheila's head came up. This was more than she could stand. Without a whit of evidence they were accusing Don — the old chivalrous Don who had never harmed a cat. Mistakes he might have made in an impetuous moment — but not this. It was unthinkable, and her whole soul revolted at the foul suggestion.

'You talk of justice,' she said angrily. 'Justice! Why, you are already engaged in putting a rope round his neck. For all the evidence you possess it might have been I who did it. Please — please excuse me. I — I need air — air.'

Fergusson winced as she went out.

'I had forgotten they were old friends,' he said.

'Friends! More than that. She loves him,

father, but she is not sure about him. If I could only make her realise that he is a bad character I should be content.'

'It looks as if complete disillusionment is coming. Poor little brave-hearted woman. I'm sorry for her.'

10

The Danger Line

A week passed and still Willeton was missing. There was no doubt now in the minds of anyone that the rancher had been the victim of foul play. The Sheriff at Albany had got into touch with the police, and had been promised assistance in clearing up the mystery. But the man whose name was associated with the assumed tragedy went on with his work in complete ignorance of it. He had not been to Albany for ten days, and no one had whispered the news common to his neighbours.

Once he met Lee on the boundary of his land, and was greeted with a murderous scowl, and an unintelligible murmuring. And he noticed that the stockmen riding in close proximity to Lee wore expressions scarcely less dark than the foreman himself. He recalled the incident of the cattle, and felt a queer pain in his back to remind him of the upshot of that business. But he was content to bide his time. He passed on.

It was on the following day that Slocum

borrowed the dog-team and paid one of his periodic visits to his relatives at Albany. When he returned he sought his master immediately, and found him smoking reflectively before the fire.

'So you're back, Slocum? Family all right?'

'Ver' well. But Slocum 'ear strange things in Albany.'

'No doubt. What's the latest lie?'

'Mr. Willeton — him missing.'

Donald took his pipe from his lips and gazed at his informant with furrowed brow.

'Missing? How long?'

'A week — and more.'

'Hm! Strange!'

But Slocum's eyes were still fixed on his face, and in them was a significant light.

'Well, what are you staring at?'

'Slocum hear a beeg lie whispered. They say — they say that someone shoot Willeton and bury heem — someone who hate him ver' much.'

'Well?'

'Someone he use a whip on. You savvy?'

Donald's big fist came down on the table with a thump. Then he stood up and stared hard into space. For over a week Sheila had stayed away from him. Was this the reason? Had this foul rumour reached her ears?

'I never knew,' he said slowly.

'They keep it from you because they t'ink mebbe you run if you 'ear — '

'Run!' He seized Slocum by the shoulders, as an idea came to him. 'What do you know about this, Slocum?'

'Nothing. One time I feel like keeling heem and the dog Lee, but Slocum do nothing — nothing.'

'You swear to that?'

'Yes.'

'All right. I believe you. Better forget all about it. It is nothing to do with us.'

'By gar it is. They send for the police, but if the police do nothing they will come here and — '

'Let them. Clear out now. I'm tired.'

Slocum slouched out muttering to himself, and Donald resumed his seat by the fire and turned things over in his mind. He could well imagine the state of mind of the neighbouring community. The incident of the horse-whipping had been spread far and wide. If murder had been committed a motive was there ready-made. Even Sheila might believe it, for the force of public opinion was great in isolated districts.

He cared little what Lee or Rose or Fergusson believed, but Sheila was another matter. He did not want her mind poisoned, nor her trust in him shattered. Perhaps she was waiting for a word from him to ease her suffering mind? He resolved to visit her on the morrow — Fergusson or no Fergusson.

After a disturbed night he harnessed the dogs to the sled and set off down the lonely trail that led to Black Rock. The snow now lay thick in the valley, and the ice was forming on the creek. On all sides were leafless, frozen trees — beech, maple and poplar. Only the conifers looked prim and proud in their winter glory. But he was not in the mood to appraise Nature. To him the world was one of black lies.

In half an hour the Fergusson home came to view — a quite artistic timbered house standing high amid beautiful pines, with the rough outbuildings practically obscured by timber. The sound of the leader-dog's bells brought Rhoda to the door, and he saw her lips tighten as she recognised him.

'Good morning! Is Sheila about?'

'I'll see,' she quavered, and disappeared.

Two minutes later Fergusson came to the door. He gave Donald a curt nod.

'Miss McLeod has gone for a walk,' he said shortly.

'Do you know where?'

'No.'

'Then I'll hang around.'

'Just as you wish.'

The stout door slammed in Donald's face, and he felt the sting acutely. Could it be doubted that this kind of antagonism was infectious? He laughed bitterly, and then talked to his dogs for comfort. A little later he caught a glimpse of a pink woollen coat and a tam-o'-shanter in the distance. Leaving the dogs he trudged through the snow, and waved his hand to the advancing Sheila.

They met under a great fir that completely shut out the house. Eagerly he scanned her face, to read if possible the state of her mind, but its composure baffled him.

'I didn't expect you, Don,' she said in a level voice.

'It's over a week since I caught a glimpse of you.'

'So long as that?'

'It seems longer. I came to-day because of what I happened to hear yesterday.'

She remained silent, but her breast was heaving tumultuously.

'You know about — Willeton?' he asked.

'Yes.'

'Have you also heard — certain rumours?'

He saw her mittened hands close tightly.

'There are some things one tries not to hear.'

'And is that why you have avoided me, Sheila?'

'Avoided? No — no. I have been worried — that is all. I — I have wanted to be alone — to think.'

'You are not quite sure — what to think?'

'No — you are wrong,' she said hastily. 'I know it is all a terrible lie. Nothing could ever make me believe it, but Don — there is danger — great danger. However innocent you are, you must realise that what has happened is bound to place you under suspicion. Even Fergusson is inclined to believe that you — you — He tries to be just — unprejudiced, but all the time he sees things through the eyes of the mob. My constant dread is that they will find poor Willeton's dead body. If — if that should happen it — it may go hard — '

He was astonished at the emotion with which her words were charged, for he himself did not take quite so serious a view of the situation. However much mud-slinging there might be it required evidence to convict a man.

'You are exaggerating things, Sheila,' he said. 'I know I am a kind of dog with a bad name, but it will require more than Lee's fuming hate to bring this home to me.'

'But Rose too is convinced.' She hesitated for a few moments. 'Don, were you ever in love — with Rose Willeton?'

'Never. Why do you ask?'

'She said something — recently, and I heard from a neighbour that you and she — '

'I know. But there was no truth in it. Can you imagine me in love — with Rose?'

'Are you proof against Cupid's dart, Don?'

'I hope so.'

'You hope so!'

'I don't think I'm the sort of man to make any woman happy. Years ago I put an end to such dreams — for ever.'

'Then you did dream — once?'

'Doesn't every man, when he sees a beautiful girl, and lets his imagination run riot? Then he finds his balance, and knows that all his swans are just geese.'

'You talk so strangely. Sometimes I wonder if I really know the real Don Fraser.'

'Sometimes he doesn't know himself,' he replied with a short laugh. 'But about Willeton — you needn't worry. He wouldn't be the first man to disappear and then turn up again. I refuse to believe that anything tragic has happened to him.'

'I wish I could think that.'

'You must. Sheila, you are letting this matter spoil your holiday. It mustn't do that.'

'I don't think you quite understand, Don — what it means to hear your name besmirched by people who have scarcely seen you. Already they take you for a thief, and now — What a cruel, unjust world it is.'

'It would be worse but for women like you — who can still nurture faith and trust. For all you know I might be lying to you. I had good cause to detest Willeton. In a moment of madness I might have — shot him.'

'Don!'

'Hadn't that possibility occurred to you?'

'Yes, but you couldn't look at me — like this, if you were guilty.'

He removed his gaze, for the deep soft eyes were discomfiting to him. The desire to take her and tell her that he loved her madly, that he had never ceased to love her since the day when he had first been conscious of her beauty and charm, was checked by thoughts of Angus. Even now he could not abandon the idea that she was Angus' destiny. Trouble there might have been, but one day it would all come right. Yes, he still envisaged bonnie nieces and nephews, and because of that the burning love within him had to be controlled.

'Have you heard from home?' he asked.

'Yes. Father is interested in the life here, but he is still hesitating. It is hard to make a break with the old life.'

'And you — do you want that?'

'I — I am not sure.'

'You told your father — about meeting me?'

She shook her head.

'Why not?'

'I didn't know whether you wanted that.'

'It doesn't matter now, for I have written myself. Perhaps I should have written before.'

'Yes — you ought to have done. They were waiting on a letter from you, Don. Did you think they could forget you — that they would have no desire to know where you were, and what you were doing?'

'I left home under peculiar circumstances, Sheila.'

This confession was accompanied by a searching look, and he found his gaze held by her.

'I know,' she said softly.

'That was why it was best to — to let time pass. You — you must understand.'

For the first time they had reached the subject that had tormented her for two long years. She was hanging on his words — waiting for a denial of the deed of which he had been accused, and which, it was alleged, had caused him to leave his home suddenly — without a single good-bye.

'I have been trying to understand.'

'Thank you, Sheila.'

She winced at this bald rejoinder. In the matter of the stolen cattle he had been quick to vindicate himself. Why not now when a graver charge was revived — the charge of robbing his own father?

'Don, I want to ask you something,' she said impulsively. 'You may hate me for it, but I must know. Was it true — what they said about you at Culm — was it?'

He turned his head away and stared through the forest of still pines.

'Tell me — for God's sake, tell me!'

'Wasn't — wasn't it made clear?' he asked hoarsely.

'Nothing is clear. I'll believe no rumours — no vulgar gossip.'

'Not even when the facts are so — so evident?'

'Why — why do you vacillate?'

'Because I want to forget the past.'

'Then — then — !'

He caught her firmly and looked deep into her startled eyes.

'When I left Scotland I shut a door upon the past. Don't ask me to open that door now, and rake over old bones,' he said tensely. 'Is it fair — after all this time?'

It silenced her effectively.

11

The Pendulum

The next few days found Donald greatly disturbed in his mind. Sheila's direct question and his inability to answer it as he would wish had placed an abyss between him and her. He could have cleared himself by taking her into his confidence, but he was not built that way. To him the pact made with Angus was sacred. So far it had achieved nothing, but that did not alter things in the least. There was always the possibility of a rehabilitation between Angus and Sheila, and he would have cut out his tongue rather than utter a word that would operate against such a dénouement.

In addition there was trouble nearer home. A curious illness had fallen on certain of his stock. Steers that had been strong and healthy began to wilt. Slocum was as puzzled as his master, and hunted in vain for some cause.

'Two die this morning, boss,' he said.

'Bad! You have separated the sick animals?'

'Yes. Maybe the sickness go soon.'

113

Donald hoped so devoutly, for he could ill afford to lose valuable stock. But on the following day there were three more dead animals, and Slocum informed him that one steer was suffering so intensely it was better to dispatch it.

'See to it then.'

Slocum shambled out, but came back a few minutes later and asked for the humane killer.

'It's in the bin — in the shed.'

'Slocum no find 'eem.'

Donald went out with him, but the lethal instrument could not be located. In the end a rifle had to be used. Followed more losses, until Donald calculated that his profits for the season were completely cancelled. It was a heavy blow, coming as it did without warning, but he managed to smile.

'We'll have to put our backs into it, Slocum,' he said. 'Has anyone else's stock been affected?'

Slocum didn't know, but he had not heard of any trouble elsewhere. Then there came signs that the worst was over, and Donald thanked God it was no worse. But the set-back was so serious it called for extra effort in some direction. He turned his mind to hunting — even lumbering — to tide him over the winter.

During the past week the cold had intensified, and there was every sign of an unusually severe winter. The ice now reached from shore to shore on the river, but he kept a few holes open through which to fish. At times he walked towards Black Rock, and saw Fergusson's house perched on the hill like a fairy dwelling. It was all the more attractive to him because of the woman it housed. He recalled her look of bitter disappointment when she heard his unsatisfactory response to her vital question. So great a part did she play in his thoughts that he almost forgot the Willeton trouble. But it was brought home to him forcefully by an unexpected meeting with Rose. She was driving a dog-team alone, and occupying almost the whole of the narrow path. He stepped aside to let her pass, but she had no intention of doing so without expressing the loathing she now had for him.

'Back from love-making?' she sneered.

He winced and made to pass the dogs.

'Slinking away, eh? Well, you will run faster yet.'

He swung round with his face inflamed.

'I don't quite understand you.'

'Oh yes you do, Donald Fraser. You've been pretty cunning, but you are not going to get away with it. You've taken your revenge, and very soon I will take mine. Now you're playing up to that McLeod girl as you once played up to me, but I'm not going to sit still and see her happiness ruined by a man of your type.'

The words, spat out with all the venom of which she was capable, made a deep effect upon him. A man he would have knocked down instantly, but she had the advantage of sex and merely laughed at his discomfiture.

'I don't think you are responsible for what you say,' he said tensely. 'This talk of revenge is foolish. When last I saw your father he was alive and well.'

'You liar!'

He gulped and pushed past her, lest he should forget she was a woman. The last thing he heard was a bitter, mocking laugh, followed by the 'woof' of a dog as she plied her whip. He guessed that she was on her way to Fergusson's and would attempt to distil more poison. Again came the feeling of revolt against cruel and persistent persecution, and it required all his natural optimism to save him from brooding despair.

When he reached home he had another surprise. A Sergeant of the North-West Mounted Police was reclining against his door-post and gazing at a bill which he had just affixed to the door. It read:

$250 REWARD

The above reward will be paid to anyone giving information as to the whereabouts of James Willeton, who has been missing from his home since the night of November 22. Height — 5 feet 10 inches. Complexion dark, small moustache and short pointed beard. Last wearing corduroy riding breeches, brown coat, stetson hat. Age 53.

A separate reward of $50 will be paid to anyone recovering the horse of the above named. Dappled mare, 16 hands or thereabouts, docked tail and slight scar in left shoulder.

Apply SHERIFF, ALBANY; or HEADQUARTERS N.W.M.P.

The Sergeant switched his gaze to Donald as he approached and stretched his long form.

'Mr. Fraser, I guess?'

'That's me.'

'I've been disfiguring your shack.'

'So I observe. Come inside.'

Donald unlocked the door and the Sergeant entered. His keen eyes ranged over everything in a few seconds.

'You've heard about this business?' he asked.

'Naturally. Apparently there is no trace yet?'

'None. The Sheriff sent me up here. We've got to locate that man, and I'll be grateful for any information you can hand me.'

'I'm afraid I shan't be very helpful. I heard nothing about the business until over a week after Willeton was missing.'

'You've seen no suspicious characters round about?'

'None. We see very few strangers in these parts.'

'You were friendly with Willeton?'

'To be frank — I wasn't. We never got on well together, chiefly because there was always trouble over the boundary fence.'

'When did you see him last?'

'As near as I can remember — about three days before he was missing.'

'Hm! There's a half-breed hanging around here.'

'That's Slocum — my man. He doesn't love the Willeton outfit, but you can rule him out of it.'

'Why are you so sure?'

'Because Slocum was away on that night. He's always raising an excuse to visit his relatives at Albany, and on that occasion he

118

stayed away for two days.'

'I'll have to get that corroborated.'

'That will be easy.'

The Sergeant's whole demeanour was friendly enough, but Donald suspected that he was quite aware of the rumours that were being circulated.

'You've seen the people yonder?' he enquired.

'Miss Willeton? Yes.'

'You know what she believes? She has got it into her head that her father was murdered on that night.'

'Is that — your conclusion?'

The Sergeant pursed his lips and shrugged his broad shoulders.

'I'm not guessing anything,' he said. 'But if there has been any dirty work you can bet we'll get the fellow responsible, before we are through.'

'I hope you will.'

'You can put your shirt on it.'

He left a little later and Donald sat down and gazed into the fire. The proximity of the policeman was disturbing. Innocent as he was it was unpleasant to feel that the lynx-eyed police were prowling around, alert and suspicious. The little holding which he had grown to love was no longer the peaceful place it used to be. He wished he had

119

never seen Willeton nor his passionate-hating daughter.

The Sergeant went along the river, and ultimately reached a patch of thick timber, where a camp fire was burning, and half a dozen dogs were clearing up the remains of a meal. There was a sled nearby and sundry gear. From the direction of the river came the sound of wood-chopping, and a few minutes later a second policeman entered camp with his arms full of wood.

'Hello, Burton!' he said. 'So you're back?'

'Yep. I had a pow-wow with the Sheriff and went straight to Willeton's.'

'No news?'

'Nothing worth mentioning. Gee, that Willeton girl is a firebrand — breathing blood and brimstone. Of course she knows it all. If I had listened to her I'd have sure hanged a man by now.'

His companion laughed and put some of the wood on the fire. Then he sat down on a sack, and placed a kettle of water across two pieces of rock, raking the red-hot brands under its bottom.

'So there's nothing to get a grip on?'

'Nothing solid. There's a whole lot of rumour, but I've often had a bellyful of that. This Willeton fellow might have had good reason for beating it, or he may have

120

gone and lost his memory. Anyway, murder is about the last thing we ought to postulate. Good word that, Angus.'

'What's that girl's solution?'

'Revenge. Willeton has a neighbour — a big son-of-a-gun who was always getting his goat. It appears he took a liking for some of Willeton's cattle a while back, and Willeton caught him red-handed. Some of the boys tied him to a stake and Willeton had him welted good and well.'

'I see. And that's where the theory of revenge comes in?'

'Sure. It reads all right — up to a point. But the fellow doesn't look that sort.'

'You've seen him?'

'Yep. Got the same name as yourself, Angus, so I guess he's Scotch. You chaps from the land of cakes ain't very original when it comes to names. Now this fellow — Donald Fraser — doesn't look the sort of guy to slug a man in the dark and — '

Angus took his pipe from his lips, with a hand that was near to trembling.

'Donald Fraser!' he ejaculated.

'So. Any relative?'

'I shouldn't think so. What were you saying?'

'Well, he gave me the impression of being a foursquare man. Sort of guy who looks you in the eyes until you blink, and he looks as tough as hide. But of course one never knows,' he drawled.

'Old?'

'No — young. Big head — full of brains. Chest like a bull and a voice like brass. Put some more fire under that kettle. I'm gasping for something warm and wet.'

Angus Fraser — for it was none other — gulped and did the Sergeant's bidding. The name might have been a coincidence, but the description tallied. Was it possible that Don — dear old Don — was living within a mile of him? It seemed incredible, and yet within him was a strange intuition. If it should be Don — !

'I'll take the dogs and run into Albany later,' said Burton. 'I'd like another word with the Sheriff.'

'Shall I stay here?'

'Yep. We'll make a real start to-morrow. Our first job is to find Willeton. We want the body before we can move much.'

After the meal the Sergeant harnessed the dogs and went off in the direction of Albany. Angus loitered about camp for an hour, and then a strange impelling force set him moving along the river. In due course he saw before him a small shack lying off the frozen stream. He stopped and saw a man leave a shed and come towards the river, with an axe in his hand. It was Slocum about to keep the fishing-hole open, and he stared hard at the unmistakable winter garb of the waiting policeman.

'Who lives here?' asked Angus.

'Boss — Mister Fraser.'

'Is he in?'

'Maybe. Slocum not know,' he replied surlily.

'Then we'll find out.'

Angus mounted the long slope and soon found himself gazing at the printed poster on the door of the shack. He rapped hard with his fist and heard a deep voice bidding him enter. He raised the latch and pushed the door open. A big figure stood facing him — a figure he would have recognised among a million, though twenty years had passed instead of two.

'Don!' he ejaculated.

'Angus! Great Scott!'

A big hand was outstretched — a hand full of power, of confidence.

12

The Old Flame

Looking into his brother's face Donald saw great changes there. The dreaming lad had gone and an alert man had taken his place. There was a look of stubbornness about the chin that had never been there before, and a big development of physique generally. The well-fitting police uniform showed off his perfect figure to advantage, and he looked what he now was — a supremely healthy, fearless emissary of the law.

'This is a miracle?' laughed Donald. 'I hadn't the remotest idea you were within thousands of miles. It was only the other day I wrote to you.'

'Meeting you like this is just as miraculous, Don. Is it mere coincidence or Fate playing her own game?'

'Call it what you like, old boy, it's just as pleasant. But even now I don't understand it. What are you doing in that uniform?'

A shadow seemed to pass across Angus' countenance, but he smiled immediately after and sat down in the nearest chair.

124

'Just an impulse, Don,' he said. 'After you left things were dull. Everything went wrong. Sheila turned me down, and ultimately came out here to stay with a friend. I believe she is in this district — '

'She is.'

'Then you — you have seen her?'

'Yes.'

'She — she told you — about me?'

'Not much. How did it all come about?'

'I don't know. She gave me to understand that she had made a mistake — and taken friendship for love. I took back the ring, and after that we remained good friends. Then she got a hankering to come to Canada, and McLeod wanted her to go because he had an idea to emigrate. Well, when she left I found things deadly dull. I felt I wanted to make a clean cut with the past, and — and I believed that Sheila would never come back to Culm. Father and mother were dead against my leaving, but the urge was on me. I left within a fortnight of Sheila's departure. I tried to find work on a farm, but it was nearing the end of the season. Then I met a man who was in the North-West Police. That put me on a new tack. I joined up, and for two months they've been licking me into shape. This is my first patrol.'

'You're liking it?'

'Tremendously. You've no idea how it gets into your blood. Service! That is the slogan of the corps. A fellow soon gets the idea that he is both useful and necessary. All the fellows are splendid. I wouldn't change it for anything in the world.'

'That sounds good.'

'But, Don, was there ever such a ringing of the changes? You and I and Sheila all brought together again like this!'

Donald agreed, for he, like Angus, was quite ignorant of the fact that Sheila had known beforehand of Donald's location.

'And what are you doing up here?' asked Donald.

Angus started, for in the thrill of this reunion he had overlooked certain grim facts.

'The Willeton business,' he said tensely. 'It was that which led me to you. I came up with Sergeant Burton at the request of the Sheriff of Albany. He mentioned your name, and that set me wondering. Don, I hope it isn't a betrayal of confidence to warn you that the Willeton girl is making all kinds of assertions — about you.'

'I know.'

'You needn't tell me they are not true. But all the same, Don, it is serious.'

'Until the truth is discovered.'

126

'Yes. We're out to learn that. Burton's a good fellow, and as smart as they make them in the force. He won't listen to any wild rumours. We're going to find Willeton — dead or alive.'

'The sooner the better.'

'Tell me about Sheila, Don. I can't stay long. Is she — does she appear to be happy?'

'Yes.'

Angus' expression was a queer mixture of gladness and disappointment. Donald gripped him by the shoulder.

'Is it still the same with you, old boy?'

'You mean — as regards Sheila?'

Donald nodded.

'Just the same. I'll never cease to love her. I gave her my word that I would accept friendship in lieu of love, but it's all a masquerade. I chose Canada because she was here. Of course I never hoped to meet her, but there seems some force operating to keep us three together. Where is she now?'

'With the Fergussons at Black Rock — a few miles from here.'

Angus nodded and his gaze went past Donald — into space. Donald realised that the old love was as strong as ever, and wondered what the effect of Angus' presence would have upon Sheila — if and when they met.

'There's something else, Don,' said Angus. 'We've got to put that other matter right. I would have told the old people before I left, but you made me promise not to speak. I want your permission to explode that lie. It can't go on — '

'Better let things remain as they are.'

'No. I am almost sure to meet Sheila. I want to tell her that you took my burden over — '

'Say nothing, old boy.'

'But before she came here she knew what had happened in Culm. The story about a quarrel wouldn't hold water. She thinks that you — that you — '

'Does it matter?'

'Matter! Great Scott! It matters tremendously. It is time for the truth to be told, and I want to tell it.'

But Donald shook his head stubbornly. In his heart was the feeling that that old love affair would be patched up, and he wanted that to happen as much as he wanted anything in the world.

'It wouldn't do, old boy. The old fester is healing slowly. Why start a new one?'

'In the cause of truth.'

'Truth may sometimes hurt more than a

lie. We've gone so far along a certain road, and there is no turning back.'

Angus began to argue afresh, but Donald was adamant — as firm as a rock. He held Angus by a solemn promise, knowing that Angus would be bound by that, and hoping that the end would justify it.

'How are you going on, Don?' asked Angus when the painful subject was shelved.

'Not too badly. Things were actually blooming when I struck a bad patch. My cattle have been sick with some unknown disease, and it has put me back a year. But I'm going to make leeway.'

'I'll warrant you do.'

Angus stayed for over an hour, during which time he and Donald revived old memories, and the one outstanding fact that emerged was that Angus was just as deeply in love with Sheila as ever, and tremendously excited at the thought of meeting her. It caused Donald to reflect upon his own feelings in that direction. Despite Sheila's recent coldness towards him the old passion was there — a glowing spark that was prevented from becoming a roaring flame by his own repressive attitude. It had to be killed, he thought. That good-natured, handsome brother of his would soon win back what he had lost — and more. He himself had to be the looker-on, content with reflected joy.

It was late in the evening when Sergeant Burton returned to camp, wearing an expression of deep disgust. Angus wondered what had caused this, and Burton soon enlightened him.

'There was a message for me,' he growled. 'We've got to separate, Angus.'

'Separate?'

'Sure. Some fool trapper has knived an Injun down at Cool Springs, and caused a whole lot of bother with the local tribe. I'm ordered there at once, and you're to take over this business, solo.'

Angus whistled expressively.

'It's a mighty big compliment — for you,' mused Burton. 'And it's a fine chance to show what you can do. All the same I'm selfish enough to wish that trapper to blazes. I like this part of the country better.'

'When are you leaving?'

'Now. Lee is loaning me a horse, so I'll be able to leave you the dogs and sled. Anything you want to know?'

'I don't think so. It's clear that my first job is to find Willeton, or the horse, before I can make much progress.'

'Sure! And better keep your eye on your namesake. I'm not suggesting he had anything to do with it — but you never know.'

Angus bit his lip as he realised the novelty of the situation. So far Burton was ignorant of the fact that Donald was his brother. But that fact could not be long hid, and he wondered what would be said when it was discovered. His own conscience was perfectly clear, for nothing in the world would have shaken his loyalty to the corps. Moreover the idea of Don being guilty of, or being party to, murder was ludicrous. All the same, gossip was a cruel adjudicator. In the end he decided to keep his own council.

On the morrow he started on the quest for Willeton, working up all the snow-covered trails that radiated from the Willeton ranch, searching under snow-drifts, among the timber, and even under the ice on frozen pools. It was an arduous business, and a lonely life. At nights he pitched his camp, and fell back upon his own mind for entertainment. The loss of Burton made all the difference in the world, for a comrade was a most desirable being in this northern wilderness.

After spending three days working round in a great circle, he came again upon the river, and within sight of Fergusson's house. There was no real need to interrogate Fergusson on the matter, since Burton had already done that, but the thought of seeing Sheila was too much for him. He drove the dogs up the hill and, entering the garden, knocked boldly on the door. It was Sheila herself who answered the summons, and she blinked at the apparition as if she doubted her senses.

'It's me all right,' said Angus. 'Perhaps I ought to have warned you.'

'A policeman!'

'Why not?'

He gripped her hand and held it for a few seconds. Sheila's face and neck were crimson, for she had not been prepared for this.

'I'm glad to see you, Angus,' she stammered confusedly. 'But — have you come — in the cause of duty?'

'Yes — no. Don told me you were here, and I couldn't resist the temptation. Burton has been recalled and I'm left in charge of the Willeton case.'

Sheila's eyes opened wide, and then something like an expression of horror entered them.

'I — I'll come out,' she said ultimately. 'I'll just get my hat and coat.'

'Do. I've just come back from scouting, and am entitled to a few minutes' relaxation.'

When she reappeared she seemed to be anxious to get away from the precincts of the house, and they soon reached the sled.

'I'll drive you to my camp,' said Angus. 'Jump in!'

She sat in the sled and was drawn swiftly over the snow, to the spot where Angus had cached certain stores. All the while her mind was active. The coming of Angus agitated her, for she foresaw a painful situation.

'Here we are,' he said cheerily. 'Not even a front door, nor a carpet, but not a bad little nest.'

'Angus, I'm still bewildered. I knew that Burton had another man with him, but I never dreamed it could be you.'

'Miracles do happen, you see. I thought that both you and Don had vanished for ever, and here we are again, just as if we had arranged a rendezvous.'

'Then you've seen Don?'

'Yes. We had a long yarn.'

'Oh, it's awful!'

'What is?'

'Fate selecting you for this job. Don't you know what they are saying — about Don?'

'Yes, but it doesn't disconcert me much. No one but a born lunatic would think that Don had anything to do with Willeton's disappearance.'

'You are wrong, Angus. There are many people who are not at all insane, who suspect Don. He — he has a bad

133

name — undeservedly, of course. Willeton once thrashed him — '

'What!'

'It is true. He accused Don of cattle stealing, and used brute force. Don't you realise what a strong motive that appears to be? Even Fergusson, who has no personal cause to dislike Don, is full of suspicion.'

'It is all the more reason why I should get this matter cleared up.'

'Yes, of course. Oh, Angus, I'm worried — filled with all kinds of horrible apprehensions.'

'But you have no cause to be.'

'It wouldn't be the first time that an innocent man has suffered through public feeling. Rose Willeton hates Don, and Lee hates him too. I am sure they are both convinced that Don murdered that man, and they have enough influence round about to work on the passions of Don's enemies. I dread that they will take the law into their own hands — before long.'

Angus' mouth tightened at this.

'They had better not try,' he said grimly.

'There is something else too, Angus,' she said after a long pause. 'If they discover that you are the brother of Don they will suspect — suspect — '

She halted as she saw the look of

resentment in his face.

'Sheila!' he protested.

'It is human nature. I hate to hurt your feelings, but the truth must be told.'

'Then it is time to disillusion them,' he growled. 'But the fools, to think that of Don! I would as soon believe that you were guilty, Sheila.'

13

Adventure

The result of Angus' meeting with Sheila was to cause the latter strange heart-flutterings. For two years she had believed that her former intimacy with him was one of friendship — that real love had never entered into it, and that it was Donald whom she loved. But this new Angus, fired with the sense of duty to the corps he already revered, was vastly different to the dreaming, careless boy at Culm. Drill and hard work had performed miracles already. As upright as a gun, and fearless as a lion, he was a romantic figure. She wondered whether she herself was not lacking in self-knowledge.

This Donald, to whom in secret she had given her whole heart, was still the dominating figure, but the incident that had caused him to flee his country rankled in her mind. It took away some of the gilt from the image which she treasured, and had the effect of putting Angus higher in her estimation. Yet while her reasoning powers urged her to repress this love for the elder brother, her heart seemed to be unaffected. She had heard of women who loved even when the object of their love was proved to be unworthy — rotten to the core, and now she was coming to sympathise with them.

Notwithstanding she was convinced that Donald was innocent of causing Willeton any bodily harm. One thing he was not — a liar. She thanked God for this saving grace. He could have lied — or tried to lie — about the forged cheque, but he had not. Had he done so doubt might have been born. As it was she felt sorry for him, and found a rather flimsy excuse for the reprehensible act of the past. But the ideal was tarnished — she had to admit it.

Intermittently she saw Angus, scouring the neighbourhood, as indefatigable as any sleuth-hound. Time passed and all his efforts proved vain. But still he would not admit defeat, and the bitter winter days found him still seeking.

'The snow has made things harder,' he said. 'It means endless labour.'

'It looks like murder now?'

'Well, it is strange he has not turned up.'

'The body might have been sunk in the river.'

'Yes, that is highly probable. But the horse could not have been moved.'

'Angus, I'm worried.'

'Why?'

'Rhoda has seen me talking to you. She — she teased me. Ought I — ought I to tell her that you are Don's brother?'

'Why not?'

'Don't you realise how strange that would appear?'

'I only realise it is the truth. I have not attempted to conceal my name. It is true no one has asked me, but if they do I shall tell the truth.'

'It might mean your recall to headquarters. Rose Willeton would raise a storm.'

'You don't quite understand the North-West Police,' he replied. 'The Commissioner would take no notice of such a complaint. Until a man proves himself unworthy he is trusted. He may already know. I hope he does.'

'A man would be expected to arrest his own brother?'

'A member of the corps would be expected to arrest his own mother — if she were guilty.'

'I admire you for that, Angus, but somehow it seems opposed to human nature.'

He laughed and caught her hand playfully.

'Why dally with useless enigmas? Don doesn't come into this at all, so we are

138

wasting words. I saw him yesterday — laying traps in the woods. He told me he hadn't seen you for quite a long time. I am to reprimand you.'

'Did he say that?'

'No. But it is necessary, all the same.' His face grew more serious. 'Sheila, you don't think that Don is in any way culpable, do you?'

'Of course not.'

'Then why have you quarrelled with him?'

'Quarrelled! We haven't quarrelled.'

'You are close neighbours but you see very little of each other, and he is not very happy about it.'

'How do you know that?'

'I know Don. There's a kind of sympathetic bond between us. Instinctively I know when he is fretting. Friendship with Don is an ideal. Be nice to him, Sheila.'

She was breathing heavily, deeply shaken by his words.

'I think he is one of the best men in the world,' she said slowly. 'But — '

'But — what?'

'There is something — difficult to forget.'

'You mean — ' Angus' face grew as tense as she had ever seen it. 'You mean — something that happened — long ago?'

'Yes.'

'You ought not to judge him — on that.'

'Why not?'

'Because — because you may not know all the facts. Even if you did — even — '

He could not go on. It was impossible to perpetuate that damnable lie, with Sheila's great eyes focussed on his face. He lapsed into silence.

'It was terrible,' she said huskily. 'I had hoped it was not true, but now I know — '

'Say no more,' he said sharply. 'You — you do Don the greatest injustice.'

'Angus!'

She left him in a huff shortly afterwards, and Angus bit his lip in vexation. When he had taken a meal he walked over to Donald's farm, and found his brother sawing logs, with his coat off in a temperature of twenty below zero.

'Hullo, Angus! Any news?'

'No.'

Donald went on sawing, with the energy of a steam-engine.

'Stop that for a bit, old man.'

'Can't loiter. Anything wrong?'

'Yes — everything.'

A twelve-inch log fell off into the snow, and Donald mopped his perspiring brow.

'Let's hear the worst, old boy.'

'I'm going to cancel a promise, Don.'

'Eh?'

'For over two years I have been living a lie. There's a solid reason why it can't go on. Sheila knows what happened in Culm. It is poisoning her mind. I mean to tell her the truth.'

'Don't be an idiot.'

'Idiot! Do you think I am going to let her continue to think that you are a — a forger and — ?'

'What does it matter what she thinks — about me?'

'The thing that matters is that a monstrous lie has been uttered and kept alive. The time has come to let the people concerned know the truth. I want to tell Sheila, and to write to the old people, and I will not be deterred.'

It was evident he had made up his mind resolutely, but he had scarcely bargained for Donald's pugnacity. He saw his brother's jaw projecting — the blue wide-set eyes gleaming with all the gigantic determination of their owner.

'So promises mean nothing, Angus, eh?'

'Promises! Such a promise can never be held sacred.'

'You can't differentiate. We made a pact to save certain people pain, and I'll never allow you to break it.'

'But the circumstances are different now.

Sheila believes that — '

'Will it comfort her to know the truth? Will it help those at home — just when they are getting over the first rude shock? Will it help you?'

'Me! It's because I can't stand this shameless masquerade that I am asking you to release me from — '

'I won't.'

'Don!'

'I've played the part for so long — I like it. In my last letter I enclosed — fifty pounds.' His face softened as he saw Angus flinch. 'Dear old boy, I'm a bit older than you. I know it would do no good to rake over old bones. Let them rest, and let us keep our vows — you and I.'

He held out his hand. Angus hesitated to take it, for the desire to take over his own burden was great, but the dominating personality of Donald won — as it always had done. Angus sighed as he gripped the big muscular hand.

'That's better,' said Donald. 'Now tell me what you have achieved.'

'Absolutely nothing. There is not a clue of any kind. But I've not given up hope.'

'I believe Willeton disappeared of his own accord. All this talk of murder is nonsense.'

'But why should he?'

142

'There might have been a reason. Queer how that little vixen yonder got it into her head that I had designs on her father's life. She used to be quite milk and water.'

'You knew her pretty well, Don?'

'I knew her even better than she imagined. Intriguing little hussy! I suppose she doesn't know that the 'body-snatcher' of the police is my own brother?'

'No one appears to know — yet.' Angus' brow became furrowed. 'There'll be more gossip when that comes out.'

'Yes. Some will be mean enough to think that that fact might influence you in your duty. Seriously, Angus, I should not like to get in your clutches.'

Angus winced and then smiled.

'Thank God, that isn't possible. Well, they seem to have provided me with a Chinese puzzle for my first job. I don't want to fail them. I'm going to produce something soon or — or bust.'

'That's the spirit.'

'It took the Police Force to engender it. I was a bit of a weakling in the old days. If I could only get that other thing off my mind — '

'No more of that. We have said the last word. You — you have seen a great deal of Sheila?'

'It is — inevitable.'

'How are things in that direction?'

'I don't know, Don. When — when we broke the engagement she gave me the right to hope. Since I have been here I feel that she has warmed to me — just a little. I don't want to build too much on that, but it is impossible not to feel it. What I have to guard against is the impulse to rush in impetuously, and ruin things.'

Donald nodded reflectively.

'It will all come right, old boy,' he averred. 'It takes a woman a long time to know her own mind.'

There were grounds for this remark, for Sheila at that moment was wrestling with her emotions. Angus had brought with him pleasant memories of courtship in the Scotch hills, and time had a way of gilding them. She recalled many a scene in that distant land that was pleasant to dwell upon. Angus and herself picnicking by the side of the loch; Angus and she whispering delightful secrets amid the green bracken. But obtruding over all this was Donald — the big reliant Don who had fastened on her imagination only to deal it a blow from which she believed it would never recover.

It was patent to her that she was near to loving both of these fine men. Hitherto the scale had dipped greatly in Donald's favour, but now her whole outlook was changed, and she wondered whether Fate had sent Angus back to her in the nick of time. Thus her innate idealism sought to keep from her the real truth, and it needed a jolt to bring her face to face with facts. That jolt came a few days later.

She was out walking, somewhat aimlessly, when snow began to fall heavily, and a bitter wind swept down from the mountains. It was so evident that a blizzard was working up, that she decided to retrace her footsteps immediately, for she was miles from home. The river took a serpentine course from where she was and she resolved to cut across the big bend and thus save a mile or so.

Through the driving snow she caught a glimpse of Donald's shack, and the sight of it set her heart beating fast. She was conscious of having avoided him of late, and her contrition was greater than she thought it should have been. Nervous of the rapidly increasing wind and the awful cold, the vague form of the shack drew her towards it. Donald would unquestioningly be glad to escort her home, and the circumstances made that rather desirable. She resolved to drop her scruples.

She was within fifty yards of the shore

when a figure emerged from the trees. From the size of it she knew it was Donald himself, and she raised her voice to him. He turned, and to her surprise made frantic gesticulations.

'Keep away from — !'

A nerve-shattering crack prevented her from hearing the rest of the warning. To her horror the ice heaved up and then subsided. In that terrible fraction of a second she saw black water gushing up, and the next moment she was immersed up to her neck, and clinging desperately to a slab of ice.

'Hold on!'

It was Donald's stentorian voice, and she saw him rushing towards her with an axe in his hand. But the ice to which she clung was turning under her weight, and her frozen hands lost their grip. Down she went into the icy depths.

14

A Discovery

When Donald reached the scene of this disaster there was nothing visible but floating slabs of ice on the disturbed water. He realised in an instant that time was terribly precious, for no human body could long withstand the low temperature of the water. The hole through which Sheila had fallen was but a few feet in diameter, and to attempt to dive into it would be akin to suicide. He got to work with the axe on the ice, dealing smashing blows with his powerful arms. Glistening chips flew up into his face as he hacked his way through it. In less than a minute he had enlarged the hole to treble its size.

There was still no sign of Sheila, but he nurtured the hope that there was no undercurrent at that spot, for it was on the inner arc of a curve. Acting speedily he lifted out several great slabs of ice, and then lowered himself into the water. It stung like something hot, and seemed to expel all the breath from his body. An instant's hesitation and his head went under the surface. Half unconscious he groped about with his arms, but came to the surface again after thirty seconds of vain hunting. Once more he went down — this time under the ice-rim. Desperately he flung out his arms, and a great thrill went through him as his hands encountered a soft, resisting substance. In a vague way he knew it was Sheila, and he was dimly aware that she was some few yards under the ice, and that his lungs felt like bursting.

What followed he scarcely knew, for the cold was eating into his vitals, and the greater half of his brain seemed to have stopped functioning. But he fought his way towards the light — and when he believed that all was lost his head suddenly emerged into thin air. Like a limpet he clung to the edge of the ice with one hand, while he supported Sheila with the other. Then exerting every ounce of his remaining strength, he managed to withdraw his body from the water, pulling Sheila after him.

She was quite unconscious, and he feared that she was past recovery. With a short grunt he commenced to run across the frozen river towards his shack, and ultimately stumbled into it, with ice forming all over his drenched clothing. Forgetting himself completely, he set to work to bring back life into the half-drowned girl — and ultimately succeeded. She opened her eyes, and blinked at him in bewilderment.

'Why — where am — ?'

'Good!' he ejaculated. 'Phew! That was a narrow shave.'

'Donald! I didn't come — Oh, the ice!'

'Take another nip of this.'

She took the brandy somewhat reluctantly, but it had the effect of bringing colour to her pallid cheeks, and she sat up on the couch and stared at her wet garments.

'You must change those,' he said. 'Anything will serve until I can get them dried. I'll round up something for you.'

He went into the small bedroom and hunted up a suit of warm pyjamas and a dressing-gown of enormous length. These he threw into the living-room, and bade her change quickly. Five minutes later she called him, and he joined her. She was sitting in front of the fire — Arab fashion, with the saturated garments already steaming before her, and the capacious dressing-gown taking the semblance of a balloon above and below her waist.

'Better?' he enquired.

'Y-yes. I can't quite think what happened.'

'You stepped on to the thin ice over one

of my fish-holes. I ought to have marked it in some way.'

'And then — you came in for me?'

He nodded, and saw her shudder as her imagination got to work.

'I — I can't remember anything,' she said. 'Except the terrible paralysing sting of the water — then the blackness. But aren't you going to change? You're still wet.'

'Almost dry now. I won't hurt.'

The grateful eyes surveyed him so intently that he turned his head away.

'Don!'

'Yes.'

'You — you saved my life. I know I must have been near to death. How can I ever thank you? What can I say?'

'Nothing. It was just a stroke of luck — on my part.'

'Luck! Why, I was under the ice — I must have been. You risked your life to get me out. Why — why do you make so light of it?'

'You weren't far in. I caught you almost first time.'

'It must have been awful — diving in there — ' She gulped and held out her hand. 'Oh, Don, I shall never forget.'

Her hand was warm now — as warm as the heart that was expressing its gratitude. Donald held it for a second or two, and then smiled and let it go.

'Were you coming here?' he asked.

'Y-yes. I was rather nervous about the snow-storm. I thought you would see me home.'

'I will — as soon as your clothes are dry. I hope you haven't taken cold.'

'I never have colds. Ugh! That was a horrible experience. I have a dim recollection of a kind of panoramic past which swept across my mind. There were you and I and Angus playing around by the old loch and . . . I was living it all again — in a few brief seconds . . . '

'Better forget it,' he advised.

She touched his coat and found it still saturated.

'I knew it,' she expostulated. 'Change at once. I don't want you on my conscience.'

'All right.'

For her the pendulum had swung back again. This courageous act set at naught — temporarily at least — the spectre that had haunted her. Here was the same reliable, modest Donald, holding lightly the fact that he had undoubtedly saved her from certain death — and at tremendous risk to himself. Many a man would have counted the probable cost before attempting what he had successfully achieved. Dear Don — dear black sheep! How could she prevent that out-going of admiration — and love?

Half an hour later she was able to don her dried clothing, and as the wind was still shrieking down the valley Donald harnessed the dogs and drove her home. *En route* they encountered the camp of Angus, and found him confined to his tent, reading before a kerosene lamp. His eyes opened wide when he saw the two travellers. Sheila explained quickly.

'What an awful experience,' said Angus. 'Don, you old water-spaniel, your luck was in.'

'I agree. What about yourself — anything to report?'

'No. It's like blind man's buff. I came in only an hour ago. I hope this storm will soon pass.'

'Isn't he splendid?' asked Sheila, as they resumed their journey. 'His whole heart is given to his work. I — I hope he won't fail.'

'I'll bet he doesn't. He was always full of grit, though he never showed it. He'll climb up and up — you'll see.'

'I hope so with all my heart.'

The tone of her remarks was non-committal, but Donald believed that she was finding a recrudescence of the old love for Angus, and was utterly blind to the fact that it was himself who occupied her heart and mind. He left her near Fergusson's house, feeling that she would prefer it, for the antagonism of the Fergussons had been made abundantly evident.

That same evening, when the blizzard had blown itself out, the thing which Sheila feared came to pass. Rose turned up in a sled, driven by Lee. When she burst into the room Sheila prepared herself for a shock of some sort, for Rose's face was ugly with repugnance.

'I've just discovered an extraordinary thing,' she said. 'It — it is almost incredible.'

'What is it?' enquired Rhoda.

'That policeman — the man who came with Sergeant Burton — by a remarkable coincidence he is Fraser's brother.'

'Fraser's brother!' gasped Fergusson. 'Impossible!'

'It isn't. It is true. His name is Angus Fraser, and he came from Scotland only a few months ago, and joined the police. I have just heard it — in Albany.'

'But he need not be a brother. Fraser is a common enough name, and — '

'I met a man who knew them both. He swears — ' She stopped as she saw Sheila's pale face. 'Why, of course you can prove this. You have known the Fraser family for a long time, and you've seen that policeman — haven't you?'

'Yes,' quavered Sheila.

'And are they — brothers?'

'Yes.'

'Then why didn't you tell us before?' stormed Rose.

'I could not see the need.'

'Need! This is an impossible situation. No wonder no clue has been discovered. No wonder the murderer of my father is still at large!'

'You mean to suggest — ' commenced Sheila angrily.

'I suggest that blood-ties are strong, and that this man — Angus — is not likely to unearth anything that will place his brother's life in jeopardy. I know that Donald Fraser is guilty and — '

'Careful, Rose,' warned Fergusson. 'The North-West Police is an honourable corps. You have no grounds for what you are suggesting.'

'I will find them,' retorted Rose. 'I am going to lay this information before the Sheriff. Either Sergeant Burton must be recalled or this policeman must make place for another man. It is infamous — most unnatural.'

154

'See the Sheriff by all means, but act discreetly.'

But discretion was not Rose's strongest quality. Full of prejudice and preconceptions she hurried away. Fergusson drummed the table with his fingertips.

'A strange coincidence,' he mused. 'And you knew all the time, Sheila?'

'Yes.'

'You might have told us,' said Rhoda rather tartly.

'Put yourself in my place and tell me what you would have done,' replied Sheila. 'I know that Donald Fraser is not capable of harming a fellow creature. I know that his brother, Angus, is the soul of loyalty. I foresaw that this revelation — if it ever came — would give rise to foul suspicion, but I hoped that Angus would achieve his end before his relationship with Donald was discovered. If Rose should get her way and have him recalled it — it will break his heart.'

'But if you are wrong, and that man is guilty?' asked Fergusson. 'What then?'

'He is innocent. I know it. All my life I have known him, and would pledge my soul for him.'

She came under the gaze of Rhoda's keen eyes, and blushed as she realised that

Rhoda was drawing inevitable conclusions. Fergusson too looked astonished at the impassioned defence.

'We must leave the law to decide,' he said.

'What will the Sheriff do?' asked Rhoda.

'Nothing, if he is wise. The honour and loyalty of every member of the force is above suspicion. The Commissioner would resent any imputation of disloyalty. It is up to young Fraser to prove his mettle. Gad, I would not care to be in his shoes.'

'He has nothing to fear,' said Sheila stoutly. 'In any case he places duty before everything.'

Despite her brave words her heart was sorely troubled. She believed that Rose's interference would bear no fruit, but the knowledge that Angus as well as Donald was under suspicion was painful indeed. Now she wished she had divulged the truth earlier. It would at least have cleared the air.

'You are annoyed with me, Sheila,' said Rhoda later. 'I'm awfully sorry that we see things in different lights.'

'I don't blame you for holding certain opinions,' replied Sheila. 'If I were you, and had no knowledge of Donald, I — I might think as you do.'

'You know him — intimately?'

'I told you — we were boy and girl together.'

'Can a woman always be sure of a man? Aren't you led astray a little by — by your heart?'

'What do you mean?'

'I'm a woman. I understand.'

'I don't think you do.'

'You love Donald Fraser.'

'No — no.'

'Yes you do, but there is something which prevents you admitting it even to yourself. While you defend him so stoutly you have a little doubt in your mind.'

'No doubt concerning the cruel and unjust allegations that are made against him. Nothing in the world will ever persuade me that he would kill a man in cold blood.'

'But a quarrel, Sheila — a fierce passage of words, a quick but fatal blow — isn't that possible?'

'No — no. Donald is not impetuous. Though Willeton humiliated him he would not nurture hate. Justice is another matter. Donald would seek justice — not revenge.'

'I fear you are in for a bitter disappointment, and I wish I could shield you against it.'

'Thank you,' said Sheila shortly.

15

Murder

On the following day, while Rose Willeton was riding to Albany to apprise the Sheriff of what she had discovered, Angus paid a visit to Donald's shack. He found the place vacant, but saw Slocum farther down the range and interrogated him.

'Boss go hunting,' said Slocum. 'Business ver' bad — lose many steer through illness. Boss t'ink he get plenty good pelt and make some money.'

'When did he leave?'

'Sun up.'

'Will he be back soon?'

'Slocum not know. Maybe boss stay away long time, maybe he come back soon with full sled — yes.'

Angus frowned. He knew quite well that Donald had suffered a serious set-back through the recent cattle sickness, but he had not imagined the loss he had sustained was so great as to make such a trip as this necessary. He waved his hand to Slocum and went down the river towards his camp.

The recent blizzard had played havoc with the accumulated snow, heaping it into deep drifts and ornamenting the surface with series of waves and ripples. At the end of Donald's holding was a steep fall towards the river, and Angus had to pull up the dogs sharply to avoid a mishap. He was about to turn the sled when he noticed a strip of black leather projecting from a snow-heap below. Leaving the dogs he swarmed down the bank and found that the length of leather was part of a horse's rein, uncovered by the force of the wind. He removed some more snow and brought to view part of the dead body of a horse. It was frozen as hard as rock, but its markings told him at once that it was the missing animal, ridden by Willeton on the night of his disappearance.

His heart bounded at this first-fruit of long labour, though it seemed ironical that he should make this rather important discovery by accident. A closer examination of the beast revealed a deep wound in its temple. He judged it had been killed instantly by some kind of firearm. Going back to the sled he brought a shovel and commenced to turn over the snow in the neighbourhood of the stark animal. For two solid hours he worked steadily, and then came upon a human body. It was Willeton — as frozen as the horse, and with a hideous wound in his back!

'Murder!' he ejaculated.

Still he worked on, hoping to find some article that might serve as a clue to the murderer. His luck still held, for twenty yards from the spot he found an empty cartridge, and also a humane killer, with a second cartridge in its chamber. The short weapon bore the address of a gunsmith in Albany, and a number engraved on its barrel.

That afternoon he rode into Albany with the dead body of Willeton. Rose Willeton was sent for, and identified her father. The news spread like a forest fire, and within two hours all Albany was agog. The bullet was extracted from the corpse and it was established that it was fired from the humane killer.

'Find the owner of that, and we get the murderer,' said the Sheriff.

'It carries the dealer's name,' replied Angus. 'I'll go right along.'

He found the store just off the main street, and hunted up the proprietor. Fortunately the man carried on his business on business-like lines, and he possessed records of every firearm sold. In two minutes he had traced the purchaser.

'This yere weapon was traded to Donald

Fraser who lives up the river,' he drawled. 'Here's the date — over ten months ago. Yep, I recall it now.'

'Donald — Fraser!'

Angus felt a great stab at his heart, and a mist rose before his eyes. Was it possible — ?

'You're sure?' he asked.

'You bet. I remember him coming in through that door. Big fellow, with a voice like a trombone. Ain't that the fellow they've been connecting with the crime ever since it happened? Guess this sort of puts the kybosh on him.'

'Did he buy cartridges at the same time?'

'Sure! A box of fifty.'

'That's all I want to know at the moment.'

Angus left the place in a state of bewilderment. Never in his most imaginative moment had he guessed that such a situation would develop. That Donald had purchased the humane killer he had not the slightest doubt — and the dead man was found on land closely adjoining that held by Donald. Then the motive — it was all conclusive enough. But there was yet another factor to be considered. Slocum too had hated Willeton, and Slocum would have access to the instrument which fired the fatal bullet. Before making any report he went to find

161

the half-breed. As soon as he set eyes on him he divined that Slocum had heard the news of the discovery of the corpse, for the dark face was as set and expressionless as a piece of wood.

'I want a few words with you,' said Angus.

Slocum gave a slight nod and stood rigidly.

'You remember the night when Willeton was missing?'

'Sure!'

'Where were you on that night?'

'In Albany. Sleep there with budder.'

'Why are you so certain of that?'

'Slocum 'member day ver' well. Daughter have birthday and Slocum go to sing-song. Get ver' drunk and stay there all night.'

'When did you come back here?'

'Sundown, next day.'

'And then you heard that Willeton was missing?'

'No, Slocum know not'ing for two-tree days.'

'Well, Willeton has been found. Do you know that?'

'Slocum hear — jus' now.'

'He was shot in the back. Have you any suspicion as to who did it?'

'No. Why you look at me lak that? If I hate a man much I keel him lak this — but not in the back.'

162

He whipped out a knife and stabbed the air swiftly.

'And you are telling me you never saw Willeton after you left this place for that jag?'

Slocum shook his head emphatically, but his eyes were restless, and when he saw Angus take the humane killer from the sled there was a visible tightening of his features.

'Look at that,' said Angus. 'Have you ever seen it before?'

'No.'

'You are sure?'

'Ver' sure.'

'Careful!' warned Angus. 'You may be asked to swear to that before a judge.'

Slocum made no response, and Angus terminated his questioning. He returned to Albany and found where the half-breed's sister was living. From her and her uncle he established the fact that Slocum had spoken the truth about being in Albany on the night in question. In horror he saw the sword of justice hanging over Donald. The evidence so far as it went was damning. Who in the face of these facts would believe that Donald was innocent, save those who knew him and loved him?

He got into touch with headquarters and

then interviewed the Sheriff. Stiff-lipped he narrated what had taken place, and he saw the burning eyes of the Sheriff attempting to probe his soul.

'You want a warrant?'

'Yes.'

'For the arrest of Donald Fraser?'

'That — is so.'

'Very well.'

The document was filled in and signed, and the Sheriff handed it across the small table.

'Same name,' he said, lifting his eyebrows.

'Yes. My — my brother.'

'I happened to know that, but I'm glad you told me. This is a painful business.'

'Yes, but there is a flaw somewhere. Anyway, it isn't for me to express opinions here. All Donald will want is a square deal, and I guess he'll get that.'

'Sure he will! Gosh, I admire you for your spirit. Go and get your man, and leave the rest to justice.'

Angus marched out, and made for his late camp with a view to packing up. Again he interrogated Slocum with the object of learning Donald's objective. But Slocum feigned absolute ignorance. The boss had not mentioned the trail he was taking. He might be north, or west, or east.

'Why you wanna know?' he asked finally.
'That's my business.'

There was a flashing of dark eyes, and a grinding of white teeth, but no response. The half-breed's loyalty to his master was no less than Angus' for the Royal Mounted. In this brother he saw an enemy, and he did not disguise the fact.

Before Angus was ready to hit the lone trail Sheila put in an appearance. She was breathing heavily from a hurried journey, and she winced when she observed the signs of his impending departure. One look at the grim face was enough for her.

'Then — it's true?'

'What — is true?'

'I heard — there was a warrant issued for Donald's arrest. They said there were clues — awful clues. Angus — are you going — after Don?'

He inclined his head.

'But — Oh, it's horrible. Don is innocent — I know it. If you take him it may mean — it may mean —'

He caught her and held her closer than he had held her since the old engagement was broken off.

'Yes, Don is innocent, but duty is duty. I know there has been a lot of vile gossip around here. It's going to be the hardest thing I have ever tackled, but I pledged my loyalty, and I mean to go right through with this.'

'I wouldn't have you prove disloyal, Angus, but my heart is full of fear — for Don. Things look so black, and innocent men have suffered before now. It is cruel to make you do this thing — '

'It is an opportunity to prove that justice comes even before blood-ties. Most men are someone's brother. I mustn't cry out because chance has chosen me for this. In any case Don will be glad of an opportunity to prove his innocence.'

'Suppose — '

'No conjectures, Sheila. There are certain points to be cleared up. Don will help us do that.'

'Then the evidence is not so bad as I supposed?'

'It doesn't carry us far,' he lied.

'Please God it will all come right.'

'I am sure it will. Now I must go.'

'You know where he is?'

'No. But I must stay out until I find him.'

'Well, good-bye, Angus.'

He was glad to get away from her sorrowful eyes, and hoped he might be forgiven for causing her to believe that the threat to

Donald was less than it really was. Not for one moment did his own trust in Donald waver, but he saw clearly the pit that was dug for his brother. There were people who wanted a hanging, and the excuse for this one was very strong. And he of all the far-flung members of the corps was selected to bring the man he loved best in the whole world before his relentless accusers.

Arduous as his work had been hitherto he realised that worse was to come. There were dense forests to the north where a man might hide himself as completely as a needle in a haystack. There would doubtless be weeks of terrible loneliness, during which even the bark of a dog would be a comparatively pleasant sound. And added to the daily miseries was the ever-present realisation that he was hunting his own brother.

Sheila had the imagination to see the thing in its full horror, but Angus' assertions had comforted her a little. She tried to persuade herself that she had exaggerated the danger to Donald. This quest might even have the effect of clearing up the whole business for ever. But on the following day she heard something that killed her hopes, and drove the steel deeper into her heart.

16

Seeking

Fergusson and Rhoda had been invited to spend the evening with Rose Willeton, and Sheila was included as an afterthought. She had no desire to renew the acquaintanceship of the woman who bore Donald such unremitting hate, but Rhoda had begged her not to refuse, and Sheila took the line of least resistance. The topic which everyone in the neighbourhood had at heart was destined to be revived before the evening was out, and it was Lee who started the old hare.

'We got that half-breed talking,' he said. 'I knew the skunk was lying.'

'You mean Slocum?' put in Fergusson.

'Sure! He knew all about the humane killer.'

Sheila pricked up her ears, for she had not heard that instrument mentioned before. She understood that Willeton's body had been found near Donald's farm, and that death was due to a gun-shot wound, but it was news to her that a humane killer had been used.

'The Sheriff told me that Slocum denied all knowledge of its existence,' said Fergusson.

'He would,' said Rose. 'He was merely trying to shield his master. The lie was obvious after Crosby's evidence.'

'Who is Crosby?' asked Sheila.

'The storekeeper at Albany who sold the humane killer to Donald Fraser.'

'He — he said that?'

'No doubt about it,' growled Lee. 'Crosby had it entered in his book, and he swears he remembers Fraser calling. When that dirty breed was interrogated he denied that Fraser ever possessed such a thing. Well, we made him talk up.'

Fergusson winced at the significance of this remark.

'He — confessed?'

'Sure he did.'

'You used force?'

Lee laughed shortly.

'It's the only way when a guy is a born liar. He knew all about the killer. It was kept out in the shed, and it disappeared mysteriously about the time of the murder.'

'Had you the right to take that step, Lee?' asked Fergusson rather stiffly.

'I'd go further than that to get justice done,' snapped Lee. 'It's up to us to help ourselves in this matter. Why did the policeman swallow a lie like that? Do you think we will ever get a conviction without butting in? Who is representing the law here? Why the brother of the man who did the crime.'

'That's premature,' warned Fergusson.

'Premature! Will a jury think it's premature when they know that a man who was hated by another man is found shot by a weapon owned by his enemy, and his body hidden away —— '

Fergusson held up his hand, for he thought that this conversation was painful to Rose, who sat close to him, stiff-lipped and pallid. But Rose had got past that.

'Lee is right, Mr. Fergusson,' she said. 'One would have to be blind not to see the truth. From the day when my father thrashed Fraser he has sought to avenge himself. The facts are as clear as daylight. Why did Slocum lie at first about the killer? He knows, and when the time comes the truth will be wrung from him. But even without that there is enough evidence to hang that man.'

'I'm not so sure,' said Fergusson. 'Would a man who shot another leave behind him the weapon that would convict him?'

'Murderers always blunder. Providence sees to that — in most cases.' Her eyes flashed wildly. 'Aren't there curious facts about this case? Isn't it strange that Fraser should leave just before the policeman made his discovery? Don't you think he knew that fine brother of his had to produce something to save his face, and that he vanished according to programme?'

Sheila gasped at the suggestion of conspiracy.

'You — you say the most cruel things,' she retorted hoarsely. 'Donald Fraser knew nothing of that discovery. He had lost money and had long planned a hunting trip. If he had known he would have stayed and faced it out.'

Lee laughed scornfully.

'Guess your heart runs away with you, Miss McLeod,' he said. 'He don't deserve your good opinions. When a man has been shot in the back it's no time for sentiment. Miss Rose here has suffered a cruel loss, and I've lost a good master. We're not sitting still and trusting to the powers of the law — not in this case anyway. A policeman who wasn't keen on getting his man wouldn't have much trouble in missing him.'

'We must trust the police,' said Fergusson.

'That's just where we differ. When the half-breed became communicative he told us where Fraser had gone. But if he thinks he is going to lie safely up in the woods all winter he is mighty mistaken.'

171

'What do you mean?'

'Other folk may be more successful than the policeman.'

Sheila stared at this significant retort.

'You don't propose going — ?' she asked.

'There are less unlikely things. We ought to be able to nail him in a day or two.'

He shut his mouth tightly after this, as if he considered he had divulged too much, and Rose shot him a swift glance. It was evident that he had wrung information from Slocum and was contemplating the pursuit of Donald, probably with the help of some of his 'boys.' That Rose concurred was also obvious. The subject was dropped after that, but Sheila's whole mind was occupied with it. These new facts in the case changed her whole outlook. Instinctively she felt that if Lee was successful Donald would get scant justice. Even if he did the evidence against him was so damning that his case would be hopeless from the start.

'Lee means business,' said Ferguson on the way home.

'Rose too,' responded Rhoda. 'She has changed completely since her father's death. I suppose it is natural to want justice done.'

'Justice!' said Sheila. 'It is vengeance they seek.'

'Lee is indiscreet to interfere,' mused

Fergusson. 'But he mistrusts everybody. I fear he maltreated Fraser's servant.'

Sheila winced, for that thought was in her own mind. She knew the devotion that Slocum had for his master, and she had a horrible suspicion that something stronger than mere argument was used to compel the half-breed to give information. Came the desire to outwit Lee — to warn Donald of the danger ahead. Even her love of justice came into conflict with the forces of impulse. To sit still and see Donald either lynched or wrongly convicted was impossible. The passive attitude passed. He had saved her life. Was it wrong to aid a suspected man when her very life belonged to him? Justice! Why, already he was as good as hanged!

A great resolution took hold of her, and she persuaded herself that it was born out of her belief in his innocence. But behind the forces that moved her was the love which even now was repressed. Early in the morning she went over to the small farm. There she learned something that caused her burning anger to rise. Poor Slocum had suffered terrible torture, and was almost incapable of speech. A lariat had been drawn closely round his throat and information ultimately extracted from him by that means.

'Lee,' he croaked, pointing to the great weal. 'One day I keel heem — yes.'

'The brute! But your master is in great danger, Slocum. To-day Lee is going to find him.'

Slocum's eyes blazed with red hate, and his hand sought the knife at his belt.

'Not that,' she said. 'It would avail us nothing. You know where the boss has gone?'

'He say he go to the Scaderacks.'

'Where is that?'

Slocum waved his hand towards the distant mountains.

'How far?'

'Two — t'ree days to the edge of the forest. But maybe he go far in.'

'We must find him.'

'Slocum have no dogs.'

'Then get some. Try to hire a team in Albany. Here is some money. Is it enough?'

He waved her notes away.

'Slocum have plenty dollars. Maybe he get dogs, then he beat that wolf to the Scaderacks.'

'Hasten then. I — I am coming too.'

'Too hard work for lady.'

'No. I must come. There is something I must tell him. Get the dogs and what else you need, and meet me at Big Bend — at

174

three o'clock this afternoon.'

Slocum nodded, but it was clear that he did not approve of her impetuous resolution. On the way back to Fergusson's she realised that some explanation would be necessary to her host, for to disappear suddenly would most certainly cause grave apprehension on his part, and Rhoda's. The truth was out of the question, and she winced as she reflected that a lie was essential.

After the midday meal she went to her room and penned a note to Rhoda. It was a most unconvincing epistle, and informed Rhoda that she had had an urgent call from down country and would probably be away for a few days. This she left on the table of the sitting-room while Rhoda and her father were engaged elsewhere, and then, taking her small handbag she stole away — and made towards Big Bend.

She scarcely dared reflect upon the effect of the brief note upon Fergusson. It would ease his mind, but would arouse his suspicions. Still, things were at such a pass that there was no time to consider incongruities. Logic and reasoning had gone. All she could think about was Donald's safety. He must have all the benefits that the law extended to an accused man. Angus would see to that, but if Lee had his way —

For over an hour she waited by the frozen river for Slocum, and at last he came, with a good sled and a team of huskies. Her heart beat furiously now, for she was about to take a step that might lead anywhere. It was a hazardous business and she knew it, but a man's life hung in the balance. Slocum pulled up beside her, and scanned her face keenly.

'So — you got them?' she asked.

'Um. Dese ver' fine dogs. We make good going.'

'And — food?'

'Plenty food.'

'Then let us go.'

'Lady not — change her mind?'

'No — no. We have to stop this man, Lee, from taking the law into his own hands.'

'But Slocum warn boss.'

'I am coming,' she said determinedly. 'It is too late now to turn back.'

Slocum muttered something unintelligible and pointed to a vacant spot in the sled. She occupied the place, and he tucked the thick bear-skin rug about her. A pistol-like crack of the long whip and away they went, down the river trail. Soon the scattered farms were left behind and the barren lands entered. North of them rolled the great hills that mounted towards the cold peaks of the

176

mountain range. It was only now that she realised fully the scope of this bull-rush adventure. Slocum to her was an unknown factor. She had Donald's word for it that he was a trustworthy fellow, but all the same the danger was there. Deliberately she had placed her welfare in jeopardy, and there was small room for regrets.

The dog-musher had his nose to the trail, which he read as easily as a more sophisticated man might read an open book. To Sheila the confused markings conveyed nothing, but the backwoodsman had extra senses.

'Lee go fast,' he said.

'How do you know?'

'It is there — in the snow. But maybe we pass him soon — if he follow the left fork.'

Two hours passed and then the trail divided. One fork went across the wilderness and the other entered the timber. Slocum nodded his head contentedly.

'He take the easy way,' he said.

'You are going to the right?'

'Um! Ver' bad trail — along de canyon. But we make heem, by gar! You trust Slocum. Many times he travel this way.'

Soon she understood his remark, for the unbroken trail led up to a narrow ridge skirting a dizzy precipice. The snow was unmarked and lay thick upon the ledge. In places the stark rock projected from the mountain, leaving but a few feet between it and the yawning abyss. Thrice the sled was stopped and Slocum walked ahead on snow-shoes to pack the loose snow. Sheila dared not look beneath her, for she felt the sickening sensation of vertigo.

Yard by yard the worst portion was negotiated, until at long last the sled emerged on to a broader and less hair-raising track. She breathed anew, but it proved to be but a temporary easement, for half an hour later the path narrowed again, and there was a repetition of the recent horror. On some of the acute bends the end of the sled hung over the abyss, and the danger to the passenger was so great that she was compelled to get out and walk, gripping Slocum's guiding hand.

'How — how much more?' she gasped.

'Two mile, and then we have gained six hours. It is worth it.'

'Yes — yes.'

The end came at last, and she thanked God that she had survived it. Slocum shot her a look of admiration.

'Lee big coward. No come this way — but lady — '

'I — I was terribly afraid.'

'All right now. We gain time through the

timber. Slocum know best trail. But we go careful lest we be seen.'

Followed a rapid descent into the valley, with no horrific abyss to freeze the marrow in one's bones. Again thick timber was entered, and all through the afternoon the wiry dogs hauled under the imprecations of Slocum, and the cracking whip.

'We camp here,' said Slocum at last. 'We nearly keel dose huskies — yes.'

Thus ended the first day, and it brought to Sheila all the excitements of the chase. Whether they had passed Lee she did not know, but the little apprehension from which she had suffered at the start had now vanished. Slocum was to be trusted. In his frost-bitten face she saw nothing but the grim determination to thwart the man he hated most.

17

The Quarry

The wooded country of the Scaderacks was entered on the third day, and during all this time there was no sign of Lee's party, nor of Angus. This was not surprising, for Slocum had broken new snow in his short cut to the objective, and the main trail by which Lee would travel lay some ten miles to the west. But notwithstanding the quicker passage it was doubtful whether they had made up for Lee's big start.

'Have you any idea where the boss would work?' asked Sheila.

'Um. He ask Slocum to tell him best hunting ground. Soon we find creek. Boss lay his first traps in the forest on the south side.'

Sheila gazed in awe at the dense timber that reached to the snow-line on the vast mountains, the trees diminishing in size until they could exist no longer, and gave way to an unbroken expanse of snow and frowning perpendicular cliffs. The scene was one she would never forget, and it filled her soul with reverence to reflect that for hundreds of miles those minarets of Nature's designing straddled the land, barring the way to the distant sea. And the silence was intense.

'Have we passed Lee?' she asked.

'Slocum t'ink so.'

'Suppose — suppose we meet him?'

Slocum's eyes narrowed, and he put his hand to the knife which was stuck in his belt.

'Maybe he try make trouble,' he said. 'It is as well he does not try.'

'But he is not likely to find the boss immediately, amid this mass of trees.'

'The trails are few, and no snow fall for many days. Sometimes the devil's spawn have much luck.'

She did not like this ominous remark, but at the same time she felt certain that Slocum would find Donald long before Lee got a clue to his whereabouts. Here in the great silence of the mountains her former fears were redoubled. It needed no great effort of the imagination to realise how swiftly a man might snatch her revenue without fear of being discovered. In the case of a man wanted for murder a comparatively trivial excuse would suffice to cover any 'accident' to the accused.

Thereafter commenced the search for

Donald. For several days time was occupied unprofitably, following trails that had not been used since the last snowfall. But at last Slocum struck the creek which he had mentioned, and an hour afterwards he came upon the cold ashes of a recent fire.

'Is it — the boss?' asked Sheila.

'Slocum t'ink so. One man only eat here.'

'How long ago?'

'T'ree — four days maybe.'

'Which way has he gone?'

Slocum pointed towards the source of the creek, and Sheila felt her heart beat rapidly. Somewhere up among the timber was Donald, ignorant of the fact that his life was in jeopardy, and that his own brother carried a warrant for his arrest. What would Donald do when he knew that?

There was a short halt for a meal, and then the dogs went forward again — following the clear-cut marks of the sled-runners. Slocum located two traps and in one of them was a dead wolf, with a fine skin. He let the animal stay and resumed his course. But as evening approached the sky became darkened and a bitter wind stirred the trees and raised the snow from the surface of the frozen creek.

'Big wind come,' warned Slocum.

'And snow?'

He nodded, and his disappointment was

182

evident. Snow would not only delay progress, but obliterate the tracks left by Donald. The dogs were hustled badly for the next hour or two, and then camp was made. While they were eating the first flakes of snow fell. All through the night the wind gathered force, but the snowfall was not enough entirely to obliterate the tracks, and despite the ominous weather outlook Slocum decided to make an early start.

Within an hour the timber thinned out, and the trail went over a great col where nothing grew. Only with the greatest difficulty could the exceedingly faint tracks be seen, and the gathering storm threatened to expunge them for ever. Once out of the shelter of the trees the wind struck them like a solid thing.

'Why did he come this way?' asked Sheila.

'Maybe he made for the good hunting in Doom Valley. Slocum tell him of that.'

'How far?'

'Ten miles.'

She shivered at the thought of making ten miles in the present conditions — over an exposed mountainside that caught the full force of the bitter wind, but she raised no protest because of the threat of a heavy snowfall which might leave them in mid-air — so to speak.

Upward went the faint parallel lines, and

the panting dogs followed them under the urge of tongue and whip. But it was soon apparent that luck was against them. They entered a realm of gloom in which the wind howled like ten thousand demons. The driving snow grew denser and denser until visibility was reduced to less than fifty yards. She felt that Slocum in his zest had committed an error of judgment, for once he stopped and hesitated.

'Ver' bad,' he mused. 'No can see tracks any more.'

'Is it better to turn back?'

'There is good shelter in the valley.'

'How far now?'

'Four miles.'

'You think it is better to go on?'

'Lady must say.'

'Yes — yes. Perhaps the wind will lift.'

But her hope proved vain. In less than ten minutes they seemed to be in the vortex of the storm. The force of the wind was inconceivable, and the cold was such that it smote through thick woollen garments as if they did not exist. Then the dogs ran into a deep drift, and she and Slocum laboured to get the sled on to a better track . . . Through the blackness they moved, towards the shelter that the yet distant valley offered. To stay where they were was out of the question.

Even she in her ignorance of this kind of life knew that. Hitherto the journey had not been arduous, but this killing wind was a new experience. It made living a misery. It rendered one breathless, and threatened to bring about a kind of coma that would prove fatal.

An hour passed and still the conditions were unchanged. With nothing to guide them but Slocum's natural sense of direction, the possibility of becoming snow-bound on that awful plateau was great. She looked at the dog-musher, but it was too dark to see his features in detail.

'Slocum! Are we — ?' she shouted.

The rest of the sentence was lost, for there was a nerve-racking subsidence of the earth beneath her. She heard a hoarse shout, and suffered the sickening sensation of falling — falling. Then came a violent bumping. She reached out and clutched nothing more substantial than snow . . .

Unconsciousness supervened, but how long it lasted she had no means of telling. When she opened her eyes she was lying in deep snow, with every bone in her body aching. Some distance away was a dark blob — and moving forms. The sled! She stood up with a great effort and fought her way through the opposing wind. The sled was intact, and the gear which had been previously lashed to it was still there. Of the team of six huskies one was dead, and one suffering from a wound in the shoulder. The others were sitting up and howling.

But Slocum was not to be seen! She put her hands to her mouth and shouted his name. She might as well have whispered it, for the shrieking wind drowned everything. Terror possessed her. She dared not venture far from the sled lest she should fail to find it again. Slocum! Slocum! The despairing cry was caught up and smothered, and the thick, fine snow drove into her eyes and mouth.

Dimly she perceived an almost vertical slope on her left, and realised that this was the cause of the catastrophe. In the bad light Slocum had driven clean over it, and only the thick snow had saved her from worse than a bad shaking-up. But the disappearance of Slocum mystified her. Was he at the summit still, or had he fallen and been caught up by a projecting rock? She moved towards the precipice and shouted again — to no effect.

For half an hour she wandered about, still hoping to find the guide, and then accepted the situation. Half frozen, and aching from her fall, she pondered the next move. To climb the precipice was impossible. The only sensible thing to do was to go on and trust that eventually she would strike Doom Valley, and ultimately be found by Slocum, who would undoubtedly follow the tracks of the sled if he were able.

With grim face she cut the dead dog free, and managed to get the sled the right way up. The whip was missing but she succeeded in getting the dogs moving, and drove forward in the teeth of the blizzard. Progress was painfully slow, for the team was tired and the snow soft and deep. A strange numbed feeling swept over her, and at times threatened to reduce her to unconsciousness. She fought against this valiantly, knowing that such a lapse would be fatal.

Whether it was day or night she could not determine. Time ceased to have any meaning. Doom Valley! The name had a deep significance now. Was this to be the end of her hazardous escapade? In that wind it was impossible to erect the tent, and to sleep in the open —

Suddenly there came a rift in the thick veil that encompassed her, and she saw ahead of her the welcome timber. A little cry of joy escaped her, but immediately the view was blotted out again. Near to exhaustion she urged on the dogs, who were lagging badly. Hours seemed to pass, and she wondered whether she had been dreaming — whether that vision of shelter from this cruel, penetrating, slaying wind was not something conjured up by a disordered mind.

At last! A great conifer loomed up, quite close to her, its branches hanging low under the encumbering snow. Behind it reared battalions — multitudes of trees, offering a stout bulwark to the blast. She seemed suddenly to come into a world of peace and quiet, and she blessed the kindly forest.

She halted on the verge of an inviting hollow, and decided to camp. The first duty was to feed the ravenous dogs, after which she proceeded to erect the tent. It was a long and laborious job, but at last it was done, and she breathed a sigh of relief and got the hatchet from the sled with the object of cutting wood for a fire. She had gathered almost enough for her purpose when her left foot fell upon something hard. There came a curious sound and two rows of steel teeth rose from under the snow and fastened on her leg just above the ankle. She uttered a sharp cry of pain and tried to prise the jaws of the trap apart, but the spring was powerful and her strength insufficient.

Almost fainting from pain she pulled on the chain to which the trap was attached, but the retaining steel peg was firmly driven into the frozen earth. She stood there helpless, and in agony. Twenty yards away was the tent, food, warm blankets . . .

'Help! Help!'

Her despairing cry rang out, reverberating queerly among the thick timber. Again and again she yelled with all the force of her lungs. And then her heart bounded as a stentorian cry came back. She turned her head and saw the form of a man breaking through the snow. She knew him at once.

'Donald! Donald!' she cried chokingly.

18

Deep Woods

Donald's face was the picture of bewilderment as he caught the swaying form of Sheila in his arms. In five seconds his strong hands had prised the trap open and released the injured limb. With the aid of his supporting arm she limped back to the tent.

'Sheila! What does this mean?' he asked.

'I — I — ' she stammered.

He looked round at the snarling dogs, and the partly unpacked sled.

'You're cold — frozen. That won't do. You had better come to my camp.'

'My — my ankle — '

'I'll carry you.'

He lifted her bodily and strode through the trees. Soon she saw a ruddy glow in the gathering darkness, and a few minutes later they emerged into a clearing, where a fierce fire was burning. Backing it was a tent, and sundry gear spread about. He put her down on a box close to the welcome fire, and looked into her eyes.

'You are in pain.'

'It is — going away.'

'I'd better attend to you. That trap was none too clean. Take off your boot.'

There was no disobeying the peremptory voice. While he obtained some hot water and a swab, she removed her high boot and several stockings. Above the slim ankle — on either side of it — were three or four deep gashes. He winced at the sight of them, for they marred the smooth white skin, and were bleeding profusely. Tenderly he bathed them, and then tied a firm bandage with his capable big hands.

'It was my own trap,' he said.

'But it was my fault. I should have been more careful.'

'How were you to know? Is that better?'

'Much — thanks.'

'Sheila — I don't understand — But you are hungry — I can see that. Let us attend to the most important matters first. Luckily my meal is cooking. There is ample for two of us. Bacon and canned beans. Can you manage that?'

She nodded, and turned her eyes to where the frying-pan was spluttering. Hunger was a very potent thing, and even the motive which had impelled her on this quest had to play second fiddle to it. She ate with him in silence, for she was starving. Coffee followed — steaming hot coffee, that was like nothing she had ever tasted before. At last their tongues were freed.

'What does it mean, Sheila?'

'I — something happened after you went. Donald, there is a warrant out for your arrest.'

'A warrant!'

'Yes — yes. They found the body of Willeton. He had been murdered — shot with a humane killer.'

'And they believe — ?'

'They found the store where the killer was purchased. The storesman swears he sold it to you.'

Donald's brow contracted as he recalled the day when he had bought a humane killer in Albany, but he had never dreamed that this instrument was connected with the crime. In the face of this disquieting news indifference was impossible.

'Was the killer found near the corpse?' he asked.

'Yes — off the boundary of your land.'

'And Angus — ?'

'Angus himself found it. Oh, it's horrible. A warrant was issued and Angus carries it.'

'They sent Angus — my brother?'

'Rose tried to get him recalled, but nothing happened. Don, that is not all. When Lee heard that Angus was your brother he — he believed that Angus would prove disloyal. He tortured poor Slocum in order to learn from him where you had gone, and he and some of his boys started off to — to get you.'

'I see. That is what I should expect of Lee.' He looked at her keenly. 'And where do you come in, Sheila?'

'I wanted to warn you — against Lee. It is not justice that he wants, but revenge. Angus does not know where you are, but Lee is close at hand. I — I had to come, Donald. Slocum was against it, but I can't bear to think —'

She shuddered, and Donald gripped her hand tightly.

'You came — alone?'

'No. I had no hope of finding you by myself. Slocum came, but we met with an accident.'

With bated breath she narrated what had happened during the past few hours, and Donald listened without comment. The thought that occupied his mind was not the danger that threatened his existence, but the slander against his brother's honour. And with this was mingled admiration for Sheila who had braved the cold and all the discomforts of that long journey on his behalf.

'I suppose they think I ran away?' he asked.

'Yes — Rose and Lee, at least. You are in great danger, Don, for public feeling is against you.'

'That is all the more reason why I must face my judges,' he said tensely. 'I know nothing of this tragedy. That humane killer which they have traced to me disappeared some time ago. I had cause to dislike Willeton, but to kill him — '

'I know — I know. But innocent as you are you stand in great danger of being convicted. Slocum made things worse. He swore you had never had a humane killer, and then had to take back his own words. Everywhere there are enemies. I'm terribly afraid, Don.'

'Don't worry. Things will come right. I shall go back to the farm immediately, and then report to the Sheriff.'

'No — no!'

He gazed at her in astonishment.

'But to do otherwise is to give grounds for their suspicions. It's the only reasonable thing to do.'

'Is it reasonable — is it human — for a man to give himself up to his judges when in their eyes he is already guilty? I didn't realise it until I went to Rose's place and heard the common gossip. Unless you can prove a complete alibi the end is certain.'

'So you really came to — to urge me to flee?' he asked harshly.

'No — yes.' She wrung her hands. 'I don't know. My first object was to warn you not to fall into Lee's hands. But now things are different — at least I see them in a new light. They will hang you, Don — I know it.'

Her voice rose almost hysterically, for in her vivid imagination she saw Donald convicted — the sober judge, and the bloodthirsty crowd. Being so near him made all that difference. She wanted no arrest now — not even on Angus' part. But Donald had no such mental problem. To him the path was clear, but to pacify her he descended to affected indecision.

'Let us think things over,' he said. 'I am troubled about Slocum. He must have been stunned by the fall, and it is our first business to find him.'

'It is impossible to do anything now. Out there the wind is terrible.'

'It may lift a little presently. Sheila, does Fergusson know — about this?'

'No. I dared not tell him the truth. I left a message that may mislead him — but I doubt it.'

'You did a courageous thing, Sheila, but

195

I wish you had not. It will embroil you.'

'What do I care? Isn't our — friendship enough to justify such a step? Everywhere I see prejudice and injustice. Why does that woman hate you so much?'

'Rose? Isn't it natural if she believes I murdered her father?'

'It isn't merely that. She once hinted to me that you and she were — '

Donald's expression stopped her.

'I'm sorry.'

'It's no great secret,' he growled. 'She's a man-hunter and set her shaft at me — God knows why. I had to be brutal to put an end to a painful state of affairs.'

'You didn't — like her?'

'No.'

'Why not?'

'What a curious question! Must a man like the first woman who looks at him approvingly?'

'She wasn't the first, Don.'

'The first one I have noticed. But why do you plague me about women?'

'I don't know — perhaps for the want of something to say that does not bear too hardly on that terrible business. How time changes everything! It seems such a short while ago that you and I and Angus were playmates together, without a care in the world; and now out of nowhere has come trouble upon trouble. What have we done to deserve it all?'

'What have we done to deserve all the happiness we have had? What shall we do to merit all the happiness that is to come to us when the storm has passed?'

'You think it will pass?'

'Yes.'

She shook her head slowly.

'I haven't your faith, Don. I'm temperamental. When things go right I am on top of the world, but when things go bad they darken my soul. It is dark now.'

'Things are never quite so black as they appear to be. But you are tired and need sleep. You had better take my bed, and I will shift your gear over here.'

'I am not tired now.'

'Your eyes tell me so. Now do as I bid you. Go to bed at once and leave the rest to me.'

'Can I safely do that when you appear to care so little about yourself?'

He laughed softly.

'You have no idea how much I am in love with myself. The sort of end that Lee visualises doesn't attract me in the least. Have no fear — I shall establish my innocence.'

But she was not comforted by this

assertion, for she was fully aware that he was simulating optimism on her behalf. Notwithstanding she did as she was bid, permitting him to half carry her into the tent where his blankets were already spread.

'Good night, Don!' she murmured. 'Thank God, I found you.'

He went back to the fire and gazed into it reflectively for a few moments. Her amazing intrusion was still giving him furiously to think, for he could well imagine the ordeal through which she had passed. Then he became active, and transported the tent, sled, and gear from the neighbouring hollow. He was anxious to commence the search for Slocum, but outside the timber conditions were unfavourable.

Sitting there alone he let his mind range over the events that led up to this crisis, and it seemed to him that Fate was playing a queer game. It had placed upon his shoulders a yoke, and upon Angus a duty that was going to test his manhood to the full. Donald recalled vividly the past when Angus had fallen from grace. That was not going to happen again. Wherever the future might lead Angus was going to play the game.

Then he sighed as his eyes rested on the tent where Sheila was sleeping. How sweet life might be if — if — ! Through the dancing snowflakes he got a vision of home — home and the old people, blissfully ignorant of what was taking place here in the frozen North. What a testing of spirit it was going to be! Here was a woman tempting him to flee before his accusers, and somewhere was Angus doubtless tortured by the consciousness of his duty.

During the night the terrible wind abated, and morning found a clear cold sky and deep snow. By the time he had reduced handfuls of snow to boiling water Sheila was up. When she emerged from the tent he was glad to observe that the limp was almost gone.

'How is the injury?' he asked.

'Much better. My leg is a little stiff — that is all.'

'Good. The weather has improved.'

'Then we shall be able to search for Slocum?'

'Immediately. It was useless last night — in the blackness. I — hope nothing serious has happened to him.'

'He had no food — nothing. Could he have survived a night in the open — in that dreadful place?'

'Slocum is half wolf. We must hope for the best.'

He passed her some food and coffee, and for some minutes she ate in silence.

'Don!'

Her querulous eyes were focussed on him. 'Well?'

'Do you — do you intend to go straight back — when we have found Slocum?'

'Yes.'

'And — and then?'

'Then we shall soon know the worst that gossip and suspicion can achieve.'

'How can you explain — about the humane killer?'

'I can't explain.'

'Then it is madness,' she cried. 'I won't let you do it — I won't let you fling away your life.'

'Look out! You are spilling your coffee.'

'Coffee!' Her eyes flashed as she put down the enamel mug. 'Is this all I get for coming up here — to help you?'

'Did you expect any different result?'

She knew not what to say. But a little while ago she was all for justice — for obtaining a fair trial, but now the spirit of anarchy was aflame within her. His passive mood enraged her. By some means or other he must be saved — from himself. He did not seem to realise that giving himself up was akin to jumping from the highest precipice in this wild region. But the way out was not easy to find.

19

Intervention

With the two dog-teams strung together Donald and Sheila made through the woods towards the place where the accident had occurred. But the snow had filled in the runner-tracks and Sheila could not assist much in the location of the actual spot.

'It was so dark,' she said. 'I saw nothing but drifting snow and blurred outlines. But we were three or four miles from Doom Valley, according to Slocum.'

'We had better try the higher trail, in the hope of seeing where the fall occurred.'

They ultimately made the higher land and Donald drove the dogs close to the edge of the ravine, but wind and snow had obliterated all sign of a disturbance. Nowhere was there a living thing to be seen.

'I ought to have marked the place,' said Sheila. 'But my mind was bewildered. He — he may be under the snow.'

'He may have got away.'

'But he would have gone on — towards Doom Valley. He would have found my tracks and reached us before now.'

'There are all kinds of alternatives. If he sprained an ankle, for example, he may have limped to the nearest shelter.'

'But where — ?'

'Slocum knows every inch of this country, and he is not the sort of fellow to be killed easily. The only thing to do is to go on.'

She kept a stiff lip and nodded her head. Instead of taking the perilous ravine path, Donald made a detour and got on to the main trail, for he guessed the other route would be impassable under its new burden of snow. Twice he stopped to examine some traps which he had laid, but neither of them had been touched.

'We saw one farther back, with a wolf in it,' informed Sheila.

'Then my luck is looking up. That is my first bag so far.'

'You are going to leave the traps?'

'Yes. I can make another trip and gather the spoil.'

'Was it necessary — this trip?'

'Yes. The cattle-sickness hit me hard. I hope Slocum left the stock well provided for.'

'I think his brother was coming up from Albany to keep things going. Don, you don't think Slocum had anything to do with the killing of Willeton?'

'No. I remember the night quite well. Slocum was in Albany. If Slocum had designs on Willeton he would have used a knife. All these half-breeds put their trust in steel.'

She shuddered at the remark, but Donald did not notice it, for he was killing space as fast as the dogs would let him. With all his self-control Sheila was a constant danger to his peace of mind. He could scarcely look at her without lapsing into wild and impossible dreams. The old love which he had tried so hard to check was as rampant as on the day when he had discovered her and Angus together whispering wonderful secrets.

From that day onward he had persuaded himself that she belonged to Angus, and even the break that had since occurred had not changed his views. They would make it up. They would be happy together — one day. For himself he asked no more than the simple joy of helping to bring about this end. As ever Angus came first, and in this deep regard for his brother he was apt to forget that the boy whose battles he had fought was now a hardened man. It was the only streak of sentimentality in his nature, and it was very deep-rooted.

'How desolate and wonderful it is,' said Sheila, breaking in upon his reflections.

'Do you find it overaweing?'

'Not so much — now. But to be alone is very different. I — I felt like a mite in an empty world. Companionship is a very necessary thing in a big country like this.'

'Yes. Men have gone mad for the want of it. But it's the land of the future, Sheila. Canada can take all those surplus millions in the old country and still ask for more. But she offers them no feather beds — at first. A man wins only through hard work. If he slacks he must go under. But it's a fair fight, with ample reward. I shall never regret the day I landed here.'

'And you never pine for — home?'

'Yes — to see it again, but not to stay. One day I shall go back and get a glimpse of the old faces, climb to the summit of Ben Tavis and swim in the loch. But it won't hold me long, I'm thinking. I'll be seeing that little farm of mine, and the great mountains. Yes, I've been permanently adopted.'

She trembled as she reflected that all this might prove but a vain dream, for the sword that hung over his proud head was keen and heavy. It needed but a snip to sever the cord. Yet he did not appear to realise it — as she did. Perhaps he did not appreciate to the full the ill-feeling that was directed at him by his neighbours? Her heart grew heavier as the day passed.

Towards evening the thick timber on the other side of the mountain was entered. The early-setting sun brought down intense cold, and she wondered that Donald did not make camp without delay, but he kept on steadily. Tired of sitting in the sled, and chilled by the inactivity she got out and walked.

'I'm all cramped,' she explained.

'But your ankle — !'

'I can scarcely feel the wound now. Shall we camp soon?'

'You are hungry?'

'Yes — famished.'

'I thought we would do ourselves well to-night. On the way up I ran across an abandoned hut. There is an old stove inside, and the roof is still intact. We are within two miles of it.'

'Then let us go on.'

'You're rather wonderful,' he said.

'In what way?'

'In a hundred different ways. Few women would have acted as you have, entrusting yourself to a half-breed, and then to me, braving all the discomforts of the trail — '

'Don't!' she begged. 'You don't know what a coward I really am at heart. I was scared to death of Slocum until I realised that he was a man to be trusted, and as for you — '

'Am I also in that glorious category?'

'I had never thought of you — like that. It would be horrid even to think in that fashion as between you and me. All our lives we have been a kind of a trinity — you and I and Angus.'

'The inseparables. Yes, there is truth in that, for it was little short of a miracle, our meeting out here.'

'Is there such a thing as Destiny?'

'I wonder!'

'If so, it works a little cruelly at times.'

He guessed she was referring to Angus, and the unpleasant duty that faced him. He became silent again.

The light went from the lowlands, but in the east the mountain tops were crimson. Sheila saw again the marvellous spectacle of alpine sunset through a vista of snow-encumbered pines. It passed, leaving a soft and mysterious after-glow on the peaks, which too, in its turn, faded out. From the north the moving shafts of the aurora borealis swept the deep blue vault.

'I can see the hut,' said Donald suddenly.

Sheila turned her head and managed to discern a squat shape not far ahead. She sighed with relief, for the day's travel had been long and arduous, and the prospect of food and rest was pleasant, to say the least. In a few minutes they were in the clearing in which the hut was built.

'The door's round the other side,' said Donald. 'Not a bad little place if one — '

He stopped abruptly as the howl of an animal rang out from close at hand.

'A wolf!' whispered Sheila.

'No, first cousin. A wolf-hound.'

'But — '

Round the end of the hut came two men. The light came from behind them rendering their features invisible, but Donald and Sheila were clearly illumined by the northern lights. Sheila saw the foremost man whip out a revolver.

'Fraser, by gosh! Wal, if that ain't luck!'

She knew the voice and recognised the tall form now. It was Lee — forewarned and chuckling with glee. He stepped close to Donald and leered at him.

'Up with your hands — and quick about it!'

Donald remained just as he was, his fine face puckered in a grim smile.

'What's your trouble, Lee?' he asked.

'You'll know if you don't put up your mitts. I can shoot you like a dog and have the law on my side, and I will, by Harry.'

'Shoot away, then.'

'Donald!' cried Sheila apprehensively.

'Your woman's got a little more savvy,' sneered Lee. 'Pretty little affair this! I surmised you two were friendly, but I'll allow I didn't bargain on finding you keeping house together.'

A low growl of rage came from Donald's throat and he moved forward a step. Lee's revolver came within six inches of his chest and the eyes behind it carried a warning he would have been mad to ignore.

'Get his gun, Wallace!' ordered Lee. 'If he moves an inch I'll let loose. Search him!'

Wallace found no firearm, but he possessed himself of a hunting knife which Donald carried.

'That's all, I guess,' he said.

'Good!' Lee turned to his prisoner. 'Come inside, and don't try running away, because I'm reckoned to be a pretty good shot.'

Donald moved round the hut with the two men close behind him, and the agitated Sheila bringing up the rear. Outside the door were dogs and a partly unloaded sled. Inside were two other men from the Willeton ranch — Brady and Lawson.

'Gee!' ejaculated Brady. 'If it ain't our particular pigeon!'

Lee chuckled and drove Donald towards the end of the building.

'Nice and kind of you to look us up,' he sneered. 'It saves us a deal of trouble. I had a hunch I'd find you long before the constable would. He had a good reason for hunting where he knew you wasn't.'

'For how long have you held powers of arrest?' asked Donald.

'Ever since the night when you plugged Willeton in the back, and buried his body. I'm going to yank you back to Albany, and there they'll put a nice new rope round your neck.'

'You anticipate too much, Lee. As a matter of fact I was on my way to Albany when — '

Lee laughed scornfully, and his companions joined him.

'You seem to doubt that.'

'I lost my milk teeth long ago, sweetie. When a man has slugged another man he usually makes for the border. If luck hadn't come my way you might have got across.'

'I could have got across a week ago if that was my intention.'

'Maybe, but then you didn't know I was after you, and you didn't know that we've got all the evidence we want to hang you, until this young woman sneaked off to put you wise. Wal, we'll deal with her too — '

'You keep her out of it,' snapped Donald.

'You're a bloodthirsty ruffian, Lee, and at this moment I'll admit you hold the cards, but I'll never admit your right to take this sort of action.'

'What you admit or don't admit doesn't matter at all. I've got you, and folks will be mighty grateful that there is someone smart enough to get on to your trail.' He turned to his companions. 'Now, boys, we fix him up so he won't start any trouble. Bring some rope, Brady.'

'Wait!' cried Sheila. 'Mr. Lee, there is no need to do that. We were on our way back to Albany. Mr. Fraser is innocent and is determined to face the thing out.'

'I get you. You just went to him to help him along, eh? It's queer you didn't think of that before you knew I was after him. You're a mighty winsome woman, but I wouldn't trust any woman who was so chummy with a man that she slept — '

Sheila's face went crimson, and Donald leapt forward and caught Lee by the throat.

'You foul-minded skunk — !'

Lee's eyes bulged, but Wallace and Brady intervened and bore Donald backward.

'Tie him up!' snarled Lee. 'By God, he'll be lucky to get a trial at all. Hurry!'

Sheila saw that further entreaty would be a waste of breath. Lee held the whip-hand by force of numbers, and his hate against Donald was such that he was not likely to spare him mentally or physically. The filthy allegations which he made sickened her. Yet she was helpless.

Within ten minutes Donald was bound securely, and flung into the corner like a sack of flour. He spoke no word, but Sheila could feel his resentment as keenly as she felt her own ignominious position.

'And now for you, missy,' said Lee. 'I'm not keen to put you to any inconvenience so long as you act on the level.'

'How considerate you are,' she retorted.

'A darn sight more considerate than the circumstances call for. Don't hand me any of your cheek.'

The hut boasted but two rooms and Sheila was given the smaller one. Food was brought her later, but she made a poor meal despite her hunger. So far as she could see Donald's plight was hopeless. Within a week he would be lodged in jail at Albany.

20

Angus Takes a Hand

Donald felt his position keenly. It had been his intention to go back and face his accusers, but he rebelled at the idea of being forcibly conducted by Lee, and the latter's innuendoes against Sheila aroused his deepest wrath. They gave him no food that night, and he was not in the mood to ask for it, but on the morrow Lee permitted his hands to be unbound and Brady brought a plate of food and some coffee.

'Eat well,' said Lee. 'For I guess your future meals are numbered, my cockerel.'

Donald shrugged his shoulders.

'Interesting finish,' sneered Lee. 'I'll admit I didn't bargain on the girl acting that way. She looked pretty respectable to me.'

'I should imagine you were a poor judge of respectability,' retorted Donald. 'You're playing a bold game, Lee. Take care you don't go too far. When I'm acquitted I may make things a little awkward for you.'

'When you're acquitted!' Lee laughed lugubriously. 'Why, if I thought that could happen I'd have you hanged from the nearest tree. No, boy, you're as good as dead at this moment. By hanging you myself I'd only rob the crowd of a little excitement. It isn't often we get a hanging in Albany.'

He spoke as if he meant what he said, and Donald could not help feeling that he was a pretty good judge of the way the pendulum would swing. The murder of a well-known and respected rancher made a fine appeal to the passions of the mob, and when the accused already had black marks against his name the jury might not be as free from preconceptions as it should be.

'Then there's Miss McLeod, who used to put on airs and graces, and — '

'Leave her name out of it,' snapped Donald.

'Not much. She's an accessory, and she's going to answer for it in the right place.'

'You fool! She has never connived at my escape. She came to warn me that you were taking the law into your own hands, and to advise me to yield up myself to the only man who has powers of arrest.'

'Your brother, eh?'

'Yes — the constable.'

'Wal, where is he?'

'Looking for me.'

Lee's shoulders shook with laughter.

'A good joke that — sending a man to arrest his own brother — on a charge of murder. The Commissioner ought to have known better, but he's so drunk with pride he overlooks human nature. Your brother is now busy looking where he knows darn well you don't happen to be.'

'You liar!'

Lee went purple with rage. He stepped closer to the prisoner and slapped him violently in the face. But Donald's hands were still free, and he managed to grip the wrist of his tormentor. The powerful hands exerted awful pressure and Lee's wrist went backwards until it threatened to break. He uttered a yell of pain, and then went reeling across the room as Donald administered a mighty shove. Brady came running in.

'What's all this?'

'I'm going to kill him,' choked Lee. 'I'm going — '

He whipped out a revolver, but Brady caught his arm.

'Steady, Lee! Hanging's better.'

'By gosh — You're right, Brady. Tie him up again. We'll get our fun later.'

Brady called Wallace and the two men secured Donald's wrists so tightly that the cord almost stopped the blood circulation. Then they all left him and went to attend to the sleds which were being packed for the homeward journey. A few minutes later Sheila emerged from the inner room.

'Don!' she said brokenly.

He smiled at her, and then looked down at his wrists.

'Try to loosen the knots a bit. My hands are getting numbed. There is no need for that.'

She used her teeth and managed to make him more comfortable.

'We — we are leaving?' she asked.

'I imagine so.'

'Is this — the end?'

'Why should it be?'

'He has everything in his hands.'

'It doesn't alter things much. I was on my way back when we fell in with him.'

'Yes — but somehow — '

'I know what you mean, and that is what rankles in my mind. It is not the ignominy of being tried that matters so much as the humiliation of being the prisoner of a man like Lee. He will exhibit me — everywhere. That is not going to happen if I can help it.'

'But how — ?'

'Don't ask me, Sheila. I do not want you embroiled in this. You must let matters run their normal course.'

'You mean I am to sit still and do nothing while the threat of — of a miscarriage of justice hangs over your head?'

'Are we sure there will be a miscarriage of justice?'

'You — you don't mean — ?' she gasped.

'Oh no — I am not guilty. But justice sometimes has a queer way of vindicating herself. The mob may want a quick hanging, but there will be a judge and jury.'

'Don't talk of them. I can't bear it, Don. Nor can I bear the horrible truculent attitude of Lee. Can't you — can't you escape?'

Donald looked round warily.

'From Lee perhaps, but not from the trial.' His voice sank to a whisper. 'I don't mind Angus handing me over. That is his duty. And I am prepared to surrender myself to the Sheriff, but this is quite a different story. If — '

Lee suddenly entered the hut and Donald left the sentence unfinished.

'You had better get outside,' said Lee to Sheila. 'I don't want you two talking together. If I see any more of it I'll gag him.'

She shot him a withering glance and went through the door. Outside she found the sleds already packed, and the dogs being harnessed. Donald's last remark filled her with apprehension, for she believed that any attempt at escape would give Lee an excellent opportunity to vent his hate on the prisoner, and she was not sure that the law would not overlook his conduct in the circumstances.

At last Donald was brought out and dumped on the leading sled. Lee intimated that she could either ride or walk, and she preferred the latter. Lee gave the word and the sleds moved forward, headed towards Albany. No halt was made until noon, when a quick meal was taken. Then progress was resumed along the well-defined trail. As the miles were covered Sheila's heart beat faster. The end now seemed inevitable, for Lee had attended to Donald's bonds after his hands have been freed in order to permit him to eat.

It was late in the afternoon when Sheila suffered a shock. She was tired and had dropped to the rear of the sleds. They were again in thick timber and she concluded that Lee would soon make camp. Happening to glance over her left shoulder she gave a start to observe a human form flitting among the trees. It acted more like an animal than a man, and the sight of it was limited to a fraction of a second. For five minutes she saw no more of it, and then suddenly it emerged within fifty yards of her. Her heart bounded as she recognised Slocum!

He had a rag bound round his head, and immediately he saw her gaze directed at him he placed one finger across his lips and vanished again. She understood that warning, and kept her glance fixed ahead of her. Hope rose anew in her breast. With the trustworthy Slocum on their side the outlook was decidedly improved. By some means she must acquaint Donald of this fact.

Another hour passed before Lee selected his camping site, and called a halt. A good day's running had been made and he was gloating worse than ever. Tents were erected and a big fire lighted. Sheila searched the gloaming for a sign of Slocum, but she neither saw nor heard anything of him. Again Donald's hands were untied and food given him.

'Another day nearer Hell,' said Lee, leering at Donald.

'I hope it won't be as bad as they paint it — for your sake.'

'Spunky, ain't ye? But you'll change your ideas when you're standing on the brink of it.'

'For God's sake, stop!' cried Sheila. 'You have no right to talk like that to a man who has yet to be tried.'

'Aw, he's been tried already,' growled Lee.

'What's left to be done is just a formality, I guess.'

Sheila shuddered and Donald shot her a glance to intimate that it was better not to engage in argument. She looked at him queerly, trying to convey what she wished to tell him, but it was a failure, for the light was bad and there were several other possible interpretations of that long glance.

When he had eaten, his bonds were fixed again, and he was carried into the smallest tent. Of the other two tents, one was reserved for Sheila and the bigger one for Lee and his companions. The dogs were hitched to a stake and slept huddled up together in the snow. Sheila looked towards the tent where Donald lay.

'Can I speak to him for a minute?' she begged.

Lee shook his head.

'But — !'

'I don't trust you,' he snarled. 'You're as cunning as a waggon-load of monkeys. You'll have lots of time to talk to him when he is in jail.'

It was obvious that no kind of argument or entreaty would move him, and soon after she went to her tent. Lee pursed his lips as his glance followed her.

'Fix up that flap in a few minutes, Wallace,'

he said. 'She's capable of helping that fellow. Better still — one of you had better sleep with him. That'll be your job, Brady. You're light on the doze.'

'I've got my sleeping bag in the other tent.'

'Then shift it — and don't argue with me.'

'All right.'

★ ★ ★

Sheila was scarcely inside the sleeping-bag when she heard the crunch of boots on the frozen snow outside. Followed the straining of canvas and the heavy thud of a mallet on the steel pegs. They were fixing her up for the night!

21

Escape

Donald lay in great discomfort in his canvas prison. Some blankets had been thrown over him, but his occasional movements removed them and the great cold ate into his marrow and numbed him. Later Brady entered with his arms full of blankets — plus a thick sleeping bag. He lighted the oil lamp and gazed down at Donald.

'I hope you don't snore,' he growled.

'Snore! I'll be frozen stiff before morning. For God's sake pull these blankets around me.'

Brady did as he was bid. He was not a bad sort of a fellow, and sincerely believed he was assisting the ends of justice in aiding Lee.

'How's that?'

'Better, thanks.'

'You're in a tight corner.'

'Not the first one. Lee is making a big mistake.'

Brady pursed his lips. He had his own ideas about that. But he was too tired to start any argument, and in ten mintues was sleeping lightly.

Donald found sleep not so easily. His arms and leg's ached most painfully, and to move them only meant exposure to the intense cold. In addition there were mental discomforts — far worse than the physical ones. To be Lee's prisoner was galling, and to realise that Sheila was exposed to all kinds of rebuffs and insults was scarcely less aggravating. He had intended making a desperate attempt to escape, but the ropes had been tied by one who understood that art.

Sleep came at last, but it was intermittent. He awoke at intervals to find himself shivering with cold. For the nth time he strove to induce warmth into his numbed body by rolling himself up in the blankets. He was engaged in doing this when he heard a queer sound near the bottom of the tent. It was like an animal trying to gain entry, and at first he suspected a timber wolf. He sat up.

'Hist!'

There was no mistaking the human sibilant. He looked down and in the light shed by a clear subarctic moon, which penetrated the canvas, he saw that one or two of the tent pegs must have been removed, for an arm was thrust under the bottom of the tent and in the fingers of a brown hand was a keen knife. He knew that knife instantly.

'Slocum!' he whispered.

A movement came from the sleeping-bag. 'Shut that noise — damn ye!'

'All right — all right.'

A long silence followed, and then slowly the arm was followed by a shoulder and part of a face. It was Slocum and his wolf-like vision took in everything. Donald understood what was required, and moved his bound wrists towards the knife edge. The blade went through the rope, and then Donald's numbed fingers took the implement. Minutes passed before his blood circulation was sufficient to enable him to get to work. But at last the rope fell away from his legs, and he found himself free. He lay there gently rubbing his muscles.

'Boss!'

He leaned over and put his mouth close to the bottom of the tent.

'Crawl in — if you can.'

Slocum came under the canvas with the lithe movements of a reptile. Then he stood up and looked down at Brady. There was a movement of his hand towards the knife which Donald still held, but Donald shook his head, and pointed to a woollen scarf. That was not Slocum's way of dealing with enemies, but he knew he must obey, and reached for the scarf, while Donald sorted out the pieces of the severed rope.

'Now!'

The scarf went round Brady's mouth, and the rope round his limbs. There came a gurgle and a futile struggle, but in three minutes Brady was as helpless as Donald had recently been — and speechless in the bargain.

'Slocum, you're a brick,' said Donald, and gripped the half-breed's hand.

'Slocum follow all afternoon. Have rifle outside and revolver here.' He tapped his pocket. 'We go quick, eh?'

'There's Sheila — I can't leave her here. Do you know in which tent she is sleeping?'

'Um. Slocum watch everything from the woods. But it is ver' dangerous to — '

'I can't leave without her.'

'Then Slocum go get her.'

'No. You stay here. Where is she?'

'Small tent — near fire. Better you let Slocum go. The knife ver' silent — '

'Sh! I want no killing. Do as you are told. Keep that man quiet, and wait for me.'

Slocum nodded and Donald took the knife. On emerging from the tent he found the camp-fire still blazing and throwing queer shadows on the snow. Beyond it were two tents. He made for the smaller one, and found the guy ropes very taut. Gently he slackened two of them and folded back the flap. The light from the fire played on Sheila's beautiful face. It was reposeful now, for deep sleep had found her, despite her mental troubles. He shook her by the arm, and at last she opened her eyes.

'Sheila!'

'Why — Don!'

'S-sh! You must come at once. I mean to get out of Lee's clutches.'

'But — !'

'Careful! Bring all the clothing you can wear. It is terribly cold, and we dare not take the sleds. Hurry!'

Still dazed, she got out of the sleeping-bag, and allowed him to help her into the thick coat which she had discarded for the purpose of sleeping.

'Boots,' he whispered.

Her mind was become active. She recalled Slocum and rightly divined that Donald's freedom was due to his intervention. But this flight in the bitter cold of the sub-arctic night was hedged about with dangers, of which she was fully aware.

'Come,' he said. 'And tread lightly.'

She followed Donald, wrapping a scarf round her head as she crossed the open space. All might have gone well, but for an unexpected sentinel. From close at hand came the eerie howl of a wolf. The dogs stirred and one of them opened his mouth and let loose a terrified wail.

'Confound!' muttered Donald.

Slocum came running at them with a rifle in his hand. He pointed towards the thick timber. Again the dog raised his penetrating cry, and a light appeared in the larger tent.

'Follow Slocum,' whispered Donald. 'I'll bring up the rear.'

He was within a few yards of the nearest trees when he heard a cry from behind. He turned his head and saw a form silhouetted against the tent. Simultaneously there was a flash and a loud report. The bullet missed him by inches and tore a strip of bark from the tree ahead of him. He plunged forward and overtook Slocum and Sheila.

'They come?' asked Slocum.

'Yes — that infernal dog gave us away.'

'Boss take revolver.'

The weapon changed hands in the darkness, and Slocum shouldered the rifle for which he had no great love. To him the knife was worth ten rifles.

'Make for some kind of shelter,' said Donald.

Slocum went off at a great pace, leaving

226

the main trail on his right. For some distance the going was good, and fairly well lighted by the moonbeams that filtered through the branches of the firs. But soon they encountered rough ground — littered with boulders and undergrowth partly hidden by thick snow. Progress became exceedingly difficult for Sheila, and she suffered a hundred minor injuries in her efforts to keep up with her companions.

'They — they will follow?' she gasped.

'Yes. Unfortunately our tracks will guide them. Our only chance is to strike another beaten track.'

'Is there one?'

'We must rely upon Slocum. But for that dog — '

Voices came to them in the great stillness. Lee had evidently raised the alarm, and pursuit was in progress. Sheila realised that she was the stumbling-block. But for her the two men might have made good an escape. Strong and healthy as she was she lacked the physical strength to surmount the rocks and bushes that obstructed progress.

'Don!'

'Yes.'

'You go on. It's the only way. I'm holding you back.'

'No.'

'Yes — please. I shall be all right. There is safety in numbers, and — '

'We go together or not at all. There is just a chance that they may fail to find the place where we left the trail.'

'But they are coming this way. I can hear their voices.'

'Hurry!' begged Slocum. 'Two mile away there is running water. We lose them there — yes.'

Through the silent woods they fought their way — now in the deep shadow, now in the incredibly brilliant light of the moon. At length — when Sheila was near to dropping from fatigue — Slocum found his running water. It was a half-frozen stream, that would freeze entirely before the winter was through, but now there was an open passage of bubbling water running rapidly over a rocky bed. Slocum stepped into it — up to his waist, but before Donald followed he turned to the weary Sheila.

'I shall have to carry you.'

'Oh no — '

'It will be quicker — and better. Come!'

It was the old peremptory voice and she knew it was useless to argue, when Donald felt that way. Lifting her in his arms he stepped into the torrent, and followed Slocum. A few hundred yards farther on the stream divided. Slocum took the left fork and worked up the stream for about a quarter of a mile. Then he made the land and waited for Donald.

'Slocum know cave through the trees,' he said. 'He come back later and cover up tracks.'

Donald nodded, and the trio moved forward. At last Slocum's objective came in sight. It was a considerable recess in an outcrop of rock, well-sheltered by timber on two sides, and by the rising land on the remaining two.

'Warm inside,' averred Slocum.

This turned out to be true, but it was exceedingly dark, and Donald possessed but a score of matches. He used a large number of these seeking a suitable place to sleep, while Slocum went back to obliterate the tracks.

'You think we are safe now?' asked Sheila.

'We ought to be, but we are faced with difficulties. I am not sure that I did not make a mistake in compelling you to come with me. We have no food — nothing but what we stand up in, and the rifle. So much for my selfishness.'

'Selfishness!'

'It was that. I was in no immediate danger from Lee. What I hated was the idea of being

229

dragged into Albany as his prisoner. Pride — pride! It must suffer a fall sometimes.'

'But I wanted to come, provided I was not a hindrance. I detest that man. At least we have Slocum. He knows the way of life amid such conditions. I wonder what happened to him?'

'He seems to have injured his head. But there was no time to ask him for details. I think I hear him coming now.'

Slocum's form was soon outlined against the opening of the cave. He came forward, seeing where Sheila thought no human eyes could see. Then he became lost in the darkness, but she heard him moving about.

'Slocum!' called Donald.

'Boss have match?'

'Yes — but only a few.'

'Slocum have candle here.'

'Splendid!'

The lighted match revealed Slocum close at hand, with a candle wedged into the mouth of a bottle. It spluttered a little and then burned steadily. To Donald's amazement Slocum was in possession of a capacious bundle, and when he opened it there came to view food of various kinds and valuable gear, including a spirit-stove and a can of kerosene. The whole was enclosed in two blankets.

'Why, where on earth — ?'

'Slocum hide him here, and watch trail from above.'

'Splendid fellow! But we both thought you were dead.'

Slocum pointed to his bandaged head.

'Big luck go with Slocum. When lady fall over precipice Slocum fall too and hit head on rock. All go dark, but Indians find him and bring him 'long. They take long trail, but Slocum trade food and things.' He scanned Sheila's face. 'Lady ver' tired. Go to sleep now.'

He spread one of the blankets on the ground, and when Sheila reluctantly occupied it, he placed the other one over her. The last thing she remembered was the warm grip of Donald's hand, and the sphinx-like expression on his strong face, before the candle was extinguished.

22

Bloodshed

The dim morning light found Slocum squatting at the roaring primus stove preparing a somewhat meagre meal. Sheila sat up and blinked at him for half a minute before she recalled clearly the incidents of the past night.

'Slocum!'

Slocum's wooden face relaxed into the semblance of a smile.

'Lady sleep?'

'Yes. Where is the boss?'

'He go to look round. Come back soon.'

'You turned up in the nick of time.'

'Lee not give up yet. Maybe he watch all trails from some place, and hope to catch us.'

'What — what are we going to do now?'

Slocum looked towards the entrance.

'Slocum guide boss across the border,' he said. 'The river go that way. Ten mile west there is good trail that go through the mountains. Boss no go back home or — '

He drew his finger across his throat and

232

Sheila shuddered at the grim significance of the gesture.

'You — you think there is no hope for him?' she quavered.

'They would hang him. Slocum know. So many people hate him. So many fools think he keel Mr. Willeton. If so be he do that, then that man deserve — '

'But he didn't,' she broke in. 'He is innocent. You know he is innocent.'

Slocum nodded his head slowly, and her heart went cold as she realised that there was the shadow of doubt in his mind. Even Slocum, the worthy reliable Slocum, nurtured doubts. It was horrible, for within her was a faith that could not be shattered.

'He will not go over the border, Slocum,' she said hoarsely. 'He means to surrender himself to the Sheriff of Albany, unless he meets the constable beforehand.'

Slocum's dark eyes flashed. He looked at her keenly.

'And lady want that too?'

It was a question she did not welcome. To answer it meant a painful heart-searching. Her love of justice, of right conduct prompted her to approve Donald's decision, but in her imaginative mind was a grim picture of a gallows and Donald — ! Slocum was merely repeating the opinions of others. Albany spelt death. Donald in his innocence might not appreciate that. Was it right to maintain a passive attitude and permit him to put a rope round his own neck?

'I don't know — what I want,' she demurred.

'But Slocum know what is best. To-day we go through the mountains and — '

Donald suddenly entered the cave, and Slocum closed his mouth and began to dish up the cooked food.

'All clear,' said Donald. 'Well, Sheila, we have to thank Slocum for our breakfast, and for our delivery from the hands of our enemies.'

'You can see no sign of Lee?'

'None. If he ever got as far as the river he must have found a dead end. Now we will race him back to Albany.'

'You mean to — to go there?'

'Of course.'

Slocum shot her a glance over Donald's shoulder. It conveyed the unmistakable fact that the half-breed had no intention of taking that route if he could succeed in hoodwinking his master. The meagre meal took but little time, and then Donald and Slocum made the food and other oddments into two packages.

'Lead on, MacDuff.'

She marvelled at his cheerfulness in the circumstances, and wished she could assimilate some of his amazing optimism, for to her the outlook was black indeed, unless Slocum could pull off his stratagem and ultimately succeed in bringing Donald to his senses. They struck the stream again, but did not cross it. Slocum began to work up the western bank, keeping well ahead of his companions to avoid questions. But it was not long before Donald realised that they were not heading for Albany.

'What is Slocum at?' he mused. 'Albany lies in the other direction.'

'I expect he wants to avoid Lee.'

'He can do that without wasting so much time, Slocum!'

The half-breed turned his head, but still walked on stolidly. Donald ran forward at a dog-trot and caught the guide by the arm.

'Half a minute! Aren't we going wrong?'

Slocum shook his head silently.

'But we ought to be going downstream, not up. What has come over you?'

Slocum looked at him steadily.

'No good — that way. Slocum know.'

Donald's brow contracted as he gazed at the frowning mountains. Then he turned on Sheila and saw the blood mount swiftly to her cheeks.

'I see,' he muttered. 'So that's it! Slocum, about turn and keep your nose to the east. You've wasted a good hour.'

'I tell boss — '

'You can tell me nothing I do not know. We're hitting the trail for Albany. Do you get that?'

'Slocum no go to Albany.'

Donald caught him by the collar and pulled him round so that their faces came within two feet of each other.

'You'll go where I tell you, Slocum,' he said. 'You've been a good servant so far, and a good friend. You'll lead the way to Albany now or we part — for ever. Make up your mind. I've no time to waste.'

Sheila came between them and laid her hand on Donald's arm. He released Slocum and met her moist appealing eyes.

'Isn't he right, Don?' she asked. 'In going to Albany you will throw your life away. Don't blame him because he is trying to prevent — that.'

'I'm not blaming him — nor you for taking his view of things. But my mind is made up and nothing will change it. You must accept that, Sheila, for it is final.'

'Won't you — won't you be reasonable?'

'I am the only reasonable being here. The man who runs is usually a guilty man. I

236

am not running.' He turned his head to where Slocum stood in a somewhat dejected attitude. 'What is it to be, Slocum?'

'The boss has said. We go back.'

'Good!'

They thereupon retraced their footsteps, and ultimately passed their recent camping place, but they did not cross the river, for Slocum was of the opinion that the western side was more sheltered once the timber thinned. Donald and Sheila walked together, but a tense silence reigned almost continually. At noon they came into the brilliant sunlight of the unwooded foothills, and Slocum took advantage of the undulations to keep hidden, for on the more elevated land the visibility was wonderful.

But as Slocum had surmised Lee had not yet been beaten. They were crossing a wide, treeless space when Donald uttered a low cry. Sheila soon saw the cause of it. About two miles away, on a vast shelf, were the black forms of men and sleds. And as she looked the still forms became active — ominously active.

'Lee!' said Donald.

'Um!'

'He — he has seen us?' gasped Sheila.

There was no need for Donald to reply, for the distant figures were coming at them at a great pace, on a long down-gradient. Slocum looked back, but between them and the friendly timber was nothing but blinding snow.

'Well, that's that!' said Donald with a grim laugh.

'What are you going to do?'

'What is there to do — except wait for them?'

'But if — ?'

She stopped and winced as Slocum unslung the rifle, and opened the breach of it. Donald frowned and took the weapon from the half-breed.

'You are — not going to fight?'

'I hope it won't be necessary. Lee may have the sense to realise that we are armed and can take care of ourselves.'

During the tense minutes that passed the oncoming men made great progress. They were lost to sight for a short while and then reappeared in the valley, but half a mile away. Slocum's hand went to his knife, and he moved from foot to foot in agitated fashion. Sheila waited in an agony of suspense.

At last the sleds came to a halt about a hundred yards away from the trio, and Lee came forward alone. He grinned in sinister fashion as he stopped a few yards from

Donald, whose arms were folded across the muzzle of the rifle.

'I've come for you, Fraser,' he said. 'Better avoid trouble and walk this way. The others can come or go as they please.'

'Thanks!' replied Donald. 'But we are quite capable of finding our way back.'

Lee ground his teeth.

'I came up here to get you, and by gosh, I'm not going back without you. Have a little hoss sense. We're four men to two.'

'Listen,' said Donald calmly. 'I intend to get to Albany without delay, but *not* as your prisoner, Lee. If there is any trouble it is not of my seeking. Go now, and leave us alone.'

'Not much! I'm taking you — dead or alive, and you'd better decide which way it is to be.'

'It will not be alive.'

'You fool! Are you wanting to get shot? Do you prefer lead to rope. That lank-haired son of Hell helped you to get away last time, but he won't help you now, and I'll feed him to the wolves if he — '

This was more than Slocum could stand. A cry of inarticulate rage left his lips, and without the slightest warning he whipped out his knife and leaped at Lee. There was a flash of steel in the sunlight, and a cry of horror from Sheila. Lee saved his life by a finger's breadth, and as he leaped aside, drew his revolver and shot, almost blindly. Slocum stood still for a fraction of a second and then coughed and fell on his face. Donald ran at him, but the life seemed to have gone out of him.

'Dead!' muttered Donald.

'Serve him right!' snarled Lee. 'If I hadn't got him he would have got me. Now I'll deal with —— '

Donald, taken unawares, found himself covered with Lee's revolver, with Lee's determined face behind it. Ordinarily he would have been discreet enough to have accepted the situation, but the death of his faithful servant momentarily unhinged his mind. With a growl of rage he flung himself at Lee. Again the revolver spoke and Donald collapsed across the dead body of Slocum. With a wild cry Sheila went to him. She saw the blood welling from a wound in his breast.

'Donald! Don! Don!'

But no reply came, and the hand which she fondled was limp in her own. She dashed away her tears and shook her fist at Lee.

'You — you brute! You've killed him!'

'He forced it on me. But maybe he ain't —— '

He made to approach the still form, but she drove him back with the ferocity of a tigress.

'Don't you touch him! Don't come near — '

'He's alive, I tell ye.' He turned and beckoned his men towards him, and while he did so Sheila felt the heart of Donald beating faintly.

'Not dead!' she muttered.

'So I told ye. Brady, lend a hand. Get the sled up here. We'll save him yet for what's coming.'

Sheila was suffering a reaction now. She felt sick and faint and could do no more than sit down helplessly. One of the sleds was brought up and Donald was lifted on to it. Brady tried brandy, but although the pulse quickened Donald still remained unconscious. As in a dream Sheila saw them place some rugs over Donald. Then Lee came to her.

'We're ready. If you're feeling faint you'd better take a seat in the sled.'

Somehow she got there, and an hour of semi-oblivion supervened. Whether they had buried Slocum or not she did not know. She was moving over the snow in a world of imagery. Here was Scotland — Culm, the rugged peak of old Ben Tavis, and the blue still waters of the loch.

'A policeman — by gosh!'

This remark broke upon her dazed brain. She pulled herself together and gazed ahead of her. On the narrow trail between the rocks a dog-team was approaching, and the musher wore the familiar winter garb of the North-West Police. Then a low cry left her lips, for she recognised the driver. It was Angus!

'It's *the* constable,' said Lee. 'Now ain't that jest wonderful! Wal, we've put one over on him anyway.'

The sled stopped suddenly, for Angus was blocking the way. Sheila jumped out and ran at him, and a look of amazement passed over his face as he saw her.

'Angus! Angus! — Thank God!'

'This is — extraordinary,' he said. 'I had no — Why are you so pale and agitated? And what is Lee — ?'

'It's Donald,' she cried chokingly. 'They've got Donald — there in the sled.'

23

Duty

Angus turned his gaze from the distraught Sheila to the group of men facing him. In the foremost sled he saw the unmistakable shape of a human form, and projecting above the rugs part of Donald's head. Leaving Sheila he walked across to the leering rancher.

'What have you got there?' he snapped.

'A mutual friend,' sneered Lee. 'I reckoned you might miss him, so came out for him myself.'

Angus pulled back the top rug and his lips became compressed as he saw in full the immobile countenance of his brother, and the crimson stain on the breast.

'You — you did this?' he said hoarsely.

'Sure! He went for me, and I guess I'm entitled to protect myself against a murderer.'

'Hold your tongue! Who are you to bring accusations against — anyone? You've meddled too much, Lee, and if anything happens to him you may have to answer for it.'

'I know where I stand. This man's wanted, and it's up to honest folk to see that he gets his deserts.'

'That's what I'm here for,' replied Angus tensely.

'You!' Lee laughed scathingly. 'I guess we know all about that, Mr. Policeman.'

Angus turned on him with his fists clenched, and Lee retreated before the outraged constable.

'I'm going to know more about this affair — later,' said Angus through his clenched teeth. 'You've acted without any kind of authority, actuated only by hate — '

'By a sense of justice,' cut in Lee. 'But for me he'd have got clean away.'

'That's not true,' said Sheila, stepping forward. 'He had no intention of escaping. We were on our way to Albany when Lee saw us. It is true Donald attacked him, but only with his hands. He was shot — callously.'

'He was shot in self-defence,' snarled Lee. 'I've enough witnesses to substantiate that. Anyway, what's done can't be undone. I've got him and I'll hand him over to the law.'

'You'll hand him over to me,' said Angus.

'I'm damned if — '

Angus put his hand on the butt of his revolver and looked at Lee and his companions.

'If there's any interference from any of you I'll shoot. This man is my prisoner, and it's my duty to deliver him up. That I intend to do.'

Lee looked as if he was ready to dispute this, but Brady and Wallace had more sense and a few whispered remarks caused Lee to shrug his shoulders and give way.

'Take him then,' he said. 'But we're here to see you do the duty you talk so much about. If you ask me it's a pretty sort of conspiracy.'

Angus turned his back on him, and enlisted the aid of Brady. Donald was carried to Angus' sled and laid in the end of it. Sheila winced as she gazed at the pallid face.

'Angus — I believe he — '

'We must attend to him at once. Which is his team?'

She pointed out the dogs and sled which Lee had taken over, and some time was spent in hitching the two teams together.

'There are Slocum's dogs too,' she said.

'Slocum!'

'I came with him. It is a long story. He — he quarrelled with Lee — and Lee shot him.'

'If I hadn't I'd have been a pretty sort of corpse,' put in Lee who had overheard her. 'Anyway his team is safe with me. Now we'll

245

all hike back to Albany.'

'You keep away from me,' said Angus. 'I'm not in love with your habits.'

'Maybe not,' sneered Lee. 'And I've no great idea of your sense of duty either. Anyway, I'll be on your tail, just to remind you. I presume the young lady will go with you, seeing she's so blamed interested in the pair of you.'

The last thing Angus heard was a raucous laugh behind him. He looked at Sheila who walked beside him, and saw that her face was ashen.

'Once we get clear of that gang we must attend to Don,' he said. 'I'm worried about him.'

'Angus — this is terrible.'

'Yes. I never suspected that Lee would take matters into his own hands. How did he find Don?'

'He tortured poor Slocum to make him give information. Slocum lied to you to prevent your arresting Don. Afterwards he told me the truth. We — we came to warn Don.'

'Warn him?'

'Against Lee. I dreaded that Lee in his bitter enmity would find an excuse to shoot Don. That has happened already.'

'You came up here — alone with Slocum?'

Angus was still cogitating on this astonishing fact.

'What else could I do? He went away not knowing how black things were against him. But I heard that if captured he would have no chance. The evidence is too damning — and yet he is innocent. I wanted to tell him the truth — '

'Then it wasn't entirely due to Lee's interference?'

'No — no,' she demurred. 'I won't lie to you, Angus. I tried to persuade myself that I merely wanted to save him from Lee. But it wasn't so. If he is taken to Albany and tried, he will be convicted. Nothing can save him, and it is left to you — his own brother — to put a rope around his neck. It's cruel — cruel and inhuman.'

Angus was breathing heavily. He had had time to go over the pros and cons of this affair, and his conclusions were very similar to Sheila's. The iron had struck down into his heart, but he had gone on seeking, earnestly striving to do his duty, though inwardly he prayed that Providence would spare him this painful task.

'We — we must hope, Sheila,' he said.

'Hope? For what? For a change in the hearts of the mob? For a better knowledge on their part of the man for whose blood they are craving? Angus — you can't do this.'

'What are you saying?'

'It oughtn't to be expected of you — not of his own brother!'

'It may seem hard — to us. But you cannot possibly understand the traditions of the force. Perhaps elsewhere a man placed as I am placed might have been recalled, but the Commissioner is not built that way. He expects of each man unswerving allegiance. He trusts every man to put duty before every other earthly consideration. It is such occasions as this which provides the acid test. I am facing it now.'

A little later they halted and Donald was attended to. The wound was deep and large, and the leaden bullet was in his breast. It was Angus' task to remove this, and a difficult task it proved to be. But at last the misshapen thing came out, and the wound was washed and dressed. All the while Donald lay like one in a trance.

'He'll do better now,' said Angus. 'Cheer up, Sheila, Don is as strong as a horse. He'll pull through.'

'For — for what?' she demanded.

'To prove his innocence.'

'To be the victim of hate and injustice. Everyone is against him, because of a lying rumour that was spread some time ago. Lee and the Willeton girl would even lie to see him hanged. I think — I think it would be better if he were to die now from his wound.'

'Sheila!'

'I — I can't help it. Somehow — somehow — '

To his surprise she dissolved into tears, and her convulsive sobs tore him to the heart. But he let her give vent to her feelings, believing that she would be the stronger for it afterwards. At the same time it gave him much food for reflection. Were these the tears of a friend or the lamentations due to a closer understanding? Angus' eyes were being slowly opened, and as the scales fell from them his agony of mind became the more acute.

They resumed their journey, with Lee not far behind, watching them like a lynx, and at dusk they camped amid timber. As Sheila anticipated Lee camped within sight of them. She bit her lip as she realised that two more days at most would see them at their destination unless some utterly unexpected incident supervened. That evening Donald regained consciousness. Angus had brought the sled close to the fire, and Donald's low cry reached Sheila's ears. She ran from the tent and leaned over the helpless man.

'Sheila! I thought — '

'Thank God you have revived,' she said. 'Angus will be back in a minute. He is cutting wood.'

'Angus! What are you saying?'

'He is here. After you were wounded we ran into him. He took you from Lee and — Don't try to move.'

'It doesn't look as if I can,' he replied with a wan smile. 'Lee must have got a good line on me.'

'The beast!'

'What happened to Slo — ?' He stopped and winced as he recalled the events of that morning. 'I remember now. Poor old Slocum! Such a good fellow too — '

Angus suddenly appeared with wood in his arms. He dropped it when he saw Donald smiling at him, and ran to grip the rather limp hand.

'Good old boy!' said Donald. 'So you got me after all?'

'Yes — I've got you.'

'Well, that's better than being Lee's guest. Did he make any fuss?'

'He is not two hundred yards away at this moment. Don, this is a sorry business.'

'Hard on you, old boy. But don't worry. I want nothing better than to face this thing out, and I'm glad to see you here.'

'I oughtn't to let you talk.'

'It won't hurt me. Quite a relief to lie here and do nothing while others work. I suppose that human wolf has a notion that I may try to escape? If so, he underrates the power of his own gun. Lord, how he hates me!'

Despite his former assertion speech exhausted him. Sheila saw his breast heaving under the strain, and marvelled anew at his toughness and optimism. She saw, too, that Angus was far from emulating his brother's example, and guessed that he was recalling the distant past, and all that the big brother had done for him.

'Hadn't we better get Don into the tent?' she asked.

'Yes — yes.'

'I will attend to his wound while you prepare the meal.'

But Donald objected. He wanted to lie there and watch the burning logs, and he looked so comfortable that he was allowed to have his own way. Later Sheila fed him with a spoon.

'Back to the nursery,' he joked.

But neither of his auditors reflected that mood.

'Why are you worrying — you two?' he demanded after a long silence.

'Is it a time for rejoicing?' asked Angus. 'This is my first job — the thing that was to win me my spurs. Don, could Fate deal more brutally with any man?'

'Can't see it, old boy. Any man you might arrest is probably someone's brother — and certainly some woman's son. It doesn't make much difference in the long run, and it allows you to prove to that skunk yonder that his mind is rotten.'

Angus kept a taut face and Sheila's breast heaved under her emotion. Don was trying to make it easier for his brother, but without any great success, for Angus was fully aware of the animus against his un-welcome prisoner. Later he and Sheila placed Donald in the tent, and dressed his wound before they left him.

'He — he doesn't understand,' said Sheila.

'He does.'

'But the way he talks.'

'His way of letting me off lightly. He knows as well as I know that his chance of being acquitted is not one in ten. The whole neighbourhood is against him, and the motive they will impute is strong. Proof? There never is any proof. Men are hanged on circumstantial evidence.'

Sheila's face was pallid, for it was the first time that Angus had really uttered his thoughts. It was fuel to her already deeply rooted fears.

'Angus, it can't go on,' she cried hysterically. 'You can't give him up — to be hanged like a dog with a bad name.'

'We are powerless to avert the danger.'

'You mean — because of Lee?'

'Yes — and because of my own oath of allegiance. If it were not for that I would fight to the last ditch for him. But you know Don. Even if for one moment I thought of shirking my duty, Don would not have it so. He'd sacrifice himself for others, but will accept no sacrifice in return. No, we are caught up in a foul web that offers no way of escape.'

'Must duty come even before justice?'

'We must not assume that justice will fail.'

'But it will — you know it will. Not from malice but from ignorance. We know Don — you and I. Whoever perpetrated that crime it was not he. Isn't there anything we can do — anything?'

He looked into her eyes and read the pleading of her soul. What she desired was as plain as the stars above — it was Donald's life in the face of vows, oaths — anything. Slowly he took her hand and compelled her to face him.

'Sheila, there is something I want to know. Do you — do you love Don?'

The red lips quivered and then the beautiful head dropped.

'Sheila! You mean — you do?'

'I — I can't help myself,' she admitted in a strangled voice.

'And Don — doesn't he guess?'

'No — no.' She turned her moist eyes towards the tent and lowered her voice still more, until it was but a husky whisper. 'Forgive me, Angus.'

'Forgive! I have nothing to forgive. When — when did this start?'

'Long — long ago.'

'Before he left home?'

'Yes. I was scarcely aware of it then, but when he had gone I knew — I knew.'

'And that is why you — you gave me back that ring?'

She nodded, and Angus drew in his breath with a sibilant sound. At last it was all clear to him, and the little hope that still lingered was shattered. He sat there in silence for some minutes — steadying himself.

'I never dreamed of that — until recently,' he said slowly.

'You knew then?'

'A suspicion came when I met you up here, and realised the length to which you had gone to — to help him. That was so grave a step that even friendship seemed not to warrant it. And Don — dear old Don — doesn't know!'

254

'S-sh!'

'Why shouldn't he know!'

'We have never talked of love — he and I. He doesn't know that our meeting in Canada was not entirely a chance reunion. I heard from Rhoda Fergusson that he was living near her. She invited me to stay with her — but it was Donald's presence that caused me to accept. I'm ashamed to tell you this, Angus. But it's true. Don means everything to me. I know he went away in disgrace, but that oughtn't to count against him all his life. Out here he has done wonderfully well, and it wasn't long ago that he saved my life. Can you wonder that I want to save his?'

Angus winced as she introduced the subject that was so painful to him. In his mind he registered a vow that that old lie should be nailed to the counter ere long.

★ ★ ★

He sat alone in the great silence, shoulders hunched and hands clenched. Hitherto his duty had been hard enough, but now — The idea of hurting Sheila was no less painful than to contemplate handing Donald over. What a strange world it was! Men like Lee could strut at their ease while the loyal and magnificent Donald was threatened with a felon's death, and women like Sheila placed upon the rack.

'God help them both,' he murmured.

24

Desperation

The following morning showed a great improvement in Donald. His temperature, which had been a little high, was practically normal, and there was a look about him that promised well. Sheila's confession of the night before caused her a little embarrassment to remember, and she could not meet Angus' eyes without blushing. Donald was carried to the sled to be fed, for he hated being shut up in the tent, and the morning was cold and beautiful.

'I'm actually getting an appetite,' he said. 'Angus, you are an admirable cook.'

'None for you,' said Angus. 'I have prescribed for you — slops.'

'How mean! Sheila, I appeal to you.'

'It is no use. I am a menial, Don.'

Donald laughed and turned his head.

'Is Lee still away back?'

'Yes. He won't give us much rope.'

'He's likely to give me some,' said Donald. 'About six feet of it, I'm thinking.'

Sheila shuddered at this grim jest, and

Angus winced. While Donald was being fed Lee himself strolled into camp and leered at them.

'Thought I'd jest see how things were going,' he said.

'Well see — and then be gone,' retorted Angus sharply.

'So you've still got him?'

'What did you expect?'

'Nothing else — when I'm so close at hand to prevent any kind of — accident.'

'Beat it!' said Donald. 'The sight of you isn't calculated to improve my health. But there is going to be a reckoning one day. When that comes — '

'A man in your position oughtn't to talk about reckonings. What sort of reckoning do you imagine a fellow gets after he has shot a man in the back?'

Angus swung round on him with furious eyes.

'Get out!' he said. 'Or I'll fling you out. This is my affair and will be until my prisoner passes out of my hands.'

'You're right,' snapped Lee. 'But I'm taking good care he don't pass too quickly. Anyway, I'm glad he's doing so mighty well, and being nursed with such devotion. I wouldn't have him dead for a whole lot of money.'

He marched off after that, and a silence fell over the three friends. With another day starting Sheila could scarcely control her feelings, and Angus wore an expression that was eloquent of his mental agony. Donald was by far the most hopeful.

'You two look and act as if the judge had passed sentence on me,' he said. 'Why pay any attention to what Lee thinks, or gives us to believe he thinks? He'll say anything that is likely to annoy us. He and I have always been like cat and dog.'

'He'd hang you if he could, Don,' said Angus. 'Don't underrate his influence. He has used that incident of the alleged cattle-stealing to inflame public opinion against you.'

'Will that count for much?'

'Up here — yes. I don't want to paint things blacker than they are, but you have to prepare to face violent antipathy and deeply rooted preconceptions.'

But still Donald smiled and made light of it, and the reason was clear enough to Sheila. It was all done to make Angus' task easier. Here was the stout Donald acting up to his chivalrous nature — because he could do naught else. Sheila had too fine an opinion of his mentality to be hoodwinked by his indifference.

While Angus finished packing the sleds she gazed at the map of the neighbourhood which was lying with his gloves, and she realised that their route lay parallel with the United States border, which was less than twenty miles away. An idea entered her mind, but she had to abandon it. Angus would never play traitor — and even to plead with him to that end was more than her appreciation of him would permit, though she had once hinted at it. Again, there was Lee to consider. Lee would be watching.

They started off and for some distance the trail was easy to follow. Then came broken country over which the sled bumped and creaked. It must have been painful to Donald, but he raised no complaint. The nearer they got to Albany the blacker the outlook became. Away in the distance was Lee's outfit.

'Hanging on,' growled Angus. 'But we are gaining on him. I'd like to shake him off. If I can only draw away round the mountain yonder I have the choice of three routes to Albany, and it is quite likely we could lose him.'

Donald heard this and beckoned Sheila to him.

'Tell Angus to take the right fork near the creek,' he said. 'It will take us to Albany, and we can lose Lee in the folds of the hills.'

She communicated this to Angus, who consulted the map, and then agreed to follow this advice. An hour later they struck the diverging trails and Angus struck off on the right side of a narrow creek. Soon they were hemmed in by great hills, and the trail wound about in serpentine fashion.

'Are we far from Albany now?' asked Sheila.

'We ought to make it to-morrow evening, if this fine weather continues.'

'So — soon!'

'Would you prolong the agony?'

'I would defer for ever the terrible ordeal which Don has to face,' she replied. 'I'm afraid, Angus — terribly afraid.'

'There is a chance.'

'Yes — the chance that a cornered rat has against the terriers who are hemming him in.'

'S-sh!'

He looked towards Donald, but Donald had fallen into a sleep, for he had spent a bad night.

'He knows,' said Sheila hoarsely. 'He knows that Lee's cruel jibes are based upon reason. And we are only one day from Albany. What hope is there now?'

Angus set his teeth and stared ahead of

him. It was useless to lie to her when all the facts were so clear. What comfort could he give her in the circumstances? Unlike her he was anxious to reach his objective, in order to probe deeper into the mysterious tragedy of Willeton's death. Somewhere the real murderer was lurking, and the best way to help Donald and the woman who loved him was to concentrate his mind on bringing that felon to book.

'Giving up hope will not help Don,' he said. 'We've got to save him — somehow.'

'He's asleep,' she said. 'Sleeping while we take him nearer and nearer a horrid — Ugh!'

She saw him wince and reproached herself for adding to his pain. Then she noticed a narrow track leading through a rocky valley and managed to read the inscription on a signboard covered with snow and ice 'To Montana.' Again there surged up a wild impulse to save Donald, but a few minutes later the board was lost among the trees. Ahead of them was Albany!

From a slight elevation Angus looked back across a tumbling wilderness of stunted conifers and snow. Not a living thing was to be seen, and the intervening mountain obscured the easterly trails.

'We've given Lee the slip,' he said. 'Our

dogs are better than his and we ought to make Albany well before him. That is a satisfaction, anyway.'

On they went again, with Donald still sleeping. Sheila went forward and put the rugs closer around him, compressing her lips to save herself from giving way to tears of compassion. A little later, to Angus' surprise the trail bifurcated, and the map gave him no clue as to which road he must follow.

'The map doesn't help,' he mused. 'It won't do to make a mistake here, or we may find ourselves landed hopelessly.'

'Don may know.'

'Better let him have his sleep out. Poor old chap! The only way is to scale that hill. If I can locate Sedge Lake I shall know what to do. I'll take the binoculars.'

'It is a good way up,' she said, gazing at the towering slope.

'It will save time in the long run. Rest yourself while I reconnoitre.'

He went through the scattered trees and Sheila saw him mounting the heights. Then she went to Donald and gazed into the immobile face. How calm it was! Calm — while her heart was beating so furiously. To the south-west were towering mountains, intersected here and there with trails. 'To Montana'! She remembered the sign-post — not a great way back. There lay a chance to beat Lee, to save Angus from the mortification of giving up his beloved brother — perhaps to the hangman. And why not? Why not? It was not justice she wanted to cheat, but black lies and hate. She scanned the dogs — twelve of them in all. With the best eight and the light sled Angus could never overtake her, and Don himself was powerless to stop her!

For a moment her heart quailed as she reflected. But another look at Donald's face put reason out of court. To stay passive and let things drift was impossible. Angus had his duty to consider; she had nothing but her love for Donald. That love was big enough to laugh at danger, to set at naught all risks to herself both from Nature and from the forces of the law. She would bring Donald to his senses. She would make him see that facing this thing out meant death, that life was too precious to be flung away thus.

Trembling with pent-up emotion, she looked for Angus. He was climbing steadily — hidden at times by trees. From where he was he had no view of the trail back to the border trail. Eight dogs! Eight good dogs! Quickly she made her choice, and soon had the eight hitched to the sled on which Donald lay. Going quickly through the gear and food, she put into the sled certain things that were necessary. Then, feeling somewhat like a thief, despite the goodness of her motive, she turned the sled and went back along the trail.

From a bend she got her last glimpse of Angus. He was a mere dot on the snow — standing quite still, and apparently gazing into the distance to locate Sedge Lake. Then he was lost to view. The sled moved down the incline faster and faster, then through a rock-strewn wood, until at last she saw that enticing board before her.

To Montana.

She went past it, breathing hard. It was done. Regrets were useless now. Having so far committed herself she must go on. She tried to imagine Angus' surprise. What would he say? Would he understand to what extremes love could drive a woman?

25

Refuge

Donald awoke from a long and invigorating sleep to blink at the brilliant snow and the waving dog-tails ahead of him. He knew he was still weak and incapable of helping himself, but there was within him the conviction that he was making rapid progress. Then it occurred to him that the team was considerably smaller than before, and he counted the wagging tails. Eight!

That brought him to full consciousness with a start, and he turned his head with a view to enquiring of Angus the meaning of this sudden diminution of dog-power. But instead of Angus he saw Sheila wielding the whip, expression in her eyes that puzzled him.

'Where is Angus — and the other sled?' he asked.

'We've separated.'

'Separated!'

She nodded and gulped.

'Sheila, what does this mean? Has anything happened to Angus?'

'No. He is all right.'

'Won't you explain?'

'Presently.'

He stared ahead of him to where the twisting trail struck through a canyon. To the left of it towered a mighty peak — a vast pyramid of snow, with a snake-like glacier gleaming blue on the northern side.

'But we are on the wrong trail, and — !'

His speech was suddenly arrested as his gaze fell on a sign-post. Snow and frost had partly obliterated the wording, but he was able to read 'Eagle Crossi — '

'Eagle Crossing!' he ejaculated. 'We are heading for the border. Stop!'

But she had no intention of stopping, and cracked the whip over the dogs' backs as successfully as any old-timer. Donald drew himself into a sitting position and stared at her grimly.

'Are you going to stop?'

'No.'

'Then I will get out.'

He attempted to do so, but she uttered a cry of alarm, and pulled up the dogs.

'Now,' he demanded. 'Explain.'

'We are making for United States territory — that is all.'

'All! And Angus — where is Angus?'

'I — I ran away from him.'

'You ran — ! Sheila, have you taken leave of your senses?'

'No. I am doing this because — because I will not see you throw away your life. You haven't a dog's chance, Don. Everything is against you — the evidence, public opinion and — '

'And you expect me to — to run?'

'I pray that you will come to see this is the wisest course. We shall be over the border before sunset. There will be a chance for you to get well — and get out of the country. I have food and a tent — '

'We are going back,' he said determinedly.

'We are going on. There are limits to chivalry — to duty. We have passed that limit. Whatever happens I am going on.'

'But I won't let you.'

'You can't prevent it, Don,' she said with a smile. 'Things are in my hands now.'

'If — '

She looked behind her apprehensively and then took the reins again. The sled moved forward and Donald sat motionless, and helpless, for his feeble attempt to leave the sled had caused his wound to set up a dull ache. Mile after mile was covered and then Sheila stopped for food. She came round the sled to meet his resentful, yet admiring, eyes.

'Slops again,' she said.

'When will sanity come, Sheila?'

'It is here now, Don. Do you think I am regretting this step? You and Angus were caught in a net partly of your own weaving. I am going to get you out of it.'

'Do you imagine I am always going to be as helpless as this? Sheila, be reasonable. You have done a courageous thing, but it is useless. No purpose can possibly be served by it. I implore you to go back now and find Angus.'

'The spirit stove,' she mused. 'I'll swear I brought the spirit stove.'

'Do you hear what I am saying?'

'Perfectly, Don. But why do you say it when my mind is made up.'

'You are a stubborn little fool,' he said angrily.

She turned away and he knew that he had hurt her deeply.

'Sheila!'

'Never mind,' she murmured.

'Come here!'

She hesitated for a moment and then approached him. His hand came out and caught hers.

'Forgive me — for what I said. I know that you have acted according to your point of view. But I believe that point of view to

269

be wrong. Won't you give up this escapade
— for my sake?'

'You are making it harder and harder for
me,' she replied.

'There is yet time to put matters right.'

She shook her head and left him, to
search for the spirit-stove. This she ultimately
found, and a meagre meal was prepared. She
fed Donald, then the dogs, and took but
little herself. In all there was less than half
an hour's delay, after which she hit the trail
again. Four hours of slow progress followed,
for the trail went up and up through deep
snow. At last — on reaching the highest
point — she came face to face with what
she was anxious to see. It was a sign that
marked the boundary-line.

'Montana!' she said, stopping the sled.

'And now what do you propose to do?' he
asked.

'Camp — as soon as possible. I'm
— tired.'

Despite his complete disapproval of her
conduct, he could not but admire the spirit
that moved her. He tried to see in her the
rollicking care-free girl of the past, but she
had gone and in her place was a woman
— as self-willed and determined as any he
had ever encountered. But it was no time
now to debate the matter. As she averred

she was tired from the long journey, and the arduous work of footing it up miles of trail. To-morrow there might come a more balanced outlook. He hoped that would be the case.

In a sheltered, wooded fold of the mountain Sheila found a suitable spot for erecting the tent, and she accomplished this task successfully. With business-like precision she got the dogs settled down and built a fire.

'Problem number one — how am I going to get you into the tent?' she mused.

'I can get myself into it.'

'I forbid you to try.'

'Then I will sleep in the sled.'

But she shook her head at this suggestion, for the cold was intensifying as the sun declined.

'We will attend to that later,' she said. 'Food is the pressing need.'

'For heaven's sake, give me something substantial. I am getting past the invalid stage.'

She nodded, and later he made a fairly good meal. Most of the time his eyes were on her — he could not take them away. Being alone with her like this was disconcerting enough. The love which he had tried so hard to repress leaped to fuller life, yet the circumstances were such he dared not utter one word that would give her an inkling of the truth. Apart from the fact that he still believed she and Angus would ultimately patch things up, he looked upon himself as a doomed man.

The darkness came down and the glare from the fire fell on their two reflective faces. Both were full of determination — his to play the game as he saw it, and hers to save him from himself. And both of them were adamant.

'I must attend to your wound,' she said. 'But first of all I must get you into the tent.'

'The wound can look after itself.'

'I know best. Come!'

She pushed the sled as near as possible to the opening of the tent, and then attempted to lift him bodily. But he removed the encircling arms, and with a great effort managed to stand up and grasp the tent pole.

'Don!'

'I'm — all right. A bit dizzy, that's all.'

He tottered forward and managed to occupy the bed without accident. The wound was dressed in silence, and an hour later she was occupying the other half of the tent. In these strange circumstances they slept the sleep of the weary.

★ ★ ★

Donald awoke first, the next morning, and tried his legs again. They seemed to be very mutinous limbs, but he felt his strength slowly returning, and blessed the fine constitution that Nature had given him. Sheila opened her eyes to find him sitting on his mattress, with his big chin propped on his hands.

'You shouldn't,' she complained.

'I'm not half as bad as you imagine. To-day we are going back, Sheila.'

'No — no!'

'Yes. Your brief spell of authority is over. You do see things differently now, don't you?'

'How are they different? Nothing has changed — except that you are a free man — temporarily.'

'Yes — temporarily. Now listen! Yesterday you were agitated — carried away by emotion. It was no time to argue things out. But now we must face facts.'

'I have been facing them all the time,' she replied.

'I doubt it. You did a great thing, believing it to be the right thing. But there is a factor which I am positive you did not take fully into account. It is Angus.'

'Yes — yes I did. They had no right to

send Angus on this mission. It was an error of judgment — and inhuman. At first the relationship between you two was unknown, but when it was known Angus should have been recalled.'

'We are in Canada — not England. To recall a constable hundreds of miles away from his station is not an easy matter, and would necessitate a delay that might be favourable to the culprit. Anyway, Angus was not recalled. In him was placed implicit trust. Would you have it said of him that in the time of need he played the part of traitor.'

'But he didn't. He meant to take you back with him. It was I who prevented him.'

'Yes, you — his friend. The situation is almost exactly as predicted by Lee, and the rest of them. They will see in it a dirty conspiracy. Angus' name will reek in the nostrils of his comrades. He will be a broken man.'

'Don!'

'That is no exaggeration. Sending Angus for me may have been an error of judgment in the first place, but ironically enough it was a brilliant move, for though I might have attempted to evade capture in the ordinary way, I can't let Angus down. I can't see them fling mud at him just as if he really connived to let me slip through the meshes of the net. In this test of devotion and loyalty Angus must come out clean. You see that, don't you?'

She could not help seeing it, for he put the case with such brutal clearness. But she was yet far from conversion, for the weak point in his argument was his personal rights. Was brother-love justified in demanding this big sacrifice? She felt she was incapable of holding the scales fairly. In different ways she loved them both, and the cloak of dishonour was almost as repellent as the shroud of death — for death seemed like the probable price that must be paid for Angus' vindication.

'I — I can't think, Don,' she said. 'I dare not think. I can only act.'

'We should tackle our problems as they present themselves,' he said. 'The first thing to do is to save Angus' name.'

'And then?'

'The rest is on the knees of the Gods.'

'You are content to leave your life there?'

'I have no choice.'

'Don't you want to live?' she cried. 'Doesn't life mean anything more to you than a — a forfeit?'

'I will not have it at the expense of those I love. No life is worth living purchased that way.'

275

She rose slowly and passed by him. At the door of the tent she stood looking out upon the magnificent scene. For all their problems the earth was fair yet. To it a broken heart or two meant nothing. Far away to the south were great bustling cities — millions upon millions of men and women all ignorant of the drama that was being played here amid the frozen mountains. She envied those who had never loved — as she loved.

'I must think,' she said. 'I must think.'

26

Defeat

From the vantage point of the mountain slope Angus was enabled to see the flat expanse between the hills which he knew to be Sedge Lake, and it settled his problem. Unquestionably he must take the left fork of the dividing trail. The right one apparently led into the mountain fastnesses. He commenced the steep descent, and ultimately reached the spot where he had left Sheila and the sleds. Amazement was engendered when he gazed upon four dogs only, and the heavier sled.

'Sheila!' he raised his voice in a loud call, but heard no response. Then he realised that he was wasting his breath, for there could be but one explanation. The missing sled and dogs and gear told their own story. She had gone and taken Donald with her! He examined the ground and saw the curves made by the runners of the turned sled. Obviously she had gone back on the trail by which they had arrived. He recalled her agitation — the hints which she had thrown out, and he remembered the sign-post which they had recently passed. She had made a bid for Donald's liberty!

He sat down for a few minutes, stunned by this revelation. There was method in it too, for if she succeeded in getting Donald over the border it would require an extradition order to have him apprehended, and that would take time. In the meantime here was he, frustrated by a woman's wile.

The thing which he had secretly hoped would happen had occurred. Donald had an excellent chance of evading capture, provided his wound healed rapidly as it promised to do. But his face grew gloomy as he pondered the circumstances. Lee would justify his suspicions. His chief's faith in him would be shattered. Even if he made his story good it could never remove the stigma or blot out the stain.

And Donald? Don did not desire this. Sheila had taken advantage of the prisoner's helplessness — impelled by a love that was all-consuming. Somehow that thought did not hurt as much as he would have expected. True, he loved her still, but this life with the North-West Police was rapidly opening up a new world to him. Service was a worthy substitute for love. Service!

He winced again. They had expected so

much of him — more perhaps than they were entitled to in the circumstances. They had put him on his mettle and he was going to fail them, because the human equation challenged duty. Had he believed Donald was guilty the problem might not have been so vexed, for then any wavering would be tantamount to the lowest treachery. But now — !

Time was passing — valuable time. There was still a chance of overtaking the fugitives, even with his sadly reduced team. He had to make the choice — now. The greatest moment of his life had come. He could let Don go and possibly make good his story. And Don under the influence of Sheila's love might ultimately evade capture. But in his heart he knew that such a passive act would spell his eternal damnation. Even Donald, if he chose to take that way of escape, would despise him, and never again would he be able to hold his head high. Donald did not desire that — he knew it.

He stood up and looked back along the runner tracks. Then, with a gulp, he made his decision. In a few minutes he was mushing the short team, urging them on with whip and voice, and running in the snow to lighten the load. When he reached the fork where the sign-post stood he saw

Sheila's tracks on what had been unmarked snow. His conclusions were correct. She was making for the boundary line!

Up the steep inclines his poor team laboured badly, but he lashed them onward, and hated himself for it, for it was not his habit to belabour his dogs. Now and again a lonely trail crossed his path, but always the deep tracks acted as guides without choice of a mistake. Before him he saw the mighty mountains, magnificent in their aloofness, and as he progressed he began to see things more clearly, and was glad he had not hesitated too long. It seemed to him that women were not so responsive to idealism, and that where a man would place duty first a woman would unhesitatingly put love. Doubtless Sheila had acted on that pretext. She saw the man she loved in danger of being unjustly convicted for murder, and no argument was big enough to deter her. Life to her came first — and Donald's life first of all.

He did not blame her, but regretted the set of circumstances that had brought about this vexing situation. Donald would understand that it was no selfish motive, no overweening sense of authority, that had caused him — his brother — to put aside his natural repugnance. Yes, Don would understand, for it was Don who had set this example years ago.

Despite his fierce energy and deep-set resolution the pace was slow. One dog was contributing nothing to the work of hauling and was almost being dragged along. He soon realised that night must overtake him before he could reach the border — and this eventually happened.

But in the morning he was off again — and still hopeful, for he considered it quite probable that the fugitives might have been compelled to camp on the Canadian side. It was during the last few miles that bad luck overtook him. The sky had become overcast and he felt snow beating into his face. In ten minutes the landscape was blotted out — and he drove through a dense veil of wind-driven flakes. Little by little the tracks were filling up.

'Mush!'

For a little while a better pace was maintained, but the clogging snow was a determined obstacle, and when at last he stood on the border line the tracks had disappeared, and nothing was to be seen but a few vague firs in his near vicinity.

'Gone!' he muttered.

A little joy was born of the thought that he had done his very utmost to overtake them. Nature had decided — in Sheila's favour. Then he visualised Lee — perhaps back in Albany by that time — vilifying him for all he was worth, and boasting of his own prognostication. It certainly would look like a conspiracy with a woman at the back of it.

Hungry as a wolf he stayed where he was and prepared a meal. He tried to imagine what was taking place between Donald and Sheila. There would be a conflict there too, and he feared that Sheila might win. Would Donald, with all his fine spirit, and stubborn temperament prevail against the barbed darts of Cupid? He imagined himself in similar circumstances — on the one side capture and perhaps death, on the other the possibility of escape, with the most adorable woman in the world — ?

A little sigh escaped him, and he stared into the whirling snow as if he saw the two there — enclosed in each other's arms. Perhaps — perhaps there was justice on earth after all. Unwittingly he was repaying his brother for that act of chivalry in the past. Whether he had sought it or not he was surely going to foot the bill. Lee would leer at him, and many others would point an accusing finger. None would believe that things had happened just as they had. A woman to fool a constable!

He finished his meal and packed up the gear. It seemed there was nothing to be done but make for Albany and report what had transpired. Like a great blanket unfolding the thick cloud about him passed away. Firs and rocks and snow leaped to view again as the sun smote down — a veritable mountain miracle! Far below him he saw thick timber and on the fringe of it the smoke from a fire.

He brought his binoculars to bear upon the spot, and was able to discern Donald and Sheila through the trees — the former sitting in the sled. A moment's hesitation and he set the dogs moving down the decline. He had covered about half the distance when Sheila came running from the trees, and obstructed his passage about a hundred yards from the camp. He pulled up the dogs and looked intently into her face.

'You — you can't touch him now,' she said. 'He's on United States soil. You have no right — '

'I'm not so sure,' he replied slowly.

'Angus!'

'Would anyone question my right if I took him back?'

'I — I am appealing to you — to your sense of honour. If you did that I should hate you. Back there it was different. You had your duty to do — '

'I still have my duty to do, Sheila.'

'You — you would use force and violate — .'

'An-gus!'

She turned at the faint sound of Donald's voice, and saw him leaning against a tree waving his hand.

'All right. All right,' she said brokenly. 'Go to him. You — you have beaten me.'

Her clearly expressed humiliation touched him to the heart. This love which she had placed first seemed to have broken like a rotten stick. Donald had disillusioned her. She saw now that these two men worshipped another idol.

'Bear up,' he begged. 'All is not lost — yet.'

He left her sitting on the sled and went to Donald, who gripped him by the hand, and grinned at him.

'Good old boy! So you made it?'

'God help me — yes.'

Donald turned his gaze to the still form on the sled and his mouth twitched.

'She acted for the best, old boy. But she didn't understand. I never imagined that friendship could go so far.'

'Friendship!' ejaculated Angus. 'Is that the name you give it?'

'Well, call it what you like, Angus. She

284

thought she was helping you to evade a painful duty. But she doesn't quite understand even now that in doing that she was merely assisting Lee and all the other wrong-thinking folk.'

Angus stared at him incredulously. That Donald could be so dense was amazing.

'Don, are you blind?' he demanded.

'I don't get you, Angus.'

'You've been with her for days together, and you don't realise that it is you she loves — not me?'

Donald's brow became wrinkled, and he looked as if he could not believe his own eyes.

'You — you must be crazy, Angus,' he said.

'No. It's true. She told me so with her own lips.'

'She told — ! But it was understood — I always thought you and she — '

'That ended two years ago, after you had gone away. I didn't know then — the real reason why she broke with me. But when I came here I began to suspect the truth. It wasn't merely to save me from carrying out a painful duty that she did what she did. It was to save the life of the man she loves.'

'Angus! This — this is incredible!'

'Do you imagine you are the kind of man

no woman could love? She's lucky, Don.'

'Lucky! Why, I — '

Angus seized him by the arm.

'You don't mean you can't return her love?'

'I wish to God I could. But the situation makes it impossible. If it wasn't for this thing that is hanging over me — It wouldn't do, Angus. She mustn't know that I love her to madness. It will hurt less if — if things go badly. You must help me to keep that from her — you understand?'

'Is that wise?'

'Yes — yes. It's true I have been blind. I've tried to hide my real feelings. She doesn't guess even now. I'm not such a fool as not to realise how thin my chances are of proving my innocence. This is no time to ventilate the truth.' His eyes brightened as he glanced at the distant figure of Sheila. 'When the verdict is given, then perhaps — perhaps — '

'But you are not caught yet, Don.'

'What do you mean?' he snapped.

'Whatever people may think, I have done my duty. Yesterday I was determined to get you — before you crossed over. I have no power to make an arrest at the moment.'

'Not on this side. But yonder, yes.'

Angus stared down at his boots in his perplexity.

'Why not — why not make a bolt for it, Don? It is a square deal. I shall go back and report — everything. We may get you — and we shall try, but at this moment you hold a winning card. Why not play it?'

'You — you ask me that!'

'Yes — because of — her.'

Donald hesitated for a moment and then shook his head stubbornly.

'It wouldn't do, old boy. Even if I got away neither she nor I could snatch a moment's happiness, knowing that it was due to a trick.'

'A trick?'

'She tricked you — with the best of motives perhaps. Your conscience may be clear, but will others take that view? You and I have always tried to play the game. Let us go on like that to the end of the innings. I am crossing into Canada — at once.'

'I — I shall arrest you.'

'Of course you will — you old duffer. Go to her now and tell her we have fixed matters. But don't let her suspect — you understand?'

Angus nodded sadly. The passionate love of his brother was not hid from him, and his old admiration for him was increased a hundredfold when he reflected what he was willing to sacrifice in the cause of loyalty and honour.

27

Lee Proposes

Three days later Angus and his companions looked across the snowclad country, from a dominating eminence, and saw in the distance the familiar buildings of Albany. Two days had been lost through a prolonged blizzard which had made travel quite impossible, and during that time Donald had taken great strides towards recovery.

'Albany!' said Angus. 'Less than four miles.'

'Let us make it,' begged Donald.

'It is better to eat first, for it is past noon.'

Donald sighed, and Angus tried to light the spirit-stove, but he had run out of methylated spirit, and the alternative was a wood fire. He took the axe and went towards a patch of spruce. Donald beckoned to Sheila, who was feeling the situation keenly.

'Cheer up,' he murmured. 'You can trust me to put up a good fight. I'm not so near death as I was a few days ago. In fact, I am feeling quite lively.'

'Don!'

'Seriously. Of course old Angus is gloomy. But you mustn't take your cue from him. I'm glad the trip is over, for it must have been arduous for you.'

'You did wrong, Don,' she said, clenching her hands.

'Oh no. We couldn't let Angus down like that.'

'You — you can let yourself down.'

'Do you think I have?' he asked quietly.

She felt the mild rebuff and hung her head. When she raised it again there were tears in her eyes.

'I'm wrong,' she said. 'I'm always wrong. You men — I don't understand you. I think no woman ever can hope to. Our lives are pitched to a different key. We — we can't help ourselves.'

'Don't regret it. This is rather a matter of hard logic.'

'You can't exist on logic.'

'I think one can. You see if Angus had gone back empty-handed his disgrace was certain. On the other hand my being found guilty is by no means a certainty. So we win on the balance of probability.'

'You let innate optimism play too large a part. You do not take into consideration prejudice and even hate.'

'Do you think Lee's enmity will carry much weight with a jury who are trying a man for his life?'

'Yes. That — and the evidence, plus the alleged motive.'

'We shall see.'

He was smiling as if the prospects were quite rosy, instead of being jet-black. But she was by no means deluded by that. It was always the other person Don considered first, and in this case he was trying to mislead her and Angus — striving to give birth to a spirit of hopefulness that was by no means warranted.

'I — I wish I had your courage, Don,' she said.

'Courage! There's nothing like that about it. It is an innate faith in people's good sense. Why should I want to murder Willeton, when I could have satisfied myself by giving him a good walloping — like he gave me?'

'Why do some people commit murder?'

'I don't know.'

'But the jury will know — or think they know. Oh, Don, to think of all the happy days we've had together — we three, and then to end like this.'

'This is not the end. Better to think of the triumphs. Here is Angus giving the lie to the gossips — letting them know that the North-West Police force is a greater thing than some of them imagine — utterly incorruptible. If we all did what was best for ourselves we should soon find how little real pleasure one got out of it.'

Angus came back to interrupt a conversation that led nowhere. To Sheila the curtain was about to fall on the first act of this distressing drama, and she was reluctant to look far into the future, to anticipate the terrible days of anxiety that must follow. Her mind was a maze of conflicting emotions, hopes and fears. In addition she had to go through the ordeal of facing the Fergussons and explaining her absence. But that was a trivial matter compared with the other. Looking into the distance she saw not shacks, spires and chimneys, but the wide-open doors of a grim jail!

* * *

Lee's mortification at losing Donald was mitigated to a small extent by the pride of having made an apparently correct prophecy. On reaching home he apprised Rose Willeton of what had transpired and then went into Albany to interview the Sheriff.

'I told you so,' he said. 'A fine hash the

police have made of things.'

'What's wrong?'

'I had a hunch that constable wouldn't act on his orders. He didn't. Fraser has made a get-away.'

'How do you know?'

'I went after him myself, with some of my boys. We nailed him, but run into the constable. Like a damned fool we let him rant about his duty and he took over the prisoner. There was a woman in it, too — the girl who was staying with the Fergussons.'

'Miss McLeod? I heard she was missing.'

'You bet she was. She and a dirty half-breed went off to warn that gink. Anyway, to cut a long story short, the three of them managed to get away.'

The Sheriff sucked at his pipe reflectively.

'Aren't you drawing quick conclusions, Mr. Lee?'

'You'll find I'm not. He knew his way home all right, but he didn't take it. I'm willing to wager they are well over the border by this time.'

The Sheriff pursed his lips, for Lee's information certainly gave grounds for that conclusion.

'I'll wait a day or two and then I'll get into communication with Police headquarters,' he said.

'Why waste time?'

'There is a chance — '

'Of what? Isn't it obvious enough? A mighty big mistake was made when that man was allowed to go after his own brother. We warned you, but — '

'That's enough,' cut in the Sheriff acidly.

The news went round quickly, and the affair was the talk of the neighbourhood. Two days passed and still there was no sign of Angus or the accused man. Rose Willeton had got over the first effects of the bereavement, but her soul was still aching for justice.

'You ought never to have given him up, Aldous,' she said.

'I know. But he was down and out, and I meant to keep close on the constable's tail.'

'That girl too — Sheila. To think of her assisting a felon to escape! Yet I ought to have expected it. She was always ready to defend him. The cat!'

Lee twisted his hat in his hands a trifle nervously, and his eyes roved over Rose's figure.

'Suppose he gets clean away? Does it mean that you ain't willing to go through with — with that other business?'

Rose stared into space and hesitated.

'Why not?' he urged. 'This ought to make

no difference. I guess I love you well enough. I loved you before that scoundrel ever came here — '

Rose winced and held up her hand to stop him.

'But that's neither here nor there. It would be a good business arrangement too. I won't say you couldn't get another fellow to manage for you, but I've been here a good time, and can handle this outfit better than most.'

'I know — I know. If you had fulfilled your part I should have carried out my promise.'

'And you aren't ready to marry me without that?'

'I told you I would not think of marriage while my poor father remained unavenged. You must leave it at that, Aldous.'

He smiled, somewhat sourly, and left her. Outside he cursed savagely, for it seemed that a great chance had been lost. Yet he was not entirely without hope, for he realised that she knew practically nothing about the running of the big ranch which she had inherited, and she hated new faces.

He went to his quarters, which Willeton had built for him some years back. It comprised a comfortable sitting-room, and a bedroom, and afforded him an outlook down the ranges, whence he could keep an observant eye on the men. Flinging off his coat he sat down and smoked sullenly. When darkness fell he lighted the lamp and went to close the inner window. But before he could reach it a ghastly thing happened. Pressed against the lower pane, strangely illuminated by the lamplight, was a horrid face — so contorted with hate that it looked inhuman. For five seconds it leered at him — and in that space of time he recognised it. It was the face of Slocum Joe!

He reeled back and opened the drawer of his desk. But when he swung round, with a revolver in his hand, the face was gone. He passed a hand across his brow. A hallucination! Just a hallucination! Slocum Joe was dead. The light had played a trick on him. Slowly he made for the door and flung it open. No one was near, but his ears caught the musical tinkle of bells, and a moment later he saw a dog-sled approaching. He slipped the revolver into his pocket, as Fergusson and his daughter reached him.

'Hello, Lee! Is Rose about?'

'In the house. Good evening, Miss Rhoda.'

'Just heard some startling news,' said Fergusson. 'They've got Fraser.'

Lee almost jumped.

'What's that?'

'The constable has come back.'

295

'The con — ! You mean he's brought back — his brother?'

'Yes. We wanted to let Rose know.'

Lee looked bewildered — incredulous. At Fergusson's invitation he accompanied them into the house. Rose saw at once that they had news of some sort.

'Well?' she quavered.

'Fraser is in custody, Rose.'

'You mean in jail?'

'Yes.'

'But Lee said — Who arrested him?'

'His own brother.'

'Impossible!'

'No, it's true.' He looked a little confused. 'Sheila — Sheila came back this evening.'

Rose's eyes flashed wildly.

'She did her best to aid him. I wonder she had the impudence to face you.'

Rhoda intervened.

'You mustn't be too hard on her, Rose. It was not to help him to escape that she made that mad trip. She got to know that Lee was going after him. She feared he might be less safe with Lee than with his brother, and she went to warn him.'

'A pretty yarn,' sneered Lee. 'Anyway, he's caged, and that is the chief thing.'

'Has he — confessed?' queried Rose.

'Confessed! Sheila says that his one great

desire was to get to Albany and prove his innocence. Upon my word I don't know what to think.'

'He's cunning,' said Lee. 'They've been framing some plot between them, but nothing short of a miracle will acquit him. It's the best news I've heard for a long time.'

Fergusson frowned at him, and Rhoda showed her resentment at his unconcealed glee. Rose displayed neither joy nor regret. The blood-lust was not so strong now. She wanted justice — nothing more. But her heart was wrathful against Sheila.

'I never want to see her again,' she said.

'I don't think you will,' replied Rhoda. 'She is leaving us to-morrow.'

'Going — home?'

'No. I think she wants to be — near him. It is evident she loves him. She will not stay with us because — because she feels that she has hurt us. We can't dissuade her from going. She had found lodgings in Albany and means to stay there until the trial is over.'

When they eventually left, Lee approached Rose again, with a gleam of expectancy in his narrow eyes.

'How do we stand now, Rose?'

'You — you want me to keep my promise?'

'I want to marry you.'

'Very — well.'

'When?'

'After the trial. I want to start a new life. This — this dreadful affair has worn me down. Leave me now.'

He was content to kiss her hand, and went back to his quarters to gloat over his good fortune. But as he sat there alone his eyes kept switching towards the window, and he lacked the courage to close the shutters lest he should see that terrible face again.

28

Waiting

Although the Fergussons pressed Sheila to stay on with them, and made it clear to her that they were quite ready to forget her recent exploit, she carried out her project to take lodgings in Albany, and found a suitable place over a small shop. Donald was subsequently charged and committed for trial, and Angus continued to follow up the case.

'There is still time to achieve something,' he said. 'We must not give up hope. Have you seen Don?'

'I am going to him this afternoon.'

'That's good. You'll find him cheerful enough. Don't let him think we are downhearted.'

'I'll try to take a bright view. Angus, what about the people at home? Ought — ought they to know?'

That very point had been troubling Angus. He wrote home at intervals, but so far he had had no opportunity to narrate his astonishing meeting with Donald. To do so now would involve telling a story that would only cause painful anxiety on the part of his mother and father.

'Better to say nothing — yet,' he suggested. 'Was it necessary for you to leave Rhoda?'

'It was better so. They are kindly people, without malice, but they believe Don is guilty. I — I couldn't endure that atmosphere.'

'Aren't they likely to write and tell your father everything?'

'I begged Rhoda not to — before I left. I heard from home yesterday. Father is not well, and wants me to return.'

'I'm sorry. Shall you go?'

'I — I can't — yet. I may be wanted at the trial. There may be a chance to say something in Don's favour. That's partly why I came here — to be near him.'

'You — you love him deeply?'

'Yes,' she replied huskily. 'Why should I not admit it? I know he left home in disgrace, but — '

'Sheila, it's all — ' he burst out impetuously. She gazed at his crimson cheeks and wondered what had caused his sudden agitation.

'I — I may have something to tell you — later,' he said mysteriously. 'Don't lose faith in Don. There never was a fellow like him. He needs your trust just now — far more than you imagine.'

He went away without futher explanation, and she tried vainly to understand his remarks. As the afternoon approached she grew very nervous. To her it seemed obvious that Donald had no love for her — except of a fraternal order. All this outpouring of her soul was like water on the desert sands — running away to nothing. Possibly he did not even guess that the old beautiful friendship had long since ripened into passion? Be that as it might, it did not check the flow. She would have lied, died, practised deception, done anything to cheat the hangman of an innocent victim. But these things were denied her. She saw herself — a mere pawn in the game, trusting in Providence to achieve some miracle.

Ultimately she was led to the cell where Donald was incarcerated, and to her surprise and relief was left alone with him. Since seeing him last his wound had received medical attention, and he looked remarkably fit — and hopeful.

'This is a great surprise,' he said, wringing her hand. 'I was getting a trifle bored.'

'Only bored, Don?'

'A bit nervy. This business of doing nothing is the most soul-searing thing in the world, and the Law is the slowest kind of funeral.

Who brought you over?'

'I'm living in Albany now.'

'In Albany!'

'After what happened it was impossible to stay with Rhoda and her father. They are friendly with Rose, and that would bring about a most embarrassing situation. I saw Angus this morning.'

'I too.' He laughed. 'It is a feather in his cap — this affair. I should like to have seen Lee's face when he was compelled to swallow his own assertions. We did right, Sheila — didn't we?'

'You — you still think that?'

'Rather! Angus has won his spurs for ever.'

'By arresting an innocent man!'

'By doing his job. That's all that matters. Look how he's changed since the old days. You remember he was always a bit of a dreamer. I had to kick him into activity many a time, when he displayed a desire to go off shooting or swimming in the loch. Work! He used to hate it. But now — he's bigger in every way, and I'm thinking he'll climb right to the top before he has finished. I suppose he has gone off getting clues?'

'I suppose so. Oh, Don, this waiting is so terrible. I — I think I shall go mad.'

He caught her hand and steadied her.

'You mustn't worry. You are taking this too much to heart. Get out and about, and let things take their natural course.'

'Natural course! It is all unnatural. If I didn't know you were innocent I might find it easier. Don, can't you possibly prove an alibi? Don't you remember where you were on that evening?'

'I remember perfectly. I was in my shack, enjoying a book.'

'And you are sure Slocum was in Albany?'

'Oh, yes. Poor old Slocum! Let him rest in peace. He had nothing to do with the crime. It was decent of the Sheriff to leave us alone like this, wasn't it?'

'Yes. He has been very kind to me. I think he did not approve of Lee's interference. That reminds me. I heard that Lee is to marry Rose Willeton.'

Donald whistled and then laughed.

'A curious match,' he mused. 'But I'll wager that Lee is marrying the Willeton ranch — and not Rose. Love seems to be a very good second name for Business.'

'Don't be cynical, Don,' she begged.

'I won't. I hope they will be happy, though I doubt it.'

'But she may love him.'

'She may. But it looks very much like a

celebration to commemorate a — a possible event.'

'You — you mean — ?' Her face went pale.

'She has a hard nature. I think she would like to be just, but hate comes quickly to her and blinds her to facts. There is nothing in life so cruel as a woman scorned.'

'Has she been scorned?'

Her deep eyes challenged him, and after a moment's hesitation, he inclined his head.

'You mean — you — ?'

'Once I was compelled to put a stop to certain gossip which connected my name with hers. That put an end even to friendship. You are acquainted with what followed. Some of Willeton's cattle was found hidden on my land. I have been wondering whether a woman's injured pride would induce her to vent her spite on the man who wounded it.'

'You mean that she — she — ?'

'It might have been Lee. He hated me because he foolishly imagined that I was interested in the woman he has now managed to capture. A word in Lee's ear and the thing could be achieved. It was very simple.'

'Don! If that could be proved it might make all the difference — to you.'

'It can never be proved. No, Sheila, we

must put our trust in other things.'

'But what things?'

'In God — perhaps.'

The Sheriff entered to intimate that the visitor must leave.

'In a minute,' she said brokenly.

'You'll come again,' asked Donald.

'Yes — yes. Every time it is permitted. Don't — don't think I am without hope. I — I am just sad to know that you are penned up here — like a brutal murderer. But Don, things must come right — they must.'

'Of course they will, little girl.'

'Then — good-bye!'

His big hands enfolded hers, and for a moment it looked as if he were going to tell her that the repressed passion of years was boiling within him. But the Sheriff entered, and he let her go, watching her until the door hid her from view.

Weeks passed and nothing transpired to change the outlook. Twice a week Sheila saw the prisoner, cheering him with her presence. But strive as he might to keep from her knowledge which he felt was better withheld, it was transmitted all the same. Sheila slowly came to realise it, and she divined what lay behind his poor masquerade.

'Dear Don!' she mused. 'Always the same!'

Then came a day that brought a tragic

message. It came in the form of a cablegram from Scotland. Her father was lying dangerously ill. If she hoped to see him alive she must go home immediately. She tried to get to Donald, but the Sheriff was away, and a visit was not possible. Angus too had vanished. For six terrible hours she wrestled with the problem. Her father was calling for her, and Donald needed her — ! A decision was imperative, for by catching the night train she could get a ship that would save three days. She packed but still hesitated.

At last the decision was made. Her immediate duty was to her father. With streaming eyes she wrote a letter to Donald, conveying the bad news — a letter with love in every word of it, though not on the surface. Surely he would understand that nothing but this calamity would have dragged her away! With heavy heart she caught the train, and was soon whirled through the night towards the distant sea.

* * *

Donald, in his cell, was also coming to a new decision. His masquerade had failed. It was impossible to see her, to talk with her and not to know that he was giving himself away. This love could not be hid. Better to tell her — to risk what blow the future might wield. Two days must elapse before she called again, but then he would lay bare his heart.

He felt better after arriving at that resolution, and slept soundly. But in the morning a note was handed him, and Fate dealt another cruel blow. He sat like a man dazed — reflecting that possibly he might never see her again. Even the few weeks' grace which he had imagined would be filled with love, were denied him. The cell seemed full of a dank mist, and things swam before his eyes. For some time he was quite unaware that Angus was in the cell — close beside him.

'Don!'

At last he looked up wearily.

'Hello — old boy!'

'Anything wrong?'

'Yes. Is there some devil that lurks close to me — always? She — she's gone, Angus.'

'Gone! You mean — Sheila?'

Donald handed him the letter, and Angus uttered an excusable expletive.

'I've just got back. I didn't know. It must have been hell for her. Have you told her?'

'No. I meant to, but I left it too late.' He stood up and laughed grimly. 'Out goes

307

another candle! Well, God speed her. I hope McLeod pulls through.'

Angus looked as distressed as Donald himself, for he knew what those visits of Sheila had meant to the accused man — bright rays of sunshine in a deepening gloom.

'I've news, Don — not much, but valuable in the circumstances. I ran into a man yesterday who had been discharged from the Willeton ranch. He told me something that lets in light.'

'What?'

'On the day when Willeton was murdered there was a quarrel between Lee and his employer. This man — Davies — was working behind an outbuilding and heard what passed.'

'Lee was always quarrelsome. He hated any kind of interference on Willeton's part.'

'This was a different kind of quarrel. Lee went to ask Willeton for the hand of Rose.'

For the first time Donald showed interest. 'Well?'

'Davies swears that Willeton flew into a rage, and told Lee he would see him to blazes before he consented to such a union. Hot words passed and Willeton ended by firing Lee.'

'Sacking him?'

'So Davies avers, and it isn't likely he would invent a story that fits in so well with facts.'

'Does it fit in?'

'Pretty well. It provides another motive for the crime. Lee was on the point of losing a good job, and the prospects of becoming boss of the Willeton ranch. What was there to prevent him from stealing that humane-killer and waylaying Willeton?'

'It is possible.'

'Where did you keep it?'

'In a bin — in the shed.'

'And when did you miss it?'

'Some time after Willeton disappeared. We never had occasion to use it often.'

'Would Lee know where that was kept?'

'He may have seen it. Yes, I remember once he came in the shed to complain about a broken fence. I was turning out the bin at the time — By jove, it looks suspicious. I had never thought of that possibility, because of the absence of a motive.'

'Nor I — until Davies started a new train of thought, Slocum had gone to Albany on that day. Lee could have stolen the humane-killer. He doubtless knew that Willeton was going to ride over to Black Rock. He had to pass the end of your land, and with the wind in the wrong direction you would not

309

have heard any report.'

'But the cartridges? The killer was not loaded and I kept the box of cartridges inside the shack. No ordinary cartridge would have fitted the bore.'

'That is the point on which hangs so much.' He gripped Donald's hand. 'I'm going to sift this matter to the bottom, Don. If Lee killed Willeton we are going to prove it — somehow. The sky is brightening a little — just a little.'

29

The Closing Net

The next few days were restless ones for Angus. He found the box of cartridges in Donald's shack — a full box with the exception of six rounds. Donald accounted for these, though he had no means of proving his assertion. The two empty cartridge cases that had been found were of the same mark and size.

'You say you bought a box of fifty rounds — and no more?' he enquired.

'That is so. The dealer will corroborate.'

'Then Lee must have bought some.'

'It looks like it.'

But the local dealer, although he bore out Donald's statement, swore he had never sold any other ammunition of that particular brand, and there was no similar stocks for hundreds of miles. This was a bad setback to Angus, for between the time of the quarrel with his employer and Willeton's disappearance there was an interval of but a few hours. Lee had had no time to get ammunition to fit the weapon used in the case, and it was established that none of the neighbouring farmers possessed a similar lethal weapon.

Angus realised it looked bad for Donald, for the only other person who had access to the cartridges was Slocum, in whose case a complete alibi was proved. Nonplussed by this blank wall, Angus decided to take a bold line. He called on Lee.

He found the foreman along the range, bullying two of his 'boys' for some misdemeanour. Lee turned and saw him, and a sneer spread over his lean face.

'I want a word with you,' said Angus.

'Fire away!'

'Better come where we can talk — confidentially.'

'I'm busy.'

'So am I. I advise you to come right along.'

'All right. But I can't give you more'n a few minutes. I've wasted enough time already on that business.'

They rode back to Lee's quarters, and ultimately entered the sitting-room. The foreman took a cigar from inside his hat and lighted it. Angus watched him like a lynx and thought he saw a lurking fear in the narrow eyes.

'Carry your mind back to the night of the

murder,' he said. 'What were you doing on that evening — from four o'clock onwards? Think!'

'Do you think I'm a blamed Datus?'

'Such a memorable day ought to be impressed on your mind.'

'So it is.'

'Then I'll be glad of details.'

'There ain't any. I was working until tea-time, and then I came in here and put in the evening on my books.'

'When did you see Willeton last?'

'At tea-time. I had to see him on business.'

'What business?'

'What the hell — !'

'I'm asking you, and you'd better tell me.'

'I — I was taking some stock into Albany on the following day. There were one or two things I wanted to ask him.'

Angus' eyes glinted at this obvious lie.

'Why was it necessary to see him about that, when you had no further interest in it?'

'What do you mean?'

'Why weren't you packing your grip?'

'Are you mad?'

'No — I'm quite sane. At four o'clock that afternoon you were fired, and told to clear out that evening.'

313

Lee gave a violent start, and his eyes narrowed until they were mere slits.

'What are you trying to pull over me?' he asked.

'I'm telling you again that you were fired at four o'clock on that afternoon, and that there was no question of your taking cattle into Albany on the following day.'

'But I did. I can prove it.'

'Yes, you did — because in the *interim* Willeton had disappeared.'

'You're crazy! He never fired me. Why the hell should he want to do that?'

'You know,' said Angus grimly. 'And I know too.'

Lee uttered a curse and stood up. He made to brush Angus aside aggressively, but Angus stood like a rock, staring into the nervous face.

'I get your game,' said Lee hoarsely. 'Trying to save your brother's neck at my expense. I warn you — '

'It is I who am warning you,' retorted Angus. 'You never spent the whole evening in this place.'

'You're a liar!'

'Steady! Shortly after dusk you were seen prowling around the Fraser farm.'

'Who says so?'

'Never mind.'

314

'Tch! What should I want down there?'

'Ask yourself. It might have been an armful of straw. It might have been something less harmless. It might have been a gun — a humane-killer, in fact.'

'By God, I won't stand this! I'll wise the Sheriff to your game, and put an end — '

'The Sheriff will be delighted to meet you — in due course,' said Angus grimly. 'For to-night he will sign a warrant for your arrest.'

Lee chuckled, but it was by no means a natural expression of amusement. Angus missed nothing — the lurking fear in the eyes, the nervous movements of the hands. His spirits rose as the conviction of Lee's guilt became rooted. He wondered now that he had not thought of that solution before. But the utter absence of motive had blinded him, for he had believed that Lee was on the best of terms with Willeton. Davies' information had altered the entire outlook.

'Have you finished with your joke?' snarled Lee.

'You'll find it's no joke, Lee. You are standing on mighty thin ice. And it was smart of you — the way you wangled that business of the cartridges.'

This was a deadly thrust. There was terror now in Lee's eyes. He gripped the back of a chair, and breathed heavily.

'Get — out!' he said in a choking voice. 'I'll have you cashiered for this. I'm wise to your game, and you'll answer for it before your superiors.'

'I've got you, Lee,' said Angus, with a triumphant voice that he knew was not yet justified. 'You've made a terrible blunder — one that is going to cause this affair to be cleared up. It is only a matter of hours — hours.'

Thereupon he left the place and rode back to Albany. After racking his brains to discover a means to establish Lee's guilt, he saw the Sheriff and opened that worthy's eyes to possibilities. Then he saw Donald again.

'A little progress, Don,' he said. 'I've got the murderer.'

'What!'

'But I can't prove it. I can't even get a warrant for his arrest on the existing evidence. It is all hypothetical — and not conclusive. I got Lee in a state of fright, but there it ends. I bluffed — more than I had the right to do — but it worked. As sure as I'm alive, Don, he killed Willeton. I got home a lucky hit — about the cartridges. Where the devil did he get them? If I could prove he obtained cartridges to fit that weapon I believe we'd get a conviction — certainly a warrant. But

316

I am up against a brick wall.'

'You are sure he could not have bought them?'

'Positive. There wasn't time, and the murder was certainly not premeditated before that afternoon. He planned it all then — remembered the humane-killer, and stole into the shed to steal it. But the absence of cartridges is the snag.'

Donald suddenly started.

'By jove, I believe — '

'Don?'

'In that bin — I told you I had used half a dozen rounds from the box. Well, the empty cases were in that bin. I had forgotten them. He may have seen them when he first saw the killer. If they have disappeared — '

'But empty cases — !'

'He could have reloaded them. There are simple means — '

Angus gripped Donald's hands — and he was trembling with excitement.

'I'm going over — at once,' he said. 'It may help — I don't know.'

He made an immediate departure, procured a fresh horse, and rode out from Albany. Arrived at the farm he went into the shed and turned out the bin. There were various implements but no cartridge cases. If there had been six and Lee had taken them, there was a possibility that some of them were still in Lee's possession. He decided to lose no time in ransacking Lee's quarters.

On leaving the shed he ran into Slocum's brother, who had been looking after Donald's affairs since the day of Slocum's departure with Sheila. Angus explained what he had been after and the man's eyes flashed.

'Someone steal cartridges, eh?'

'It is possible.'

'You go find heem — yes?'

'Perhaps.'

'Lee?'

'How do you know?'

'We t'ink Lee dirty liar and killer.'

'We!'

'Brudder and me.'

'So Slocum suspected him? When did he tell you that?'

'Li'l while ago.'

'Before he went north?'

'No. When he come back.'

Angus stared at him uncomprehendingly. 'What's all this — about coming back?'

'Slocum come back — ver' seek.'

'But he was shot dead!'

'Not die. Heem ver' hard keel. Come back and watch Lee. Now he go over dere.'

He pointed to the Willeton ranch and Angus started.

'You mean Slocum is alive, and has gone to — to get Lee?' he demanded.

'So.'

'When?'

'Jus' now.'

'Great Scott! He'll ruin everything. I don't want Lee killed. Why didn't you stop him?'

'No could stop heem. Ver' damn obstinate.'

Angus swept him aside and, mounting his horse went galloping down the trail. He saw his hope in process of being frustrated by the faithful, but hating, half-breed, who had obviously gone to settle a long overdue account with Lee. He pressed his mount forward, praying that he would not be too late.

* * *

At that moment Aldous Lee was sitting alone in his quarters, looking very ill at ease. Until that day he had imagined himself absolutely free from suspicion, for it was commonly supposed that he and his late employer were on the best of terms, and that he ran Willeton's business off his own bat, without the slightest interference from Willeton. Now this infernal constable had somehow ferreted out facts, and was threatening his very existence.

He saw before him two alternatives — one to sit tight and hope that Angus was bluffing, the other to escape while he had the chance, and neither of these courses appealed to him. He lighted one of his interminable cigars and strove to calm his nerves. The match was still burning in his fingers when the door suddenly burst open, and a dreadful apparition entered. It was Slocum Joe, and in his right hand was the gleaming blade of a ten-inch hunting-knife. Lee's face went ashen and the cigar fell from his loose lips.

'My — God!' he quavered.

Slocum closed the door with his foot.

'At las' I come for you, Misser Lee,' he hissed.

30

Home

Sheila arrived home to find her father in the throes of a serious illness. Twice his life had been despaired of, but on both occasions he had rallied. She broke down and wept when she saw his emaciated form — the lean cheeks, and the hectic flush. He did not know her. For over a fortnight he had been incapable of recognising his closest friends. A trained nurse was in the house, and her opinion was not very hopeful.

'He has one thing in his favour,' she admitted. 'A fine constitution. When I wired you I feared you could not arrive in time. But he pulled through a bad crisis miraculously, and the doctor thinks it is possible he may recover.'

'Only — possible!'

'We must do our best.'

'Yes — yes.'

The fight for McLeod's life went on with renewed zest, and Sheila had little time to think on the other tragedy from which she had escaped. Being so near death dulled

321

her mind to everything but what lay close at hand. It seemed as if Nature ordained it so — in order not to put upon her a burden greater than any human creature could bear.

Mr. and Mrs. Fraser called at times to enquire after their neighbour. They wanted, too, news of their two sons, but like the kindly folk they were they did not press these enquiries, for they saw that she was distraught. Then came a glad day when the racking fever left McLeod and his mind functioned.

'Sheila!' he whispered. 'So it is — you! I dreamed — '

'Father! Thank God! It means — it means you will recover. I — I can't — '

She broke down for the first time since the initial collapse, and it served as a necessary vent for her pent-up emotion. The doctor's next visit confirmed her hopes.

'The great danger is past, Miss McLeod,' he said. 'He will get well now. A most wonderful recovery!'

A week later McLeod was permitted to receive visitors, and the Frasers called, bringing some fruit and a book. Sheila left the old people together, and wondered how she should best answer the questions that she felt sure would be put. No word had come from Canada since she had left so hurriedly, and she concluded that by this time the trial was close at hand. To hide up facts would serve no purpose now. The truth must be told.

At last the visitors came down from the sick-room, and sat down to the tea which she had prepared for them. The mother's grey eyes were eloquent with enquiry, and at last her lips were loosened.

'Tell us about Angus — and Don,' she begged.

'You — you haven't heard anything — recently?'

'A few lines from Angus a fortnight ago. But he said nothing about Don. Is Don doing well?'

She could scarcely face those penetrating eyes. Was it better to lie and save them pain? For a moment she felt like doing that, but came the thought that soon they must know, and that to put off the evil day was no real solution.

'There — there is something wrong,' said Mrs. Fraser. 'Sheila, lass, what is it?'

'It's so hard to tell you — the hardest thing I have ever had to do. Don — Don is in terrible trouble.'

Old Fraser's lips became compressed, and his wife's face went pallid.

'Tell us, dear. We — we will bear it. Has Don gone wrong — again?'

'No — no. It's all a terrible mistake. I know it's all wrong — that he is the victim of misunderstanding. It started with — '

Summoning her courage she related what had happened since her meeting with the two brothers, choosing her words carefully to lighten the blow. When it fell she saw two tense faces — two trembling forms. It was as if something had fallen out of the blue and crushed them.

'But he is innocent,' she added. 'We know that — Angus and I. He couldn't have done that cruel thing.'

'My — Don — tried for murder!'

Fraser put his arm round his wife's frail form.

'Bear up, mother,' he whispered. 'We know Don better than that. A wild lad he may have been, but no killer of men.'

'But so far away! And we are helpless!'

'Angus is there. He will not leave a stone unturned to find the real culprit,' said Sheila.

'They sent Angus after his own brother! Cruel!'

'It was all a mistake. Nobody guessed at the time.'

'Cruel! Cruel!'

Sheila felt herself powerless in the circumstances. She could only assert — not very conscientiously — that Donald had every chance of proving his innocence. At last they went home — bent in misery and shame.

It was less than an hour later that a telegraph boy rode in from Culm with a telegram for Sheila. Her hands trembled as she took it, and for a full minute she turned it over, nor daring to open it. The boy grew impatient.

'Any reply, miss?'

'Reply? Reply? I — I'll see.'

She slit open the envelope, and three words blazed up as if in letters of fire.

'DONALD ACQUITTED. ANGUS.'

A wild laugh broke from her lips, and she kissed the buff form again and again.

'No reply,' she said.

After breaking the glad news to her father, she took the trap and drove across to the Frasers. Mrs. Fraser had gone to bed, but her husband was wandering about the farm, like a lost soul. She drove the pony close to him.

'Mr. Fraser!'

'Sheila!'

'News — news! Wonderful news! I've

just received a telegram from Angus. Read it!'

Fraser took the small piece of paper, and made a queer noise in his throat as he read the short message.

'God be praised!' he murmured. 'I — I must go to mother. She — she needs this good news.'

Thereafter Sheila seemed to be reborn. The great dark cloud had gone for ever. Don was free — dear Don. She waited on a letter in order to hear the full details, but none came. It was strange — she thought. He might know that she would be expecting to hear by what miracle he had been saved. The days passed slowly.

★ ★ ★

Mrs. Fraser sat before a letter which had just arrived by special messenger. The contents caused her heart to thrill, and her eyes to brighten, but she dared not send a reply until her husband was consulted. The hired man had gone to fetch him now from the extreme end of the farm . . . He came in, blowing his hands to warm them.

'Hullo, mother!' he said, kissing her fondly. 'What's the trouble now? Lordy, it's cold outside!'

'John — something — something wonderful has happened.'

'What is it?'

'A — a letter — from Don.'

'Don! Good! What does he say?'

'He is — he is in Culm.'

'What!'

'Yes, dear. He wants to know if he may come — here.'

The old stubborn pride of Fraser welled up. He clenched his hands and stared into space.

'I told him — ' he commenced.

'I know, John. But that was over two years ago. Are we never to forgive — and forget?'

'He's my boy, but — '

'It was a year ago — almost to a day — that you forgave me a great wrong, John.'

He stroked her grey hair.

'Wasn't that different, mother? You did what you did — for love. And it wasn't really wrong — just something held back.'

'But it was Don's one fault — the only one thing bad that we have ever known him do. He went away, and proved himself a man. He never even touched the money you left for him. If we cannot forgive, are we justified in expecting God to forgive us?'

Still he hesitated, waging a last fight against pride. But his wife's eyes were on him — soft, grey, loving eyes that even now made no less an appeal than they had done when first he met her.

'You win, mother,' he said. 'Tell him to come — and at once.' The ice broken he was all excitement. What had they got for supper? Don was keen on an apple-turnover after his meat. There was also a bottle of wine in the larder. They must open that on this occasion.

'John, you are a darling. You try to be harder than your good heart will permit. I — I feel like a young girl again. I must get that messenger away quick.'

Three hours later Donald arrived at the farm. His mother rushed to the door when she heard the noise of a motor engine. Don came running up the path, waving a bag in one hand. He found a pair of open arms — tear-flecked eyes, and his father's big form not far behind.

'Welcome, Don!'

'Howdo, dad. Gee, it's colder than Canada! Why, mother, you look younger than ever.'

'Don't talk nonsense. I've got your old room ready for you, Don. Oh, but it's fine to see you! And so big and tanned. Sheila had a telegram from Angus.'

'Sheila!' His eyes flashed. 'How is she? Is her father — '

'McLeod had made a fine recovery, and it was due to a great extent to Sheila's devotion. What a wonderful girl she is!'

'Aye, wonderful!' murmured Donald.

His mother shot him a swift glance. Wise in her years she had already probed Sheila's secret, and here was her big son confirming her belief that Sheila's love was not unrequited.

'Don't keep the boy there,' said Fraser. 'Leave the bag, Don, and come and sit down. We want all the news.'

'Does Sheila know I'm back?'

'Sheila! Can't you think of anything but Sheila?' teased his mother.

'Well — you see — '

She laughed and put her finger to her lips.

'She's coming, Don — presently.'

Later they ate together — and laughed together. The prodigal had come back, and no reference was made to the circumstances of his going. The past was buried — deep. Then Sheila came — blushing rose-red as she came under Donald's eyes.

'I — I was amazed,' she said.

'Perhaps I ought to have written, but there wasn't much time. I came straight home on

329

obtaining my release.'

'I want to hear — everything.'

'So you shall presently.'

She went with Mrs. Fraser and came down to the two men after a short interval.

'Now, Don, the story,' said his mother. 'You have told us absolutely nothing.'

'You shouldn't divert my attention by providing such wonderful fare, mother.'

'Get on with it, Don,' said Fraser.

'There isn't much to tell. I know little more than you do. I saw Angus for a few minutes only — in hospital.'

'Hospital!'

'Didn't you know?'

'No. Is he hurt?'

'Not seriously. He had written to you, but it seems that I have beaten the mail. Angus got to the root of the whole mystery. He discovered that Lee had stolen my humane-killer, and some empty cartridge cases which were with it. He went to Lee's quarters, but Slocum had got there first — '

'Slocum!' ejaculated Sheila.

'Yes. Slocum has about nine lives, and still has a few left to lose. When Lee shot him and left him lying in the snow he was as near to death as a man can be. But hate proved a fine tonic. Anyway Slocum got home, and his brother nursed

330

him back to health. His one desire was to avenge himself on Lee. He seemed to have a quaint idea that he would help me by doing it, but it wasn't what Angus desired. When he reached Lee's quarters Slocum and Lee were engaged in a death-struggle. Angus managed to knock Lee on the head, and to bring Slocum to his senses. Then the pair made a search for evidence that would convict Lee. At length they found an instrument for reloading empty cartridges, and also one of my empty cases ruined in the process. Lee must have observed their discoveries. Anyway he made a bid for freedom, and managed to get on a fast horse. Angus followed. That's all I could get from Angus. But I was told by the Sheriff that Lee died on the way back, and made a full confession, which was witnessed by two men.'

'But Angus! You said — ?'

'Angus got a bullet in his shoulder in the scuffle. But it's nothing to worry about.'

'Then he did get his man after all!'

'Yes, and now he is a hero, instead of a maligned man. I shouldn't be surprised if he gets promotion for it, for Lee was an ugly customer to face in the open.'

'Wonderful!' said Sheila, clasping her hands. 'But how fickle the public is! It was not long ago that only you and I believed in him, Don.'

'Well, we had the advantage of knowing him.'

'But why did Lee murder his employer?'

'Because he stood in the way of Lee's marriage to Rose Willeton, and had actually discharged Lee from his service. Lee saw an excellent chance of getting rid of a big obstacle — and of me at the same time.'

'The wretch!'

'He has paid the penalty. The only decent thing he ever did was to make a confession. For that at least I am grateful.'

They talked together for a long time, and then the two old folk subtly withdrew.

'I must go too, Don,' said Sheila. 'Father may be wanting me. But I — I had to come.'

'Then I will drive you back.'

'No. It will mean your walking home.'

'It will be worth it. Say no more — I insist!'

'Still the same dictator, Don?'

'The leopard cannot change his spots. But it will be fine to tread the old paths again — even in the moonlight.'

'Come then!'

31

The Rift in the Lute

They were riding together in the old trap, just as in days of yore, with the familiar summit of Ben Tavis in the distance. There was frost, and a little snow, on the road, and the pony's studded hoofs rang loudly. Away over the loch was a big, bluish moon, that was fast weaving a spell about them, and her head was near his shoulder.

'Is it true, or just a dream?' she murmured.

'Is what true?'

'Your being here — a free man, and in your own home.'

'It is something I never imagined was possible — a few weeks ago. Things looked very black then.'

'You admit that — now.'

'Well — yes.'

'And yet you tried to make believe that your chances of being acquitted were excellent.'

He shrugged his shoulders and made no reply.

'Don, are you going back?'

'To my farm? Yes. I can't leave it now.

333

Slocum is carrying on, and I must return — soon.'

'You came to see your people?'

'Yes — but not only for that.' He pulled up the pony and turned on her suddenly. 'I can't hide it any longer. I came home to tell you something which I would have told you before if — if my life had not been in jeopardy. I love you, Sheila. I have loved you ever since we were boy and girl together.'

She trembled at this confession, belated as it was. But it was not unexpected, for during those days of his incarceration she had succeeded in piercing his armour, and she knew and appreciated the motive which had kept his lips sealed then.

'I love you too, Don,' she said simply. 'I think I have always loved you — ever since I was able to know my own mind.'

He kissed her and looked into her eyes.

'How long does that go back?'

'To the days before your departure. Oh no — further. For a while I was confused. Angus came to me — when you were away at college. I really thought it was Angus to whom my heart turned. But later I had clearer vision, and when you suddenly went away I knew beyond a shadow of doubt that it was you — and that you carried away with you part of myself. I told Angus.'

334

'About me?'

'No. That was my secret. I merely told him that I had made a great mistake. It was not until recently that Angus knew. He was hurt a little, but not now. Angus understands, and he has a great new interest in life.'

'The North-West Police?'

'Yes. You helped him there, Don. I see it clearly now. If he had gone back on the police his life would have been barren of joy in the future. It was difficult for me — a woman — to understand how men regard these questions of honour. And Angus in his love for you was near to falling.'

'Never!'

'He was, Don. It needed your strength of mind, your insight, to keep him toeing the line. You two — how close you are together! There are times when I almost descend to jealousy.'

'You silly goose.'

'All women are silly geese when they love — deeply. Your people are so fine, too. I had the shock of my life when your mother sent word that you were coming home.'

'I was dubious about the reception I should get,' he mused. 'But I should have known that they would harbour no ill-feeling. Time works her own cure.'

'We must forget all about — that,' she said.

'You think you can?' he looked at her searchingly, and she inclined her head.

'God bless you!'

'He has, Don. I seem suddenly to have been lifted out of the wreckage and flung heaven-high. But what — what will they all say when they know — about you and me?'

'Mother knows.'

'You — you told her?'

'No. But she knows. I read it in her eyes the first time your name was mentioned. But there is your own father. Do you think he will approve.'

'It is my happiness that he desires. Nothing else matters to him. How long are you staying, Don?'

'It depends upon you.'

'Upon me?'

'I want to take you back to Canada — when I go. Will your father agree to that?'

'He must. But perhaps I may induce him to come, too. For a long time he has been considering such a move. We could go in the spring, and the sea-trip would do him good. Home is beautiful, but we must think of the future. And if your work lies out there, mine does too.'

The journey to Sheila's house was very prolonged, and when at last Donald gave her a parting kiss, and went trudging back to his own home, he felt he was treading on air, rather than on the frozen earth.

Followed days of wonderful courtship, in which both of them strove to make up for lost time, and not unsuccessfully. Old Fraser saw how things were shaping and looked at his wife questioningly. Wise Mrs. Fraser nodded her head.

'Made for each other, John.'

'I was thinking of Angus.'

'Angus knows. He lost her long ago and has survived it. If he is a wise lad he will know that Sheila always belonged to Don, though she never knew it.'

One day Sheila took the opportunity to confide in her father, who was now making great strides towards recovery. She did not beat about the bush, but went straight to the point — laying bare her heart. McLeod looked at her steadily.

'Ye have no doubts, lass?'

'None. Not a little one.'

'And ye can forget — what happened two years agone?'

'Yes — yes. His own people have taken him back. If they can forget, should not I?'

'I'm not wanting to scratch old sores,

Sheila. But when a lad turns round and robs his own father — '

Sheila stared at him so hard he stopped suddenly.

'What are you saying, father?' she demanded. 'Donald never did that. He got into trouble, but not that.'

His piercing glance caused her mind to work rapidly. She had been given to understand that Donald had forged a cheque, but at no time had she ever heard that it was his own father's cheque. Such a possibility had never entered her mind.

'Father — is that true?' she asked hoarsely.

'I — I thought ye knew.'

'No — no. Oh, it can't be! Don could not do such a thing. He — he could never look me in the face if — '

'It's true, lass. Fraser told me with his own lips. I'm not suggesting that it must make any difference between you and him. But it's as well to know the whole truth.'

The room seemed to whirl around Sheila. To her there seemed a vast difference between a man swindling an acquaintance — and his own father. In this case the crime seemed all the more terrible, because of the love and affection which Fraser had lavished on his sons. It was all the more incredible when she thought of Donald, with his idealism, his quiet courage, and a great loyalty. Had he been suddenly stricken with madness? She felt sick and faint, and her head drooped like a wilting flower.

'Sheila!'

'I — I didn't know,' she almost sobbed. 'But you were right, father. One should know the whole truth.'

'Poor lass!'

'Don't pity me. I — I have to think things over. You see — I love him — even now. This love is beyond reason. It will listen to no argument. Only my mind is open to reason. I oughtn't to love him — knowing that. But — '

She struggled for words to express her real feelings, but could not find them. In her own room she tried to face the situation calmly. Love was not in doubt. It was her sense of decency that had been shocked.

Deliberately she kept away from Donald for the next few days. But they were bound to meet at last, and Donald found himself before a shut door. Try as he might he could not understand the existence of this invisible, cold barrier that intervened whenever he desired to manifest the passionate love that swept him.

He had gone into Culm and bought an engagement ring, but he refrained from giving it to her until her mood changed. While in the midst of vain cogitations Angus' delayed letter arrived. It explained the delay. He had held it back in the hope of being able to give them pleasant news. Now he was able to tell them that special sick-leave had been granted him, as he would be unable to use his arm for a month or two. He was coming home to spend a few weeks with them and would probably arrive soon after the letter — if not before.

'Wonderful!' said his mother. 'And here is a postscript. He has been promoted to Corporal.'

'Corporal Fraser of the Mounted,' mused Don. 'That sounds quite good. But why didn't he give the name of the ship? I could have gone to meet him.'

'Angus never did anything thoroughly,' said Fraser.

'Don't you believe it,' retorted Donald.

The following day Angus vindicated himself by sending a Marconigram from the ship, which was nearing port. Donald consulted a railway time-table, and set off at once for the port of arrival. Twenty hours later the twain arrived at the farm, Donald shouldering a big trunk, and Angus with his right arm in a sling.

'A complete reunion at last,' said Mrs.

Fraser. 'Oh, Angus, why didn't you wear your uniform?'

Angus laughed and kissed away her disappointment.

'There's no need to advertise the North-West Police in Scotland,' he said. 'In fact, the North-West Police is Scotland. But you're all looking remarkably fit.'

'How's the arm?' asked Fraser.

'Going on well. But the surgeon had a bit of a job getting the bullet out. A fine mess he made of me.'

'You're taller,' said his mother, letting her admiring eyes range from his boots to his hair.

'And he's hungry,' said Donald, 'which is much more to the point. I've brought a bottle of fizz with me. We'll celebrate.'

That evening Angus told them the story of the Willeton affair in detail, filling in a great number of gaps. It was evident, despite his modesty, that the final capture of Lee had been a perilous business, and that the Police had recognised that fact by giving him such swift promotion.

'You'll soon be an Inspector,' said Donald, 'and after that Chief Commissioner.'

Angus flung a small piece of bread at him, with his left hand, and Mrs. Fraser laughed, for it reminded her of the old days of their boyhood when they were always chaffing each other.

'I've made your bed, Angus,' she said. 'The old place — in the corner — opposite Don.'

Donald looked across the table at Angus. He was recalling the last occasion when they had occupied that room jointly. Angus met his brother's eyes fixedly, for he had a very solid reason for coming home. Later, when they had retired, he got to business.

'What's wrong, Don?'

'Wrong?'

'Yes. In the train you told me that you and Sheila had fixed things.'

'That is so.'

'But there's a hitch somewhere. You showed a reluctance to talk much about it. Why?'

Donald hesitated and stared across the room.

'Perhaps it's just fancy, Angus. But for the past few days she has seemed strangely cold and reserved. I — I can't get close to her. I can't understand her.'

'I can.'

'What do you mean?'

'She's remembering — things. You know.'

'You are wrong. That is all forgotten. She told me that with her own lips. She was happy — I swear she was happy — that night, and for some days — '

'Yes, until certain facts — or what seemed like facts — came uppermost. You see, Don, you are an ideal to her, and when that ugly blot appears it hurts her. It is time we settled that matter for good, and I have come home to put things right.'

'No, you don't!'

'I am going to. Vow or no vow I am not going to keep silent any longer. The need for it has gone.'

'It hasn't,' replied Donald stubbornly. 'If you say a word you will only cause pain. Mother and father have agreed to let that affair lie buried in time. If you dig it up you will start another hare. They have forgiven me, and there let the matter end.'

'Forgiven you for something you never did! But there's Sheila. I'm not going to have her peace of mind injured — not one little cloud between you two. I'm going to let things rip to-morrow.'

Donald clenched his big hands.

'If you do, I'll break your neck,' he growled.

'You can't — I'm incapacitated. Go to sleep, old boy, and leave the rest to me.'

'Now see here — !'

'Rats! Good night, Don!'

32

Conclusion

During the next day Donald strove to deter Angus from carrying out his resolution but Angus was adamant. No argument or entreaty would move him. In the end Donald gave it up, and went for a long walk. Angus there-upon made a surprise visit to Sheila.

'This is — wonderful!' she said. 'I had not the remotest idea you were home. When did you arrive?'

'Yesterday. Don came to meet me. He — he told me everything.'

She blushed and trembled.

'Sheila, I've got something important to tell you — and my people. Will you come over this evening — at seven o'clock?'

'I don't think — '

'You must. It is something that concerns — all of us. Please — please, I beg of you.'

At last she consented and Angus prepared for the ordeal. Sheila turned up on time, but Donald was still away from home. Mrs. Fraser welcomed Sheila and apologised for Donald.

'Angus asked me to call,' said Sheila. 'He was rather mysterious about it.'

'I'll find him.'

Angus met her on the stairs and grabbed her.

'Is that Sheila below?'

'Yes.'

'Good! Where is father?'

'In the sitting-room.'

'Take Sheila there, please. I am going to look for Don.' His face became very grave. 'Mother, there is something I want to say — to you all. But I want Don to be present.'

'What is it, Angus?'

'You'll know presently. Trust me, mother. This thing has got to be done.'

'Very well,' she said. 'I thought I saw Don coming over the hill just now.'

'Good! I won't be long.'

But when he saw Donald he failed utterly to induce him to attend the family meeting.

'It's all wrong, Angus,' he said. 'You are going to stir up a whole lot of trouble. I'll have nothing to do with it.'

Angus went back in despair, and whispered the result to his mother.

'What's all this business, Angus?' enquired Fraser. 'Why this solemn conclave?'

'I'll explain — in a minute. But I want

Don to come, and he is as stubborn as a mule.'

'I'll fetch him,' said Mrs. Fraser. 'He'll come if I ask him.'

She went out, and Sheila's wondering eyes followed her. Some minutes elapsed, and then Donald entered with his mother. He halted and blushed when he saw Sheila.

'Sit there,' said Angus. 'Next to Sheila.'

It was the only vacant chair, and Donald was compelled to comply. A silence fell over the gathering, and Angus began to show signs of nervousness, for all eyes were on him.

'This matter concerns all of us,' he said. 'For over two years all of you have suffered under a grave delusion. I — I want to put right a wrong that was done. Donald has never been guilty of any dishonest act. It was not he who forged that cheque.'

'What!' gasped Fraser.

'Angus!' ejaculated Donald.

'Let me go on. Donald took the blame to — to save someone he loved.' He looked at Sheila. 'I — I was the culprit. I forged father's name and cashed the cheque in Culm the next day.'

'Angus! Angus!'

'I was going to leave — that night — when father had discovered the forgery, but Don was awake and saw me dressing.

346

He stopped me — he made me believe that my going would break Sheila's heart. I listened — perhaps I was a coward to listen for a moment. But Don argued — you know his bullying ways. He made me swear never to divulge the truth to a living soul. Afterwards — when he had gone — I wanted to tell you, but I — I have never broken my word to Don. When I saw him in Canada I tried again to get him to release me, but he refused. But the time has come to put matters right. I — I admit it all. Don has shouldered my burden for too long.'

Sheila could scarcely believe her ears, and sat like a statue staring at Angus, whose head was hung in shame. Fraser stood up and then sat down again, in the throes of great emotion. Donald was shrugging his shoulders uneasily.

'That's all,' said Angus. 'I came home chiefly to put this right. Now it's done.'

'Not quite finished, Angus,' said his mother in curious tones. 'Tell them the rest.'

'The rest?'

'Yes.'

'There — there is nothing more, mother.'

'Tell them why you signed that cheque in your father's name.'

'But — '

'Then I will tell them.' She gazed at

the astounded husband. 'It concerns my — my forgiven secret, John. But Donald is in complete ignorance. I will start at the beginning. Perhaps you do not know, Donald, that when I married your father I was a widow.'

'Mother!'

'I was little more than a girl when I married my first husband — very young and very ignorant. It turned out a terrible failure. I cannot speak ill of him now, but my life was made a living hell, and I had to work to keep him as well as — as my child. Within two years he died, and I discovered to my horror and pain that my little boy was mentally deficient. I — I had to put him into an institution. I must pass over that period. Ultimately I met your father. We fell in love, and I — I foolishly kept from him the fact that I was a widow with a child. I did not want that sad incident of my life dragged up, and I feared it might mar your father's love. At times I was near to telling him — but I let time pass, until it was too late. The boy grew up, and I saw him secretly. He had no love for me — nor for anyone. I saved and scraped to give him a schooling, but everywhere the verdict was the same. He was incorrigible — unteachable. One day he ran away from a Reformatory and I heard nothing of him for many years. I know that he had lived a dishonest life — that he was without shame. I decided that I could do nothing more, and that all my love must be given to those near me. One night — two years ago — my wayward son called here. Angus saw him.'

Fraser looked at his younger son, and Angus winced.

'Tell them, Angus.'

'Yes, it is true,' he gulped. 'It was on the anniversary of mother's wedding, and she and father had gone together into Culm to celebrate. Don was out and I was all alone. This man called. He asked to see mother, and I asked him his business. He laughed at me and said he was delighted to meet his half-brother. I thought he was mad, but he — he produced some old letters. They were from mother to him, and then — then I knew that he was speaking the truth. He said he wanted money, and that his mother would give him some — to keep his mouth shut. I — I nearly kicked him out, but I realised that would serve no purpose. I didn't know what to do for the best, and all the time he sat there, in that chair, scowling at me. I pleaded with him, and told him that his conduct would only bring unhappiness to — to mother. But he laughed and said he didn't care. He meant to stay and — and claim his rights. Every moment I dreaded father and mother would return . . . I talked to him again, and he told me that it was necessary for him to leave the country. He wanted fifty pounds — and meant to get it. He swore he would leave England for good if he got the money. While he was talking I heard the trap coming. I — I acted impulsively. I promised him that if he would leave at once, by the back door — I would bring the money to him on the morrow at Culm. He left just in time to avoid meeting father. You know the rest. I — I kept my promise, by the only means that was open to me — a dishonest means. Whether he kept his I do not know.'

'He did,' said Mrs. Fraser. 'He died abroad a year ago, and wrote me during a long illness regretting his wasted life, and begging my forgiveness and yours.'

'Then — then you have known this for over a year?'

'Yes, Angus.'

'And father?'

'Father knew about — him, but not about his visit here, and the great trouble he caused. You kept my secret, Angus, and I meant to keep yours until you were ready to speak.'

Fraser rose from his chair and went to Angus, who seemed a little shamefaced.

'Lift up your head, Angus,' he said emotionally. 'I — I understand — at last. There are white lies and white sins, and none whiter than those done in the cause of love and loyalty. We can forget the wrong when right balances it. Shake, my lad, and let us hear no more about it.'

They gripped hands, and Mrs. Fraser sighed. Donald went to Angus and shook his head.

'Why wasn't I let in on that, old boy?'

'It was mother's secret, Don, not mine.'

'But you gave me to understand that a bookmaker was dunning you and that — '

'That was true. I made a fool of myself, but I managed to wipe out the debt with my own money. It was that which left me broke.'

Donald's gaze went to Sheila, who was still bewildered by what had transpired. From a pinnacle of happiness she had been flung down, and now again she was being swept up — breathlessly. Mrs. Fraser was quick to come to the rescue.

'Father has befouled the room with his awful pipe,' she said. 'Let us go into the other room, Sheila.'

The girl nodded, and the two ladies retired,

but as they passed through the door, Sheila's head came round a trifle. The blushing, happy face held an unmistakable message for Donald. The storm and strife had passed for ever.

'A fine girl,' mused Fraser.

'A fine wife she'll make,' said Angus. 'Let it be soon, Don, for I mean to attend the wedding.'

Fraser laughed heartily.

'So that's how the wind blows?'

Donald nodded.

'She has always loved Don,' put in Angus quietly. 'I was just a stop-gap for a while, and I ought to have had the sense to know it. Anyway, a fellow can't have everything in the world. I've got an idea the N.W.P. is going to keep me busy for a bit. There's a whole lot of useful work to be done.'

'We're going to lose you both again, lads.'

'It is inevitable, father.'

'Yes. The old nest grows too small in time, but it's not a bad place to come back to — at intervals. Remember that.'

Mrs. Fraser entered a little later, and looked at Donald with a twinkle in her eyes.

'Sheila is about to leave,' she said. 'Don't you think you ought to see her home, Don?'

They stood in the moonlight, gazing with almost speechless happiness into each other's eyes. Behind them was the great curving bulk of Ben Tavis, dimly reflected in the still water of the loch. Far away — low down — were the lighted windows of Donald's home.

'They're happy, back there,' he murmured. 'Dear old folk!'

'And we are happy, up here — are we not?'

He kissed the hand decked with his simple ring, and then the lips that were offered him.

'What a cartload of secrets have been betrayed to-night,' he said. 'Angus was fine. And father too. How quickly he understood, and forgave! If the need arises, we too must forgive, without rancour.'

'It must never arise, Don, dear. We will harbour no secrets. Life is too, too short. Every hour, every minute must be ours to enjoy — from now onward. We will hide nothing from each other. Your life will be my life, and my life yours.'

'For ever and ever, Amen!' he added.

Back at the farm John Fraser and his wife were sitting by the fire, talking things over. Angus had just gone out to meet Donald on his way back, and there was no one to overhear.

'My last secret is divulged, John,' said the old lady. 'I was waiting for Angus. I knew he would come.'

'You're a wise mother. I was a little hard at the time, I'm thinking, but then I never knew all the truth.'

'One never does, John.'

'Your faith was stronger than mine.'

'I had an intuition there was something we didn't know. Soon the nest will be empty again, dear.'

'Yes, but a new one will be built, for our grandchildren that are to be — please God. May they run out as our two lads have. Strong enough in their love even to sin for their mother.'

'Let us hope that will not be necessary, John.'

'Yes, and somehow I think it will not.'

They sat on until the fire burned low and the room became chilly. Then he wrapped her shawl about her shoulders and led her away.

McLEAN AT THE GOLDEN OWL
George Goodchild
Inspector McLean has resigned from Scotland Yard's CID and has opened an office in Wimpole Street. With the help of his able assistant, Tiny, he solves many crimes, including those of kidnapping, murder and poisoning.

KATE WEATHERBY
Anne Goring
Derbyshire, 1849: The Hunter family are the arrogant, powerful masters of Clough Grange. Their feuds are sparked by a generation of guilt, despair and ill-fortune. But their passions are awakened by the arrival of nineteen-year-old Kate Weatherby.

A VENETIAN RECKONING
Donna Leon
When the body of a prominent inter-national lawyer is found in the carriage of an intercity train, Commissario Guido Brunetti begins to dig deeper into the secret lives of the once great and good.

A TASTE FOR DEATH
Peter O'Donnell

Modesty Blaise and Willie Garvin take on impossible odds in the shape of Simon Delicata, the man with a taste for death, and Swordmaster, Wenczel, in a terrifying duel. Finally, in the Sahara desert, the intrepid pair must summon every killing skill to survive.

SEVEN DAYS FROM MIDNIGHT
Rona Randall

In the Comet Theatre, London, seven people have good reason for wanting beautiful Maxine Culver out of the way. Each one has reason to fear her blackmail. But whose shadow is it that lurks in the wings, waiting to silence her once and for all?

QUEEN OF THE ELEPHANTS
Mark Shand

Mark Shand knows about the ways of elephants, but he is no match for the tiny Parbati Barua, the daughter of India's greatest expert on the Asian elephant, the late Prince of Gauripur, who taught her everything. Shand sought out Parbati to take part in a film about the plight of the wild herds today in north-east India.

THE DARKENING LEAF
Caroline Stickland

On storm-tossed Chesil Bank in 1847, the young lovers, Philobeth and Frederick, prevent wreckers mutilating the apparent corpse of a young woman. Discovering she is still alive, Frederick takes her to his grandmother's home. But the rescue is to have violent and far-reaching effects . . .

A WOMAN'S TOUCH
Emma Stirling

When Fenn went to stay on her uncle's farm in Africa, the lovely Helena Starr seemed to resent her — especially when Dr Jason Kemp agreed to Fenn helping in his bush hospital. Though it seemed Jason saw Fenn as little more than a child, her feelings for him were those of a woman.

A DEAD GIVEAWAY
Various Authors

This book offers the perfect opportunity to sample the skills of five of the finest writers of crime fiction — Clare Curzon, Gillian Linscott, Peter Lovesey, Dorothy Simpson and Margaret Yorke.

DOUBLE INDEMNITY — MURDER FOR INSURANCE
Jad Adams

This is a collection of true cases of murderers who insured their victims then killed them — or attempted to. Each tense, compelling account tells a story of cold-blooded plotting and elaborate deception.

THE PEARLS OF COROMANDEL
By Keron Bhattacharya

John Sugden, an ambitious young Oxford graduate, joins the Indian Civil Service in the early 1920s and goes to uphold the British Raj. But he falls in love with a young Hindu girl and finds his loyalties tragically divided.

WHITE HARVEST
Louis Charbonneau

Kathy McNeely, a marine biologist, sets out for Alaska to carry out important research. But when she stumbles upon an illegal ivory poaching operation that is threatening the world's walrus population, she soon realises that she will have to survive more than the harsh elements . . .

TO THE GARDEN ALONE
Eve Ebbett

Widow Frances Morley's short, happy marriage was childless, and in a succession of borders she attempts to build a substitute relationship for the husband and family she does not have. Over all hovers the shadow of the man who terrorized her childhood.

CONTRASTS
Rowan Edwards

Julia had her life beautifully planned — she was building a thriving pottery business as well as sharing her home with her friend Pippa, and having fun owning a goat. But the goat's problems brought the new local vet, Sebastian Trent, into their lives.

MY OLD MAN AND THE SEA
David and Daniel Hays

Some fathers and sons go fishing together. David and Daniel Hays decided to sail a tiny boat seventeen thousand miles to the bottom of the world and back. Together, they weave a story of travel, adventure, and difficult, sometimes terrifying, sailing.

SQUEAKY CLEAN
James Pattinson
An important attribute of a prospective candidate for the United States presidency is not to have any dirt in your background which an eager muckraker can dig up. Senator William S. Gallicauder appeared to fit the bill perfectly. But then a skeleton came rattling out of an English cupboard.

NIGHT MOVES
Alan Scholefield
It was the first case that Macrae and Silver had worked on together. Malcolm Underdown had brutally stabbed to death Edward Craig and had attempted to murder Craig's fiancée, Jane Harrison. He swore he would be back for her. Now, four years later, he has simply walked from the mental hospital. Macrae and Silver must get to him — before he gets to Jane.

GREATEST CAT STORIES
Various Authors
Each story in this collection is chosen to show the cat at its best. James Herriot relates a tale about two of his cats. Stella Whitelaw has written a very funny story about a lion. Other stories provide examples of courageous, clever and lucky cats.

THE HAND OF DEATH
Margaret Yorke

The woman had been raped and murdered. As the police pursue their relentless inquiries, decent, gentle George Fortescue, the typical man-next-door, finds himself accused. While the real killer serenely selects his third victim — and then his fourth . . .

VOW OF FIDELITY
Veronica Black

Sister Joan of the Daughters of Compassion is shocked to discover that three of her former fellow art college students have recently died violently. When another death occurs, Sister Joan realizes that she must pit her wits against a cunning and ruthless killer.

MARY'S CHILD
Irene Carr

Penniless and desperate, Chrissie struggles to support herself as the Victorian years give way to the First World War. Her childhood friends, Ted and Frank, fall hopelessly in love with her. But there is only one man Chrissie loves, and fate and one man bent on revenge are determined to prevent the match . . .